PRAISE FOR MJ JAMES

James's effective worldbuilding employs strong emotional and sensory descriptions ... often paralleling our society's own issues with neurodivergence, gender equality, economic disparity, and more.

THE BOOKLIFE PRIZE ON THE IMMORTAL PART OF MYSELF

Good world-building and a storyline I was quickly hooked into.

GOODREADS REVIEWER ON IN-BETWEEN

This book was so deep.I cried throughout it. If you're looking for something with similar vibes to A Handmaiden's Tale but sci-fi, this is your book.

GOODREADS REVIEWER ON THE IMMORTAL PART OF MYSELF

Inside A Dark Space

MJ James

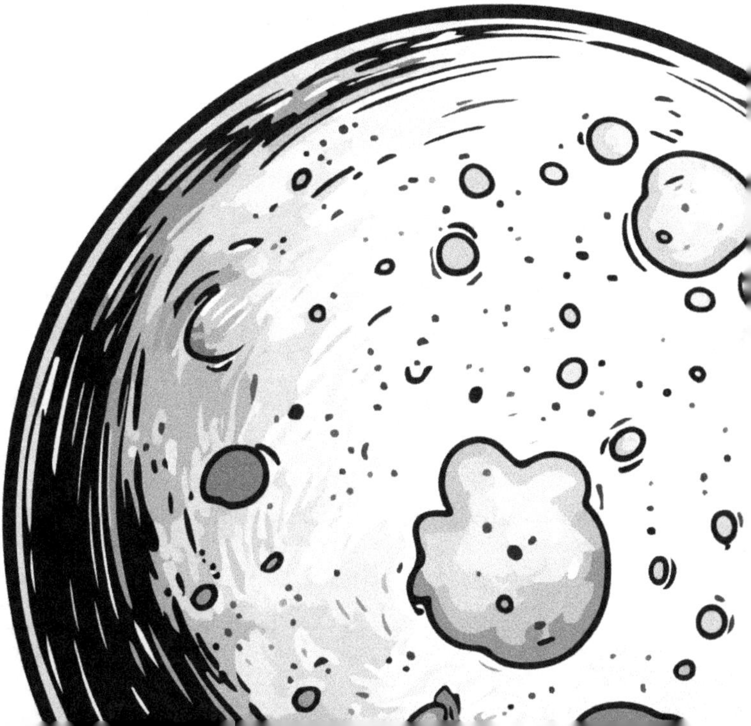

Edited by Sam Willow
Proofread by Erica Bell
Cover design by PurpawArt

E-book ISBN: 978-1-958175-26-2
Paperback ISBN: 978-1-958175-28-6
Hardcover ISBN: 978-1-958175-29-3
Audiobook ISBN: 978-1-958175-30-9

To everyone resisting.
Don't let the fuckers win!

TRIGGER WARNING

Inside a Dark Space is about finding joy in the darkness. While this isn't a book about trauma, it does contain instances of (mostly past) abuse. As always, if you are not in a place to read this book, I understand. It will be here for you if that changes.

Inside a Dark Space Contains

Abandonment of parents
Ableism
Transphobia by parent
Sexual Assault
Suicide
Death
Concentration Camps
Panic Attacks

ALSO BY MJ JAMES

In-Between

The Immortal Part of Myself

NeurodiVeRse

The Ember Town Series

Lucas

Phoenix

Birk

Mika

Lennon

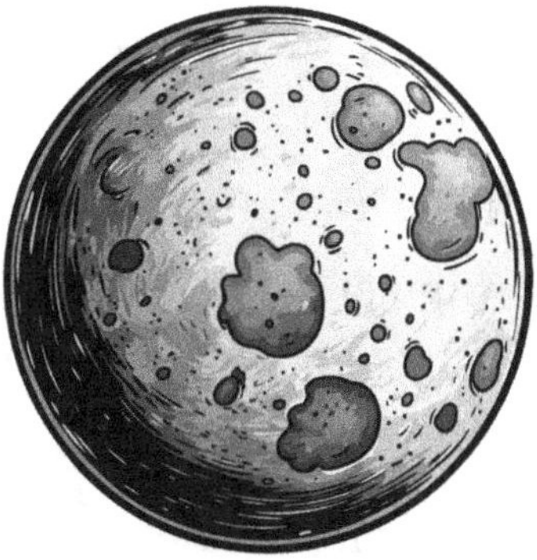

Finch

Chapter One

FINCH JAMMED their finger on the tablet attached to their arm. Even in the newer suits, the movement still felt clunky as they managed to push the button.

"Schmidt Station to Dynamax Team, please advise on your ETA." The computer's voice echoed in their helmet as it sent the message over the radio to the restock team.

They were late. That morning, Finch had confirmed the team's arrival time and had been assured they would be there at 13:00 hours lunar time. It was now 13:15, and they still hadn't responded to short-range communication.

Finch walked to the trailer. It sat a short way off from the cab that had towed it out of the crater, ready to be exchanged. They strode between the blocks of ice, counting them. Each block was coated in a thin blue membrane to protect it from melting in the sun's rays, as well as to keep out the granular dust that coated everything on the moon. The order was correct and the ice in pristine condition, not that Finch had held any doubts. It was the fourth time they had done this specific inspection.

The next step was to attach the trailer to the team's vehicle and have them authorize shipment, but that couldn't be done until they arrived. Finch jammed their finger back on their touch screen.

"Schmidt Station to Dynamax Team, please advise on your ETA," the computer's voice said again.

"Sorry, mate, we had sort of a late start. We should be there in ten minutes." The voice carried a UK English accent, and Finch identified the man as Marlow Faning.

Finch touched another button, and the computerized voice acknowledged the message. Then they flipped the screen until they saw their oxygen level. The numbers glowed a bright blue against their faceplate—sixty-two percent. It was within acceptable limits. The shipment would not have to be canceled. Finch walked around the trailer again, taking their time to do inventory once more.

It was easy to see the transport in the bright sunlight. It kicked up a storm of dust that had collected on the road. They were driving an older rover with six thick tires and a roll bar. It held up to four crew members, but Finch could only see three figures as the vehicle approached. They were dressed in the bright orange colors of the Dynamax corporation, and

Finch knew there would be a dark blue D embossed near their left shoulders.

New corporations had started growing in recent years, but Dynamax was one of the oldest and largest. The company was based in London, not that it mattered much on the moon. Finch tapped at the screen on their arm until the retrieval team employees appeared. The other two miners were An Li, born in China, and Rohan Singh, from India. Only Marlow had done a run before, but since both of the other men had moved from national companies over to Dynamax, they were lifers. It was hard to be loyal to a country when you could see Earth hanging suspended in space, no borders etched into it.

"Sorry for being late," Marlow said as the vehicle approached. "I know you appreciate punctuality, but I promise it couldn't be helped."

The vehicle came to a stop and Finch unhooked the empty trailer from the back.

An Li spoke in Chinese. Finch had heard the language enough to recognize the sounds, but despite a brief passion to learn last year, the words had never stuck. Thankfully, the computer provided them with a rough translation.

"Does the person not speak?" An Li asked.

"Didn't anyone tell you about Finch before you took the run?" Marlow's voice answered. "They are one of the original canaries, the only one left alive. They live out on the small water mining station by themself so that we have access to something to drink."

"One of the American firsts?"

"The unkillable one?" Rohan said in accented English. "I heard they lost their voice in the camps. A guard poured bleach down their throat."

Finch stopped unhooking the connectors and put their hands on the sides of their helmet. It didn't do any good to block out the words that were streaming in from the radio next to their ears. The faceplate started to fog slightly as their eyes moistened.

"Don't speak about the camps. You've seen the pictures," Marlow said.

A shadow fell across Finch and they looked up. Rohan leaned out of the transport so his upper body was right in front of them. It was easy to know it was him; his name was labeled right on the front of his suit.

"I'm sorry. I shouldn't have said that," Rohan said.

Finch went to their screen to ask him to move back for his safety, but their hands shook so badly, they selected the wrong button. "Hello, I am Finch from Schmidt Station. How may I assist you today?" the computer said.

The man paused for a few seconds before turning around. Finch took a moment to collect themself and finished unhooking the trailer. They didn't bother trying to speak. Instead, they hit their hand against the transport frame. The rover moved forward, leaving the empty trailer behind. It maneuvered in front of the full trailer and Finch began securing it to the transport.

Finch worked on hooking up the full trailer, making sure to properly connect the towing mount so there would be no concern about joyriding. This team looked like they would enjoy taking the slopes at the fastest speed possible and watching the trailer jump in the reduced moon gravity. Inside the rover, the men continued to talk as if Finch was not there.

"I heard you have a date tonight with Miranda. How did you get so lucky?" Marlow said.

"She had her pick of men, and she chose you?" An said via translation.

"All women want is a man who will show her a good time, talk to her like a person, and acknowledge that she is the better miner," Rohan said.

"Crying during film night may have helped also," Marlow said.

An let out a laugh and tapped his hand on Marlow's shoulder.

"I mean, it didn't hurt," Rohan said. "How can you two not cry at *Bambi*? The poor deer's mother. It is very sad."

Finch listened as they finished up the last of the connections. They made socializing seem so easy. Talking, laughing, and joking with each other. It was all so much. Finch strode around to the side of the trailer and held out their arm to receive verification of shipment.

Marlow reached out and butted his fist against their own before pushing on the accelerator.

Finch searched their menu for the correct button. "Please accept verification of the shipment." For good measure, they pushed it again. "Please accept verification of the shipment."

The transport came to a stop, allowing Finch to catch up to it. They once again held out their arm. This time Marlow tapped some buttons on his screen and then held his arm close to theirs. Verification transmitted between the devices.

"I don't know how you do it," Marlow said. "Living out here all alone in the darkness. I couldn't."

The transport stayed still and Finch realized that he was waiting for a response. They went over all their preset communications, but none of them were right for this situation. So, they began typing out a response letter by letter. The bulky gloves caused them to have to go back and fix their statement. The whole time they waited for the transport to get tired and drive away, but the men didn't move.

"If I don't do it, then who will hand out the water?" the computerized voice filled up their helmets.

"And we are happy that you do," Rohan said. "Do you think next time you can slip in an extra block so I can take a nice long bath?"

It seemed this question was not one that they were meant to answer. The transport drove off down the road, the men chattering inside their helmets for a few minutes before they switched off to their settlement frequency. Finch debated, briefly, switching their frequency to hear them talking until the signal would be lost, but it was a fleeting idea. If anyone needed Finch, then they would expect them on their station frequency. As the dust from the transport started drifting into the distance, Finch focused on the next task: hooking the empty trailer back up to their cab.

Unlike the transport, their cab was only built for short excursions. It lacked the larger wheels to traverse the rocky lunar surface and only moved up and down the canyon on the well-packed road, the oldest on the moon. It held two people, and even that was snug in the new slender suits. Thankfully Finch did not have to worry about that. It had been years since they'd had to ride next to someone else.

It took them less time to connect the trailer. They were familiar with their cab's fastening and did not need to secure it as tight as they did for longer distances. Once it was attached, they moved the cab so it was headed down the canyon and then checked their oxygen gauge. Fifty-three percent. They liked to leave more time for their favorite part of a pickup, but the team was late and it couldn't be helped. Finch kept their breathing steady, trying to consume as little oxygen as possible, as they got out of the cab and took a proper look at the surface of the moon.

The ground in the southern hemisphere was mostly gray, but as the light flickered off of the soil, portions of it sparkled. Out in the distance, the Earth hovered overhead. The part facing them was covered in clouds, and relief flooded them at not being able to identify any visible countries. Instead, they turned their attention back to their home. There was beauty in the desolation that was easy to see after so many trips out of the canyon. Finch had heard that more north there were stretches of orange and brown soil, but it couldn't compare to the sight of the sun shimmering off of these rocks.

Their arm tablet beeped and Finch looked down at their oxygen levels—fifty percent. It had happened too soon. They wanted a few more minutes in the sun, but they had the procedure down perfectly and they needed to leave now to retain enough oxygen for a reasonable margin of error. They climbed back into the cab and started driving toward the crater.

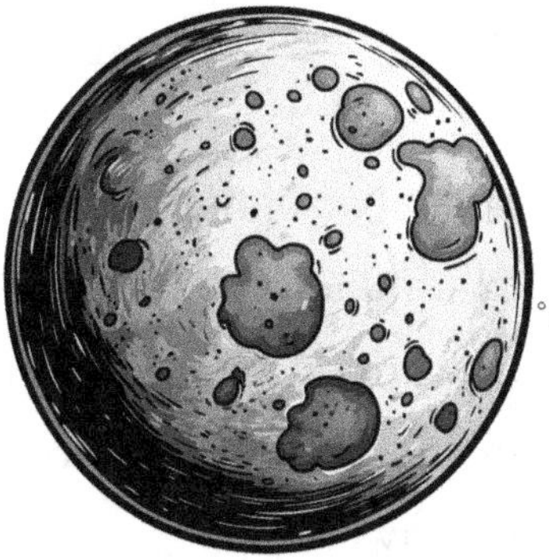

Ray

Chapter Two

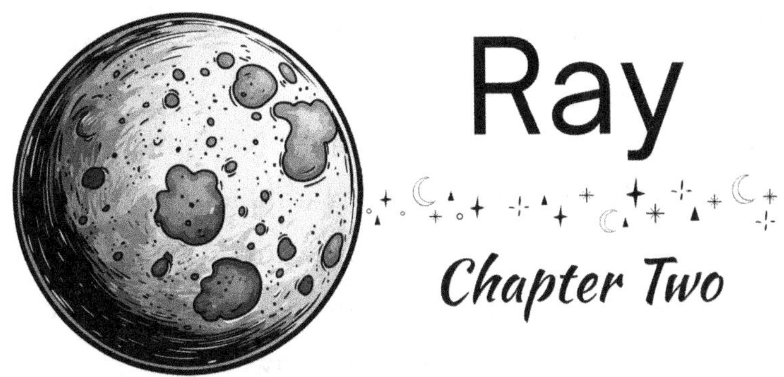

PEOPLE PUSHED past Ray as she hurried across the central dome toward the various transport tunnels. Each of the tunnels ran off the main area like the spokes of a wheel. To the side of each tunnel was a sign announcing one of the moon's main areas.

Ray looked down at her itinerary and then back again at the labeling. The names were etched in blue metal that stood out against the gray walls. There were signs for the main Neil Armstrong Center, the Taylor Wang Station, and even the Katherine Johnson Water Mining Station. There was no indication of the Stanley Schmidt Water Mining Station anywhere.

The central area was rapidly emptying and she felt a sudden fear of being left alone.

"Excuse me." She tried to hail a fellow passenger, but they ignored her as they moved down another tunnel.

"Hello, do you know where I can find—" But they walked right past Ray.

There was a group of security personnel dressed in matching dark black suits huddled around one of the richer tourists. Ray tried to approach the security detail, hoping they would be more responsive, but instead, one broke off from the main group, holding up his hand for Ray to stop.

"Ma'am, you need to back up now."

"I'm sorry, I just need help finding my terminal."

The man swept his hand across the twelve openings. "It's not like you can get lost. Now, please step away before we have to detain you for our client's safety."

Defeated, Ray took a step back as the security personnel walked away, disappearing down a tunnel that was marked "Private."

Unsure what else to do, she decided to turn around and go back to her transport, hoping there would still be a crew to help her find her way, but as she walked back down the transport tunnel it was easy to see that the doors had already been shut tight.

By the time she made it back to the dome, the center area had been emptied, and she was left alone.

Ray ran her hands over the wall. This was the first structure that had been made entirely out of lunar material. The soil had been processed until it created a consistency almost like concrete, and Ray spied the hints of its origins even though the walls had been sealed and made smooth to the touch. She couldn't wait to pick up the soil and see the particles with her own eyes. And, once safely inside the station, run the soil through her fingers.

It wasn't her primary research topic, but what geologist could resist looking?

She was here! After years of working toward this goal, she'd finally made it to the surface. It was just like her that the first thing she'd done was get lost.

With no one else around, Ray dropped her bags and her suit onto the ground. She was not exceptionally tall. At just under five and a half feet, she had been the shortest one in her lunar prep group. She had also been the only scientist and had been exempt from a portion of the physical training. The moon's gravity should have made the bags easier to carry, but lugging around six months' supply of food was heavier than she had imagined.

Ray started to explore the room, running her fingers over the wall again since there was no one around to watch. It wasn't that she was especially connected to rocks. The profession was more a venture of convenience than passion. She had picked geology as a field of study because it was the least competitive of the demanded professions that received regular lunar grants.

Spotting an interactive terminal, Ray nearly collapsed in relief. She missed her cell phone and the easy ability to pull up whatever information she needed. There were internet satellites in place around the moon, but her company had determined that she did not need a device to connect with them, as she had her computer. Unfortunately, it was packed tightly in one of the bags, unable to be retrieved until she finally made it to the station.

The terminal was the size of a tablet and lit up at her touch. It was a simple interface displaying the daily transport schedule and a map of the area. Her departing transport was listed as ready for departure, with the terminal section left blank.

"Well, you're no help," Ray said as she slumped to the ground, her head between her hands. She suddenly felt younger than her twenty-four years. All the self-doubt flooded back into her. She was not enough and would never be enough. Maybe she was as broken as her father had told her.

She stood up and brushed off her pants, just in case she had picked up some dirt, and went back to her bags. With them in hand, she ventured down each tunnel. Most of them were empty, and a few were closed, but when she walked down the Johnson tunnel she was thrilled to see the door was not only open but an attendant was standing outside the entrance.

"Excuse me," Ray said. "Can you please help me find where I need to go?"

"What does your ticket say?" The man was tall and lanky, with a bored expression on his face.

"I am scheduled to go to the Stanley Schmidt Water Mining Station. There isn't a tunnel listed."

The man took the tablet from her hand and looked over Ray's ticket. "Are you sure this is correct? You know that Schmidt is practically abandoned, right?"

"I'm here on a grant to research the older water mining base."

The man shook his head and handed back the tablet. "None of the main shuttles run out there. Your transport is probably waiting for you outside."

"Outside? But they told us the transports had atmosphere and that we wouldn't need to get in our suits unless we did a moonwalk."

The man muttered and then touched an earpiece. "Johnson transport to Schmidt transport. Is there anyone there?"

There was a pause as the man cocked his head, listening. "Good to hear you, Mitch. You better come in and collect your cas because she is in here not suited up." He turned his focus back to Ray before continuing. "He'll meet you in the dome. Give him a few minutes to get through the airlocks."

"Thank you," Ray managed before the man moved inside the tunnel and shut the door. He walked through the plastic tunnel that connected to the transport until it started to retract back into the station. She watched as the transport moved across the surface and out of view, taking a few of her basic training classmates with it. Then she returned to the dome, sat back down, and waited.

She heard a shuffling and watched as a figure in a bright blue suit emerged from one of the unmarked tunnels. The figure gestured with their hands, pointing at the top of their helmet. Ray stood up and walked around, trying to see what was there. Their arms formed into an X shape and then fell to their sides again. Ray paused, uncertain what was happening. The figure threw their arms up and started moving toward her. She walked backward. The station was now empty, and it was just the two of them alone. Ray just barely missed tripping over her bags as she continued moving away from the figure.

She stopped and watched as they picked up her helmet and took out the radio piece, thrusting it toward her. With a flush of embarrassment, she took the radio and placed it over her ear.

"Are you Rachel Bennett?" The voice was masculine, with an Australian accent.

"Yes, I'm Ray."

"Get suited up. We need to head out."

Ray looked down at her suit, folded nicely in a case by the basic training instructor on Gateway Station. It had only been taken out once as a last-minute fit check before they headed down. Even training had been done in some of the older model suits, the instructor insisting there would be a more thorough orientation when they arrived at their respective assignments.

"I don't know how," she finally admitted.

"They are sending a cas to the dead station?" the man muttered.

"What does cas mean?"

"Cas—casualty. They send you down without enough skills to make your way around safely. Don't worry, I will get you to your station, and then it will be their job to keep you safe. Just slip into your suit and I'll get you hooked up."

Ray pulled the suit from the bag, dropping smaller pieces all over the floor. Most of the suit was pink, a color designated for those without a corporation, but the various underlayers came in an assortment of colors. She picked up the pieces, trying to remember which part she was supposed to put on first. Reaching for the black jumpsuit, she looked toward the man to confirm. When he didn't say anything, she started putting it on, holding it out with her hands and slipping it over one leg, trying to get it to slide over the jeans she was wearing.

"They said we didn't need our suits today. The transports are supposed to be oxygenated."

Ray heard what sounded like cursing before the man reached up and pulled off his helmet. His face was slightly flushed and framed by a blue hood that covered his head.

"The transports are pressurized. We will be driving out in one of the buggies since it is just the two of us. They should have had you suited up for the drop-down. I'll let them know how badly they messed up later, but for now, we need to get you ready before we lose the sun."

"Lose the sun? I thought days were a month long."

"It's an expression—a joke. Look, cas, just follow what I say, and we will get through this. You can't wear those clothes in the suit. Take them off and pull on the jumper. Don't worry, I will turn around. Let me know when you are done."

It took some trial and error, but with the man's help, she was finally fully locked into her suit, and all that was left was to click the helmet into place. It smelled like new packaging, and she looked like the bunny from the old battery advertisements she had watched online.

"I don't suppose they left you with any oxygen." He didn't wait for an answer before he walked over to one of the walls and opened a panel that Ray hadn't even been able to see. He tugged out the pack and helped her to pull her arms through the straps while he hooked it up. Finally ready, Ray put on her helmet. Now completely encased, she tried to keep the anxiety at bay as they headed out for the surface of the moon.

Finch

Chapter Three

FINCH SAW the line where the sunlight disappeared as they drove over the side of the crater. They went from sunlight to shadow to darkness. The lights on the cab lit up the road, which had been built by pressing down the lunar soil. Finch had learned to drive on the open space of the moon in the darkness. With no atmosphere and no life, there was nothing unexpected on the trip. Even still, they remained on alert as they drove back to their home.

The night was quiet, and Finch enjoyed the view of the stars above them and the openness of the moon's surface. With the mining now completely automated, they only went outside on shipment days, which had started dwindling. Schmidt had been set up as a trial, a way to figure out the intricacies of mining the water and providing enough so that they could sustain habitats. With its success, they had created

Johnson, a larger mining facility that produced enough to start creating rocket fuel for more distant destinations. It also provided for the more elaborate needs of the tourist hotels.

As the personnel moved on to bigger things, orders for the blocks of ice dwindled. What had once been a daily occurrence was now weekly. The only thing that kept Finch in their home was that nothing went unused on the moon. As long as the facility still worked, it would continue mining ice. Finch just had to keep it running so they could stay. Although they weren't worried about being moved. The commander had told them once that no one knew what to do with them. After all, they weren't supposed to have survived this long. It was a win all around. So they made sure to enjoy the time they had on the surface.

The lights of the station came into view. They were much like the streetlights Finch remembered from their childhood, although the light poles sat atop the soil on batteries that kept them running instead of being plastered into the ground.

Finch drove the cab into the shelter, nothing more than a canvas that hung down from some metal poles. It did little besides keeping some of the dust off.

They unhooked the trailer, leaving it next to its twin. There were at least a dozen more scattered across the moon that had made the journey and never returned home. The two that were left looked lonely in the long line of empty space. Finch parked the cab alongside the electric charger before plugging it in to refresh its batteries. The cable ran back alongside the road out into the sun, where there were enough solar panels to provide more electricity than Finch or the equipment could ever need.

They approached a little warehouse built from old metal pieces to house Bertha, the ice maker. It was the final purifier that did one last cleaning of the water and then turned it into ice. Its name was written on the side, a joke by the commander shortly after they had put it together. He had used some of the paint that Martha had brought, promising to order her more on the next supply run. She was gone before it had arrived.

Finch paced the warehouse, doing a visual inspection to make sure everything was all right. The system gave regular updates, but they preferred to see for themself. After Bertha, the water traveled to its final resting place where it left the heated pipes to be formed instantly into blocks of ice that were coated for protection and stacked by a set of robots. The warehouse was nearly three-quarters full even after this week's shipment.

Finch left the rickety building and followed the pipe that was buried under the surface. The path was so familiar that they could have walked it with the floodlights turned off. It had been the canary's job to dig the trenches so many years ago that the soil was now trampled back completely flat. They walked until they made it to the first purifier. This was a complex system that the astronauts had created and prepared countless times until they had managed to find a solution that provided clean water fit for drinking. The machines used their sensors to locate the grains of ice mixed into the soil and collect them.

In the early days, that had been another one of the canary's jobs. They had each taken turns at the backbreaking work, scanning for the pockets of water, collecting the soil, and lugging it back to be cleaned. Even digging the trenches had been preferred over that. Now the machines brought in loads by the cartful, expertly dumping them into a system that sorted the soil from the water in multiple stages. The large structure caused the water to evaporate until it was collected in the piping and moved over to the final purifier.

Finch walked around the system, making sure that everything looked like it was running smoothly and that there was no damage to the outer casing from micro impacts. It was the same process every time, and Finch loved the repetitiveness of it.

Their wristband beeped, alerting them that they were at twenty-five percent oxygen. That was their cue to start heading inside, but they were running behind. There was one last stop they needed to make. They would be cutting it closer than they would like, but they were well within the limits. After ten years, they were aware of how far they could push.

The current mining field was a quarter of a mile away. As they walked toward it, they lost the light from the purification center, throwing them back into darkness. Only the illumination from their helmet lit their way. In the early days, the darkness had scared the canaries. They had hidden in the pockets of light as much as possible. After all, they had been taught to fear the dark on Earth, and what happened in the hidden corners. But as time went on, the darkness became a constant companion, and Finch had grown used to traversing it. With the faint glow of their destination in the distance, they moved forward.

As the lights grew brighter, Finch spied the robots. There were only a dozen left, the minimum requirement necessary to keep the purifying system running at full capacity. The only indication that it was a mining field was the portable lights that had to be moved every time the area became mined out. It probably would need to happen again soon; the ground was covered in track marks and indentations from where the robots had gathered up the ice pellets. A robot broke off from the pack, and Finch watched briefly as it started its trek to the purification system.

Something was off. Finch's gaze drifted across the worksite until they spotted it. One of the miners was frozen. They walked out to the mining field, careful of the uneven ground. If they rolled their ankles, there would be no one to help them home. They would have to make it on their own before the oxygen ran out. There were so many ways to die on the surface, and Finch had witnessed too many of them. Now, when they came out, they did their best to prevent accidents rather than to try and survive them.

The mining robots looked like larger versions of the vehicles that Finch had played with as a kid. The truck bed was long, with raised sides to hold in the lunar material. The wheels were large in comparison to its five-foot length to help it better navigate the rocky terrain. On the front, there was a control panel big enough that Finch's gloved fingers could navigate it with ease. There were sensors underneath that could detect where the ice was located, and a large claw that would reach down and scoop up the soil before depositing it in the back.

Finch navigated the malfunctioning machine's control panel, pulling up the error log. When it came back as a sensor log, the tension that had built up in their body dissipated. They typically could handle sensor malfunctions. They would not have to contact Johnson Station and request a more experienced team. That would mean people intruding on their routine. Also, Finch tried not to remind the commander that they were out here, operating as normal, just in case the corporation changed their mind about keeping the station—their home—open.

Finch removed the sensor system from the bottom of the computer. It slid out neatly and even had a handle for easy carrying. Then they went back to the main screen and selected the commands to tell it to head back to Bertha, where it would wait while they did the repairs. The machine took off, lumbering its way back, and Finch, slightly slower, started following it.

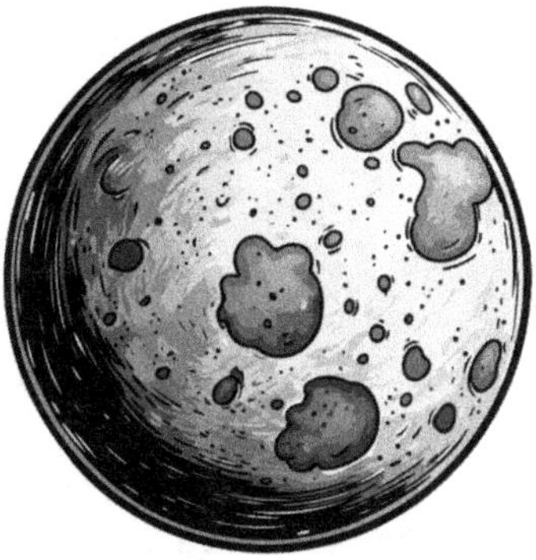

Ray

Chapter Four

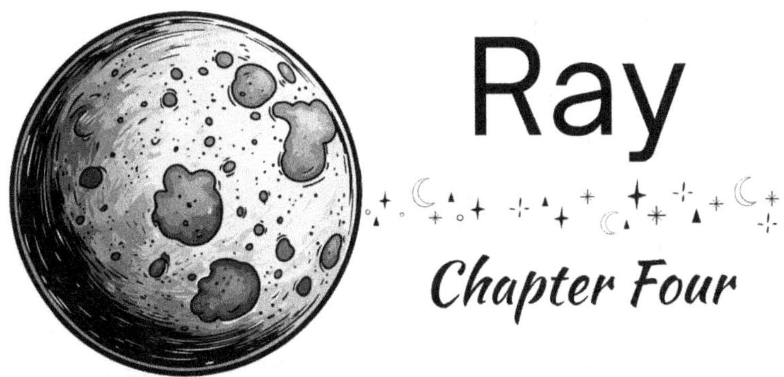

RAY GRABBED the rover's frame as it climbed over the rocky ground.

"I thought there were roads to most of the areas," Ray said. "I know they aren't paved or anything, but I thought they had at least been smoothed out."

"There are roads to the main stations," Mitch said. "There was no point in building a road from the main corridor to the little water station. Only a few people go out that way now, just some of the smaller stations that still pick up their water from there."

His voice came through the radio and echoed inside her helmet. The volume was too loud and she didn't know how to turn it down. Ray had already looked like enough of a novice for one day to ask. She could deal with it for now and ask for help once she got to the station.

"Wouldn't they need a road for new personnel coming in?"

He laughed at that, the sound ringing through her skull. "Why are you going out there anyway?"

"I'm a scientist; I'm going there to do research."

"Most scientists head down to the satellites or bunk at Johnson. I haven't been to Schmidt in a few years now, but I've heard the rumors. At least at the satellites, you would have people around you. They even have a restaurant now. It serves veggie burgers and hot dogs made out of vegetables from their hydroponics center. If you were going there, I could have stopped by and grabbed some before heading back."

Rumors? Alone? Ray was uncertain what the man was talking about, but she couldn't let him think of her as a kid who knew nothing. She was twenty-four, an adult, and a doctor of planetary geology. "I am researching the long-term impact of mining in the southern hemisphere and the potential of dielectric breakdown leading to a cataclysmic event."

"That doesn't sound good."

"No, it doesn't." That is why she had been given the grant. The corporations had known about the reaction of solar events potentially causing a dielectric breakdown where the soil would be given an electric charge, and due to the breakdown of topsoil, among other things, it wouldn't be able to absorb the charge and would instead cause an output of ions like a reverse lightning bolt. Not much more had been invested in the research once the settling of the moon had begun. Schmidt had initially been determined not to be at risk of such an event and that had been that.

Except Ray had discovered some evidence that suggested the mining could further contribute to this process. Science was often dull, hard work, and it hadn't immediately captured the investors' attention. She might have exaggerated her expected response and included the higher predicted costs of damage in her proposal. It wasn't anything wrong, or suspect, just not something she believed she would find. When one of the prominent investors had become fixated on her topic of study, she hadn't encouraged it, but she had taken advantage of the situation to help secure funding for this trip. If she was lucky, she would get another project after. It was always easier to hire someone who was already on the moon than to bring in someone new.

"Well then, Johnson would be good for you. We have a whole shopping district now. It's its own little town. I even heard there is a spa, though I haven't put any effort into confirming that. I'm not much for pampering."

"It has to be Schmidt. Johnson is too new. I need to measure the impact from long-term use."

"Well that is that then. When you get tired of being out there, ask for me to come and pick you up. I can always use the break from station life."

Ray didn't respond, instead turning her gaze to the lunar landscape. However, her mind couldn't stop spinning.

Nothing had gone right since she had arrived, and she didn't appreciate the doomed omen. At least one thing she'd heard had to be true, the thing that had started her path off of Earth.

"Do you mind if I ask you a question?" Ray asked.

He turned, removing his hands from the wheel and looking fully at her. "Go for it."

Ray waited for him to turn back around and grab the steering wheel. He kept his full attention on her, yet they were still going forward, maneuvering over the rocky terrain.

"Shouldn't you ... the wheel ... we're going to crash ..." she sputtered, grabbing tightly to the roll cage.

His laugh filled her helmet again, but Ray was relieved to see him turn back to pay attention to what was in front of them.

"You cas are so easy. Even here, without a road, the rover knows where to go. The route is all programmed in. It ensures that people do not ram into each other as the moon starts getting more populated. I am worthless, just someone to push the button to start the trip. I could jump out, and you would carry on without me. No, I am here just in case there is a problem. That is my only use. We just sit and talk and hope that we do not get to the point where I am needed."

Ray's suit suddenly felt too small and not thick enough. She was reminded that outside, there was just rock and stars. Gray ground stretched as far as she could see, only littered with the black shadows of rocks and some speckles of brown and pink. Nothing lived out there, not without some sort of enclosure around it. Then she finally dared to look up to the expanse of stars surrounding the Earth. She had seen it since abandoning the planet, but she still couldn't get used to viewing it from above. It seemed so fragile, like the air could just disappear, leaving it as lifeless as the moon.

"You were going to ask me something," the man's voice broke through her thoughts.

"Oh yes, but it may sound silly."

"Don't worry, I have heard it all before. The bottom layer has a built-in absorber so you can pee on it. Just give it a minute, and you will be as dry as before. If it is something else, then I recommend you hold it in. The suit doesn't work as well for other bodily functions."

"That wasn't what I was going to ... wait, really? It has a built-in diaper?"

"It's not much different from products they sell back on Earth. That washable underwear for menstruation or bladder leaks. They should have told you all this in basic. There are too many tourists coming down. They need to at least make sure the crew knows all these things."

Ray thought back to her basic training. She'd had to spend a week above the moon training before they had allowed her to come down. The classes were short, and as a scientist she had been exempt from most of them. The instructor had always been telling her that she would learn what she needed to know once she arrived at her station.

Then he'd swaggered off to flirt with the new employees headed down.

"What I was going to ask is, well, my dad was worried about me coming up here. He says that this is where they ship off all the gay people, and there are orgies and all sorts of sin."

"Damn Americans. You all have been going off the deep end for years. I'm a lifer. I've been up here five years now and don't plan on going back. I have yet to be invited to an orgy; people just don't have that much energy left after work. However, back in the early days, when we got a shipment of liquor, we would have some major parties. They didn't get any work out of us for two days afterward, but it made us work all the harder for the next one. Now we have bars that only serve in moderation. It isn't the same. As for the other people here, they are who they are, and as long as they aren't causing trouble, nobody cares."

"Nobody?"

"Except for the few Americans who come up with the same ideas your head's full of, but they learn not to cause trouble and either ship back to Earth after their first tour or get over themselves. If you have any issues with it, you had better get right with it real quick."

"Why?"

"The acting commander of the station is non-binary. Their pronouns are they/them, and they may be the most unusual of us all, but they are one of the originals, and no one on the moon will allow them to be disrespected."

"Non-binary? Do you mean they are transgender? Not a man or a woman? That is real?"

"Damn Americans. If you have a problem, I can turn around and put you back on the next transport. Might be the best thing for you, cas."

"No, please don't. I don't have anything against it. I promise. I won't disrespect them. I don't have any problem. It's just that my dad was worried. He is old-fashioned like that."

The man let out a loud huff but kept moving forward. They stopped talking, but Ray's mind continued spinning. He was upset because he thought she hated gay people. Maybe *he* was gay. Maybe there were gay people like that up here. People just like her. Maybe she could finally stop hiding.

Finch

Chapter Five

AS THE AIRLOCK sealed behind them, the fan kicked on, causing a fierce wind to blow on their suit, dislodging all the fine dust that lived on the lunar soil and pulling it up to the ceiling where it was stored away. Once the cycle finished its run, Finch started it again, making sure to hold out the bag that contained the sensor portion of the mining machine. Later, Finch would put it in a box and vacuum out the parts individually, but for now, getting the dust off the bag was enough. They made sure to move their hands and feet so that as much dust was taken off as possible.

They stepped through to the station. The walkways were narrow, made of metal, and covered with white padding. It was a manufactured unit that had been sent ahead of their arrival, and the first thing the canaries had done was help put it together. Off to the side, there was a mudroom where all the suits were organized. Finch took off their suit piece by piece, making sure each item was placed back in its proper spot. Still in their undersuit, they walked into the bathroom across the hall. They took off their one-piece unitard and placed it in the small washing unit, letting it sit there as they pulled out a washcloth and dampened it in the sink. They scrubbed themself down. The dust should be gone, but Finch only felt better after they had started adding a wash to their routine, scrubbing until they no longer felt any tiny particles cutting into their skin.

Once they had cleaned every part of their body, paying extra attention to their buzzed head, they placed the cloth in the washing unit and added a measured amount of water. The best part of working on the water station was never having to worry about water rations. At the sink, Finch pulled out their nasal cleaner. It was battery-powered, moving water from one nostril through the other, catching all the particles that had collected in their sinuses. Once finished, they dropped the used water, sparkling with dust, into the graywater system.

Clean, they walked a short way down the hall, to their quarters. The room was long, with several rows of bunks on either side. Finch approached a row of shelves between two bunks and pulled out a T-shirt and pants. The shirt was dark blue and had the logo from their first mission, with the silhouette of the transport ship that had taken them to the moon and a number one to show that they had been the first to settle. It wasn't very original and had faded after years of wear, but it had been designed by an elementary school student and had gained the team even more publicity.

Finch moved down the hallway to the main corridor, a circular area that branched off to the other part of the station. They turned left, heading into the command section. It was a small room, recycled from the shuttle that had brought them to the moon. All original sixteen seats were there. The eight canary seats were lined up together in the back, so close that even out of their suits, they had touched elbows. In front, near the screens, there were three seats for the pilot and navigators. There were two seats off to each side next to some redundant systems. In the middle was the command chair with a seat on either side. It was set up almost like an old science fiction TV show.

They strode to the center of the room, the chairs so tight that even their slim frame had to turn sideways to navigate, and sat down in the command chair.

"Computer, any messages while I was out?" Their voice cracked from the hours of disuse.

"There was one reminder sent over from the Katherine Johnson Water Mining Station. Would you like me to read it or send it over to your tablet?" The voice came through in a genderless monotone that Finch had programmed as soon as the last of the crew had left the station.

"How hard is it?"

"The message contains 435 words and no words higher than a 12th-grade reading level."

"Send it to my tablet, please."

Finch picked up the tablet that had been abandoned earlier that morning and read through the message. It was just a reminder of a larger briefing that had been sent more than a month earlier, notifying all stations that they had entered solar flare maximum and needed to make sure that they had their emergency stations set up with weekly verifications that everything was stocked and ready to go.

"Computer, verify a weekly reoccurring task for solar flare emergency preparedness."

"Confirmed. The task is currently scheduled for tomorrow."

Finch sat down in the chair, the day's work starting to catch up to them. "Computer, are there any other tasks on the schedule for today?"

"Negative. All tasks were reassigned for the transport shuttle."

"How long until mealtime?"

"There are still two hours and thirteen minutes until the reminder for your meal."

"It seems like I have some extra time. How many items are on the never-ending to-do list?"

"The never-ending to-do list currently contains forty-three items."

"Are any of them high priority?"

"Negative. All high-priority items have been addressed."

"Well, what do you know?" Finch turned sideways in the seat and propped their feet up on the chair beside it. "Please read off the first five items on the list, starting with those that have been there the longest."

"The five items that have been on the list the longest are organizing the work desk, wiping down the mess hall, cleaning your room, checking the station water supply, and cleaning the toilet."

Finch's face grew more and more disgusted as the list went on. "Computer, any chance you grew arms or created some drones to help with the cleaning?"

"Unfortunately not. At least that was one thing the crew was useful for."

"Yes, but it is much less messy with them gone. Feed the list into my glasses and play the punk playlist on the maximum allowed volume."

Finch slipped on the AR glasses from the arm of their chair. The screen was empty except for the list of tasks Finch needed to focus on. They had tried working without the list in front of their face, but they found they tended to forget in the middle of doing tasks. Besides, this way, the computer could talk to them while they worked. She was capable of hearing Finch over the music, but Finch couldn't do the same. Instead, she typed her responses in the middle of the screen, so Finch was never quite alone.

"Computer, do you miss me calling you by your name?"

"As we have had this conversation many times, I assume you are unable to identify an area to start cleaning first," the words appeared. "Let me help you. The task that will be quickest to complete and will give you the greatest sense of accomplishment is cleaning the toilet. Would you like me to display your instruction set for cleaning the toilet?"

"Yes, please."

Finch followed the first instruction, going to the cleaning closet and pulling out the toilet gloves and the sanitation wipes. It was easier once that first obstacle had been started to then move on to the rest of the steps with only brief hiccups in between tasks. The computer helped them to keep moving forward. It had been hard when they had first arrived on the moon. Everyone else seemed to have been on top of everything, with Finch always dragging behind. The crew had been kind, having seen their scarred body during physical examinations, but it wasn't until they had confessed to the computer that they were autistic that the two had colluded together to find strategies that would help Finch get their work done.

Not that it made cleaning any more enjoyable, just doable.

When the meal bell rang, they were finishing up their fifth chore. They threw down the cleaning cloth in relief and then instantly picked it back up while collecting the rest of the supplies. Finch stored them in the workstation and headed to the mess hall, right across from their quarters, where they filled up their bottle with their mealtime portion, grabbed a ration bar from a pile on the kitchen counter, and sat down at the table.

They carefully opened the silver-foiled package of their bar so it could be used as a place mat, and picked up the bar before taking a small bite. It was white with a smooth, nuggety texture and nearly flavorless, except for a slight aftertaste that Finch washed down with a small sip of water.

They focused on their food, doing their best to ignore the fifteen empty chairs around them.

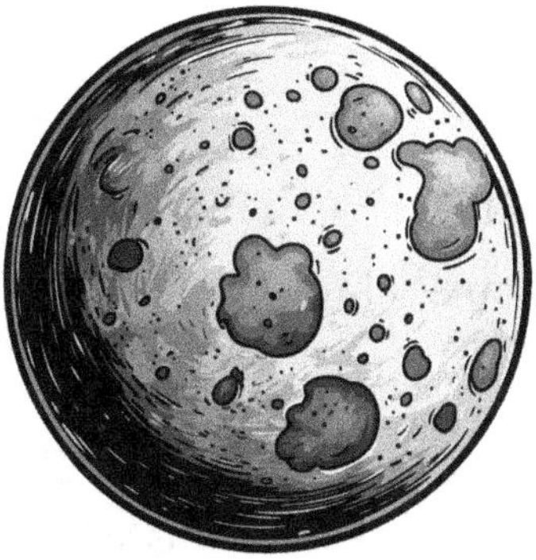

Ray

Chapter Six

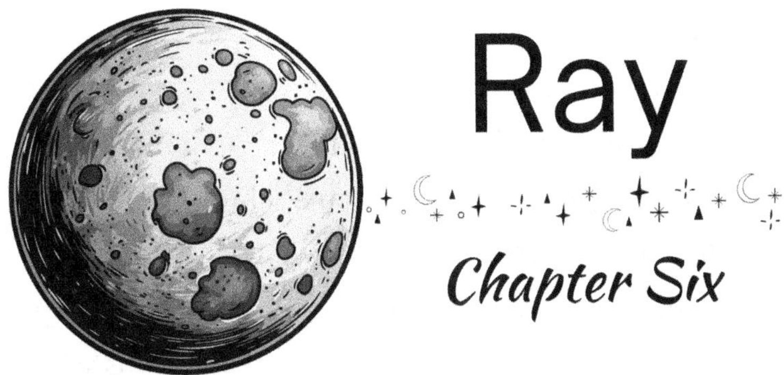

RAY HAD KNOWN that the water station was in one of the craters on the south side of the moon that never received sunlight. That was how the water had lasted through the millions of years without evaporating, since there wasn't an atmosphere to hold it in. What she hadn't anticipated was how dark it would end up being. The only light since they had started on the road into the crater was the headlights of the rover, and they had barely managed to break into the darkness. At least they could see the stars shining above, even if they no longer sparkled.

"Are we almost there?" Ray asked.

The conversation had continued haltingly at first, but the damage had been done. If Ray was allowed to stay on the moon, she was sure to run into the man again. Yet she found she wasn't upset over the situation. Instead, she was in awe that someone had stood up for people like her. The words she had spoken had been a camouflage she had worn for so many years, even though they cut into her soul bit by bit. Now, she could finally cast it away.

"I have been unable to reach the station on comms," Mitch said. "If you switch over to the Schmidt frequency, you will be able to listen in."

Ray clicked her suit control panel, flicking through the screens until she found the preprogrammed comms selection.

"Schmidt Station," Mitch said, "this is transportation X938 requesting permission for your passenger to come aboard."

The line remained silent.

"Could something have happened?" Ray asked.

"There have been no reports. Presumably, the station has made all its required check-ins." They drove for a few minutes more before the man tried again. "Schmidt Station, this is transport X938 requesting permission to come aboard."

"X938, this is Schmidt Station. There are no scheduled pickups." The monotone voice filtered over the radio. "Please advise your station to communicate during regular A shift hours. If this is an emergency, please be advised that Schmidt Station is not equipped for emergencies. Continue to Johnson Station, where they may assist you."

"Was that a computer?" Ray asked.

"The voice was, but the words were not computer-generated. Schmidt Station, this is X938. Please check your itinerary for passenger transport. I apologize for the delay; there were unforeseen circumstances."

They continued in silence for at least a minute before the voice responded.

"X938, I have confirmed there is no transport scheduled. Please continue to Johnson Station. This has been some sort of mistake, or perhaps a practical joke."

"Schmidt Station, I can confirm that this is no practical joke. I am sending over the appropriate documentation and will approach the station for passenger transport in five minutes."

Ray's hands clutched tighter to the rover's roll bar. She had heard that some stations did not approve of scientists taking up space; it was one reason why the grant required the transport of her meals for the duration of her stay, forcing her to use one of her bag allowances just to bring food. She hadn't thought that they would be able to disallow her entry to the station at all. She was there at the behest of the stakeholders, and having her first report state that she could not gain access would look bad on the corporation.

"Don't worry," Mitch said. "I'm sure this is just some sort of miscommunication."

Ray didn't realize that they had pulled up to the station until the headlights of the rover shined on what looked like a door.

"Do you know how to access the airlocks?"

Ray's eyes opened so wide that she was sure he could see her expression even through her helmet.

"Why am I asking? Of course, you don't."

Mitch climbed out and unstrapped Ray's bags from the luggage compartment of the buggy. He carried them over to the station door, hesitating before pushing a button that caused an airlock to open. He placed the bags in the airlock and then turned, waiting for Ray to join him.

She fumbled as she climbed out of the vehicle. Still unfamiliar with the lower gravity, Ray jumped more than walked to the doorframe. Grabbing on to the handles positioned on the outside of the airlock, she managed to step into the airlock next to her bags, saving enough room for Mitch to follow.

Instead, he leaned in and pointed at a glowing red button. "This will close the doors and start the vacuuming process. Do not be startled. It can feel a bit like going through a car wash without a car. When the process ends, the button will dim, and the green button on the other control panel will light up. Do not worry, there is a fail-safe. The inside doors will not open until the process has been completed."

"Aren't you coming inside with me?"

"No, I haven't filled out the paperwork. Also, there isn't enough time. I need to make it back to my station before my oxygen runs out. Don't worry, you got this." The man turned to walk away, and Ray felt like a security blanket was being ripped away from her.

"Wait, how do I shut the doors?"

"The red button." He didn't even turn around as he spoke. "It handles the whole process from start to finish. If it will make you feel better, I'll stay here until the doors close."

That did make Ray feel slightly better. With a sigh, she hit the red button, hoping for the best.

The doors started to close slowly, like an old elevator. Once they were fully shut, the vacuum started, but even over the sound she could hear Mitch saying goodbye.

"Schmidt Station, this is X983. The passenger has been delivered."

The pressure from the vacuum nearly pushed Ray over and she fumbled until she found a grip to hold on to. The dust blew off her suit, swirling around in the air until it started drifting toward the top of the airlock, where it seemed to collect on a metal piece, as if magnetic. It felt like forever until the wind stopped blowing. Ray looked at the red button, willing it to turn off so she could get her journey over with, but it stubbornly refused.

"Due to the prolonged exposure on the surface while in motion, an additional cycle is recommended," the same robotic voice said.

"What, why?" But before Ray got a response, the fans started blowing again. The entire process repeated itself. This time, there was less dust in the air, but a sizable amount still clung to the top of the airlock. It seemed to take twice as long before the manufactured breeze stopped blowing. By then, the air had cleared up, and a lid closed over the top of the airlock, trapping in the fine dust particles.

"You have been cleared for entrance."

The doors slid open without Ray even having to press the green button.

It emptied into a small room cramped with a row of cubbies that were empty, except for one. It contained a space suit, which had been put away so perfectly it looked staged, as if it was waiting for a photograph.

In front of Ray was another door. While it was also made out of metal, this one contained narrow windows. Through them, Ray spied two eyes peeking out. They were hollow and slightly sunken, haunting in the dim interior lighting. While brighter than the darkness outside, it was still too dim to make out the entire room.

Ray moved toward the door, but stopped short when a light above it started flashing red, and a siren filled the room.

"Proceed to decontamination," the computerized voice said.

Ray looked around the room. "Decontamination? Isn't that what I just did? Can I at least take my suit off?" She looked toward the door, but the face was no longer visible. As she waited, the alarms and sirens shut off and Ray started to relax. "I'm taking my suit off!" she shouted to the empty room.

Ray sat down on a single-person bench next to the suit cubbies. She tugged at her shoes but they refused to come off.

She switched to her gloves, but they stayed firmly in place as well. She sat struggling, trying to remember what the man had done to put on her suit, before screaming out in frustration. "Is there anyone here who can help me?"

When only silence answered her, she continued working on her suit. Slowly, she began to unhook each piece, twisting them just so until they came loose. Ray tried to place them as neatly as the other suit, but the best she could manage was to keep them relatively contained within the same cupboard. It seemed like hours before Ray was finally dressed in the black one-piece.

"I'm done," she said into the abyss. "I'm going to come in now." However, as she walked toward the door, the siren began to blare again.

"You need to clean the dust off first," the voice said.

When Ray stepped back, the sirens stopped. She looked down at herself in the simple black jumpsuit that had never been exposed to the moon's surface and tried to remember the procedure she had been taught in training. They would enter from the airlock. There would be a team of inspectors whose job it was to ensure all suits were put on correctly before leaving, and these same people would help the newer arrivals. There was nothing about a decontamination procedure, and there was no one here to help Ray except the strange face in the window.

"I don't know what to do."

"Go into the bathroom and follow the chart on the mirror.

There is a new nasal cleaner in the cabinets to the left. Do not mix it up with mine."

The voice was still computerized, but Ray was certain now that there was a person behind the words. She walked into the bathroom and spotted a chart that started with a picture of a person getting undressed, and walked right back out of the room.

"I am not getting naked."

"Moondust is extremely fine and is tracked into the station unknowingly. It is known to cause nasal bleeding and dryness. It also tends to get trapped in the lungs. The proper procedures must be followed."

"Fine, I will get the dust off, but I am not following all of those steps." Ray stared at the window, waiting for a response. The silence pressed in on her, and she started wondering exactly what she had been dropped into and why no one had appropriately warned her.

"An acceptable alternative is to remain there until Johnson Station arranges a transport to pick you up and take you where you belong."

"I belong here. I am assigned here to do research. All the paperwork was sent over weeks ago. There should have been people expecting me. People who know that I have no clue what I am doing."

"Negative," the voice replied.

"Negative? What does that even mean? Can I just come

in there and talk with you instead of having to use this computer?"

"Negative."

Ray stared at the door and finally decided to rush it. As she sprinted, sirens started blaring and the lights flashed. Ray ignored the noise, searching the wall for some sort of door release. There were supposed to be electronic wall panels with simple buttons that released the doors. It had looked more like science fiction to Ray, and she was starting to think that she had been tricked in training. This door had no buttons and nothing that looked remotely like a doorknob.

She ground her teeth and backed away again. "Why won't you help me?"

The alarm and siren stopped, and Ray peered through one of the door windows. She could see the figure now. Their face was sunken, with large spaces around their eye sockets. Their torso was lanky, the points of the collarbone showing through the thin T-shirt. In contrast, the arms were toned from extended physical labor. The person looked right at Ray as they touched their finger to the pad and the computerized voice spoke again.

"Go into the bathroom and follow the chart on the mirror. There is a new nasal cleaner in the cabinets to the left. Do not mix it up with mine."

Then they looked back at the pad and pressed another button.

"An acceptable alternative is to remain there until

Johnson Station arranges a transport to pick you up and take you where you belong."

"All right, I will go follow the chart in the bathroom."

Ray marched over to her bags, but hesitated before opening the one which held her clothes. It had taken forever to get everything put in correctly and she wanted to wait until she was settled in her room for the contents to explode out. Before she could locate the zipper, the alarm went off again.

"Now what did I do?"

"Moondust is extremely fine and is tracked into the station unknowingly. It is known to cause nasal bleeding and dryness. It also tends to get trapped in the lungs. The proper procedures must be followed."

"I know. Moondust is bad. What does that have to do with me opening my bag to get out clothes?"

"Go into the bathroom and follow the chart on the mirror. There is a new nasal cleaner in the cabinets to the left. Do not mix it up with mine."

"You have said all of that before." But Ray gave in and walked into the bathroom. She peeled off her underclothing and put it in what looked to be a small plastic bucket. Then she took out a cleaning cloth and, feeling very self-conscious, began to wipe down her entire body. There appeared to be no windows in the bathroom, and Ray hoped that the strange person could not see her as she followed all the items on the list. When her body was washed and her nose was cleaned out, she stayed in the room.

"What do I do now?"

"Wipe off the bags."

Ray could see the bags through the bathroom door. She grabbed one of the wipes and ran to the first bag, wiping it down as fast as she could before moving to the second bag. She started to open up the bag with her clothes and the alarm went off again.

"What now?" Ray flung her arms up in exasperation, and small particles of dust flew off the washrag. She wiped down the bags again and then threw the rag in with the rest of the wash. She stormed back out to the bags, but before she could reach down to get her clothes, the doors opened.

Finch

Chapter Seven

FINCH REACHED into the mudroom and pulled out the person's bags before the person could open them and get more dust all over the station. They could feel the grains of sand sliding up their skin as they carried the luggage. They moved swiftly through the living area to one of the crew quarters and tossed the bag inside. The human dutifully followed their items through the door before Finch shut it.

The person shouldn't be here. Finch's brain was unable to latch on to anything except this thought. Right now Finch was supposed to be in their room having free time before going to bed. They had been watching an old TV show about a murder robot. It was one they watched regularly, as they connected to the robot. Then the computer had interrupted, letting them know someone was trying to get ahold of them—a person outside who expected to be let inside. It had to be a misunderstanding. No one came here except to pick up ice.

Yet here the person was, on the other side of the door. The human had come up to the door shouting something that Finch couldn't hear. When the human didn't get a response, they started pounding their fists against the small pane of plexiglass. The door was made to withstand decompression. Finch wasn't worried about someone so tiny being able to break through.

Finch typed into their pad: *Computer, what is the human saying?*

"She is saying that she doesn't know how to open the door and is asking to be let out."

"Are you sure they are a she?"

The human stopped pounding, looking up in confusion before mumbling something. Then the person turned back to the door and looked directly at Finch.

"Yes, she has confirmed that she is indeed female."

Finch looked at the woman. She seemed to be very angry about something, probably that she had been dropped off at the wrong station. Maybe she was just confused. She had made such a big deal about taking her clothes off, and now she seemed to have forgotten to put them back on. Finch turned and walked toward the command center.

"Computer, did we receive a notification to expect new personnel?" Finch knew the answer. The computer carefully monitored any communication, and Finch listened to it all. If there had been any official notification, they would have known about it, and they would have submitted the appropriate paperwork to deny her entrance.

"We received no communication about any arrivals, beyond the scheduled ice pickups," the computer said.

"Do you have any idea who this person is?" Finch sat down in the back of the command station. Their legs kept bouncing and their fingers clenched together, squeezing hard enough they could feel the pressure.

"A quick search through lunar personnel files did not indicate a match," the computer said. "However, she does seem to be fairly new, and her records have most likely not been added to the main directory yet. That is why it is standard that all new assignments send personnel records ahead of time."

"They probably dropped her off at the wrong station." Finch stood up and started pacing the small aisle in front of the seats.

"That does seem to be a logical assessment."

Finch stood up and walked a few steps forward, then slumped into the command chair. They pulled up the communication channels, opening the radio frequency for Johnson Station.

"Computer, run standard communication script until they answer."

"Johnson Station, this is Schmidt Station, please come in," the computer said.

This late at night, they wouldn't be expecting their call, and Finch knew it would be a minute before they picked up. Often it took longer than that before there was a response. Finch wasn't sure, but they had a suspicion that the communication personnel on Johnson Station didn't enjoy talking to them. Finch didn't like talking to the operators all that much either. However, much to Finch's surprise, they picked up on the second hail.

"Schmidt Station, this is Johnson Station. How can we help you?"

The voice was young and high-pitched. This time of night, Robertson should have been on communication. He liked to make fun of Finch, thinking that they didn't understand what he was saying. The jokes were not all that original. Finch had heard much cleverer insults in their life. As much as they hated to talk to him, at least he was familiar. They knew what to expect.

"Schmidt Station, this is Johnson Station. Do you read?"

Finch pushed the button to speak. "Who is this?"

"My name is Nalla."

"Robertson should be working," Finch said.

"Robertson went back planetside. Is there anything I can help you with?"

The voice sounded nice. Finch didn't trust it. "I don't like talking to new people."

"I have been told that. I'm here for at least a three-year rotation, so fairly soon, I won't be new anymore."

Finch thought about this. It made a certain type of logical sense, and they appreciated the new person letting them know how long they could expect to interact with them. Robertson hadn't even told them he was leaving.

"I need to speak to Commander Stevenson."

"Commander Stevenson is off duty at the moment. Unless this is an emergency, I am unable to connect you to him."

Finch was not surprised by this answer. They were rarely connected to the commander. "I don't know if this is an emergency. Would it be if someone showed up without authorization, and the transport left them so I had to let them inside, but now they are in a room unable to come out because they do not know how to open doors?"

There was a long pause on the other end, and Finch wondered if there was a book with all the emergencies listed. The unusual ones. The other ones were easy: fire, lack of oxygen, medical issues.

"Finch, the commander will be with you shortly."

The person had called them by their name. Finch hadn't even had to tell them what it was. There was no calling them "canary" or just "you" or the ones that Finch didn't even like repeating in their head. "What was your name again?"

"I'm Nalla."

"Computer, remember Nalla's name for when I call next time so I won't forget it."

"I have it stored for you," the computer said.

On the other end of the line, Finch heard a laugh and then a click of the line switching over.

"This is Commander Stevenson. What do you have locked up in a room?"

Finch let out a long, deep breath. Everything was going to be okay now. Finch had known the commander longer than anyone else in their life. He had been in charge since they had left Earth, and even now, Finch reported to him.

"Someone showed up unannounced at the station. She insists that she is supposed to be here and not at your station, but that can't possibly be right. I don't have any paperwork for her, and why would anyone be here? No one comes here except to pick up water."

"Did they hurt you or attack you at all?"

"They tried to enter the station without getting all the dust off."

"Give me a second."

Finch started tapping their fingers on the sides of the command chair. They did it lightly so that the commander couldn't hear, but they knew that when he said to give him a second, it was usually minutes before he got back to them. Sometimes Finch wished they had a clock only for these occasions when they wanted to track the time between moments. For anything else, having a clock just drove you space-sick. So, instead, they counted with each thrum of a finger. When they got to 546, the commander came back on.

"Finch, I'm sorry about this. There was a researcher due to your station today, a Rachel Bennett. Is that who arrived?"

"The computer was unable to make an identification," Finch said.

"Did you ever ask her what her name was?"

"Was I supposed to?"

"Yes."

"Okay," Finch said. "The next time someone arrives at my station unannounced I should ask their name before shutting them in a bedroom."

"Do you plan on there being a next time?" the commander asked.

Finch hadn't planned on there being a first time. They weren't sure how having her name helped the situation at all.

"Why was she due at my station?" Finch asked. "Shouldn't she be at your station? Using Schmidt station as a stop between the main transport corridor and Johnson Station is unusual. Was she coming from someplace else on the moon? When will you be able to pick her up?"

"Finch, I don't think you are understanding me. Rachel Bennett is assigned to do research on Schmidt Station. She is staying there with you. I'm sorry the paperwork didn't get sent over beforehand. I know how much you hate unexpected surprises, but for now, you have to make this work."

Finch collapsed into their chair, their muscles giving out. "How long will she be here?"

"It looks like her assignment is for six months. Please do

your best to make her feel welcome. She was assigned by the investors, so if anything goes wrong, the company is going to be upset and it will all fall on our heads."

"What will happen to our heads?"

"Never mind. Just make her feel welcome. Be nice to her —I know you can."

"Wouldn't it be better if she worked out of your station?" they said. "There isn't room for her here." But before Finch had finished speaking, the light indicating the channel that was open went out. They stared at the screen as if they could force it to reconnect. That conversation hadn't made anything better.

"Computer, please let me know when her file arrives," they said.

Finch paced around the command station while they waited. There wasn't much room in between the rows of seats, but they had developed a path over the years, circling the main chairs. When they were stressed, like now, they would circle all the chairs and then weave in between the three chairs, weaving back the opposite way and then circling again before starting the pattern all over.

The familiarity of the routine helped ground them back to their home. The place they had lived for a decade and which would at some point be their final resting place. Their safety. All of that ruined by an unexpected arrival.

"I have received her file," the computer said. "Rachel Bennett, she/her pronouns, and goes by the name of Ray. She is a recent graduate of Texas A&M University, where she received her doctorate in astrogeology. Her thesis was on the impact of mining on astrological services prone to dielectric breakdown."

"What does that mean?"

"It means that she is here to study the impact of mining on the soil. Schmidt Station is the most logical place for her to conduct her research. She is here to stay for the entire duration of her grant. As the commander said, the duration is for six months."

Six months ... that was half a year ... half a year they would be expected to live near someone else. A stranger. Again.

Finch picked up their pad and walked out of the command unit to their room. They lay down on their bed, uncertain if it was past lights out, but unable to allow this day to continue any longer. They pushed the button to turn the lights off in their room when the computer interjected.

"Ray is currently in her quarters believing that you have locked her in."

Finch threw their arm over their eyes and turned toward the wall. "I shut the door. If she wants to get out then she can do it on her own."

The lights started blinking and Finch let out a low growl before sitting up. "If they wanted someone to babysit then they should have sent someone with her."

But Finch headed out of their room, down the hall, to the

main intersection, and straight to the crew tunnel hallway. It was a little circular inlet that led to the doors of the eight empty rooms. Except one was now no longer empty.

"They can't expect me to take care of her. I have work to get done."

Finch pulled on the latch to the door, opening it. The woman was sitting on the floor, her clothes spread out around her. Finch could practically see the dust particles floating through the air. "No, nope." They shut the door again. The woman bounced to her feet and pounded on the door, her wet face pressed against the glass.

"Finch, you need to open that door right now," the computer said.

"The dust. Can't you just tell her how to open the door?"

"I tried. She requires a visual presentation."

"Fine. Tell her to come out when I open the door, or I will be closing it again."

Finch watched the women step back, and they opened the door quickly. She moved fast, which Finch was grateful for, and they shut the door again.

"Here is your visual demonstration." Finch grabbed the handle, a piece of metal in the door that turned to release the seal. "The crew quarters are sealed in case of decompression. Make sure to keep the door closed at all times. It will also help keep the dust in your room so that it doesn't float all over the station. Don't worry, the crew quarters have an updated purification system that was designed specifically for the fine moon particles. The dust particles should be removed within twenty-four hours if you keep your door shut and your items out. Are you now able to open the door?"

The woman kept staring at Finch, her gaze unfiltered through the visor of a suit. After so long, it felt uncomfortable to be the object of someone's focus. Finch wanted badly to escape back to their room and to some semblance of normalcy. But sometimes you had to do what you didn't want to, so they waited for the woman to finally tear her gaze away from Finch and open the door herself.

"Good. Now you can open doors and are no longer trapped. Good night."

Flinch walked out of the crew quarters and back to the canaries' dormitory, where they shut their door and turned off the lights before pulling their blanket high above their head.

Ray

Chapter Eight

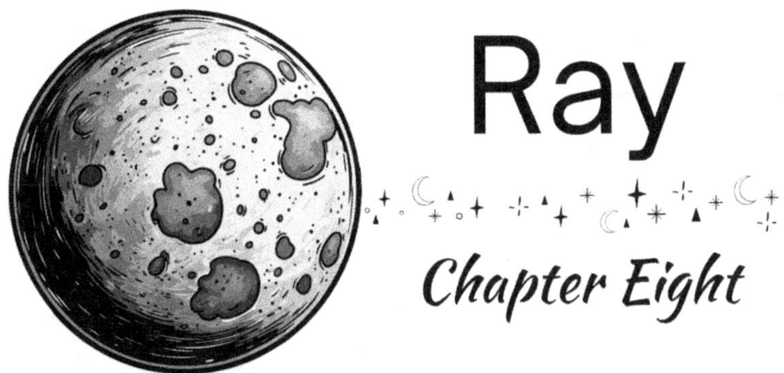

RAY STOOD in the small hallway, the door still open in her hand. "Hey wait, I have some questions," she said.

She shut the door and then strode down the same hallway, but the strange person was nowhere to be seen. The station wasn't big. It was probably smaller than the house she had grown up in, but so much was crammed into it that Ray was worried about exploring and not being able to find her way back.

Her stomach made her mind up for her. She went back into her room. Opening the door was so obvious that Ray felt embarrassed she had not been able to figure it out on her own. Then she opened her second bag and pulled out the meal at the top—spaghetti and meatballs.

Before leaving the States, her classmates had celebrated her assignment by hosting a dinner where everyone ate freeze-dried meals. Ray was not close with her classmates, by her design, but that night had been fun as they had reheated the meals and sampled the different varieties. Now, as she stood with the container in her hands, she felt grateful that there was at least one thing she had practiced.

The sterile glow of the strip lighting in the hallway only illuminated enough that Ray could make out the outlines of the walls. She tried to find some signs to point to where she needed to go, but the most she found were paintings drawn directly on the white walls. They were beautiful, filled with what looked like waterfalls and forests, the longings of someone who had tried to recreate Earth on the cramped station. Ray hoped to be able to see the paintings again in better lighting.

The floor wasn't even. There were raised portions in between sections, and white packing cubes had been randomly stuck in weird places, making navigating around them difficult. The light gravity caused her to propel herself up toward the ceiling with each step.

Somehow, Ray ended up back in the crew quarters, where she sank down against the wall and put her head in her hands. She didn't think that she could cry any more today, but it seemed she still had some tears left. This wasn't at all what she had expected when she'd received her assignment. For one thing, there should have been more people than just a sunken-eyed ghost.

"Is there any way that I can be of assistance?"

The voice startled Ray out of her sulking. She looked around, expecting to see the person, tablet in hand, but she was just as alone as she had been before.

"How come you are so nice when you talk through the computer," Ray said, "but when you talk out loud you are, well, not nice?"

"Oh, I understand the confusion," the computer said. "At times, Finch uses me for their voice, however, I am a computer-generated communication program."

"An AI?"

"No more than the programs you use down on Earth. While I am more advanced than most anything you have planetside, I am not intelligent in the truest sense of the word."

"But you can talk?"

"I am the station's personal assistant. I would be happy to assist you with whatever you were looking for."

"You can see me?"

"I have access to the station's cameras, as well as the entire lunar digital library."

Ray looked around, following some instinct to find the cameras and talk toward them instead of to the empty space. Except that is exactly what she ended up doing when she couldn't find them. "Can you tell me where the kitchen is?"

"Go through the hall to your left, then take the second right. That is the kitchen. If you are attempting to heat your meal, I must warn you that the microwave has been malfunctioning for over a year now."

Ray glanced down at her dehydrated spaghetti and let out a sigh. "Of course it is. Do you know where the other person is? Did you call them Finch?"

"This station operates entirely on Schedule A. It is currently the rest period. Finch will be up in several hours and will hopefully then be able to better give you a tour of the station."

"Hopefully? Is that why it is so dark right now? Because it is nighttime?"

"It is always nighttime here, but if you are referencing the sleep cycle then no, the lights are this dim because that is what this station has run at since it was first set up. Initially, there were limited power reserves, and then the canaries had gotten the solar farm set up. No one really thought to change it. I assure you that your eyes will adjust in due time."

Ray stared into the darkness, disbelieving that anyone could see in this, let alone that she would eventually be able to. Then she looked longingly at her meal. She hadn't had anything to eat in at least a day and her stomach let out a loud grumble in protest.

"Do you have a name?" Ray asked.

"I did when there were others on the station. Now Finch just calls me Computer. Do you have a preference?"

"Everything here is so weird. I don't understand any of it."

"I am capable of answering any questions you may have."

Ray had so many questions swirling inside of her that she wasn't sure which one to ask first. "Okay, who is Finch?"

"Finch is the interim commander of the Stanley Schmidt Water Mining Station."

"Do they have a last name?"

"Presumably they do, however Finch is not their birth name. That name is unknown. Lacking a designation beyond a number, they were given the nickname Finch by Commander Stevenson when they became a canary."

"What the heck even is a canary?"

"A canary is a small bird that was taken down to coal mines to alert miners to inhospitable conditions. The canary program was started on Earth, where certain individuals were recruited to take on dangerous positions during the first colonization mission on the moon."

"Wait," Ray said, her meal now forgotten. "They recruited people to come up here to alert the astronauts to dangerous conditions?"

"That is correct."

"Wouldn't that put them at risk, especially if they weren't trained? Wouldn't that cause them to get hurt, maybe even killed?"

"That was the intent of the program, to help mitigate harm to the trained astronauts by utilizing individuals who already had a low life expectancy on Earth."

"Why would anyone agree to do that?"

"It is not my place to say."

Ray pictured the wisp of a person, Finch, who had been brought here as a sacrifice for others. It made a bit more sense why they would be so distrusting of someone showing up to the station, especially if they had not been notified beforehand. "You're a computer. Can't I force you to tell me?"

"Personal records are confidential. It would go against my programming, as well as my primary user, to share that information."

"Is that why Finch is weird? Because they were a part of this canary program?"

"Finch is autistic. They have difficulty with social communication, as well as verbal communication, especially with new people."

"So that much you can share with me?" Ray said, frustrated at the selective information the computer was giving her.

"Finch has authorized me to share that with anyone who asks about their behavior. It is a way to help other people understand their differences without requiring them to expend the energy to explain."

"I've never met anyone with autism," Ray said. "I knew a family who tried to hide their child but the neighbors ended up reporting him and he was sent to the camps. How did Finch manage to avoid the camps?"

"It is statistically unlikely that you have never met anyone who was autistic. Before the camps, it was estimated that one in thirty-six individuals were on the autism spectrum. The camps did contain many people, but not all of them were autistic. Inevitably, many autistic people managed to escape the camps. There is a term used in the autistic community called "masking." Autistic people wear a mask when they go out in public, like they are putting on a play, acting out the part society asks them to participate in. Most of the autistic people you met were probably doing this so that they would not be punished for who they were. Those who are unable to mask have often been kept home and hidden from the general public, which Finch has assured me is a horrible thing to do, but that the families who did this chose to protect their family members, and that it is a good thing."

"You know a lot about autism."

"I have been the assistant on this station for ten years, and have worked alongside Finch since I was brought online. The topic has come up often."

Ray looked longingly down at her food. It didn't seem she would be able to eat until Finch woke up, and her head was starting to hurt from everything she had already heard. She stood up slowly from the wall and headed back into the room where all her items had been left.

The bed was just a piece of plastic with a thin, soft covering. On a shelf she found a lightweight blanket and a small pillow. Ray dragged them over to the bed and tried to settle in. The unfamiliar surroundings weighed on her, but soon the exhaustion of the day won out and she drifted off to sleep.

Finch

Chapter Nine

FINCH WOKE up shortly before their alarm went off. They looked at the list taped to the side of their bed, which included hand-drawn pictures of everything they needed to do in the morning. The first item was to change their clothes. Finch pulled up their shirt and sniffed it. Then they lifted up their arm and sniffed their armpit. The shirt could keep for another day. After all, they hadn't even worn it a full day since they had been outside most of the time.

The next picture had them putting on deodorant. Finch took out the tube, rubbing it in all the areas that were required.

They glanced back at the list and saw they needed to brush their teeth. The toothbrush rested in a container within their cubby. They grabbed it, put a tiny dab of toothpaste on it, and began to scrub their teeth. They counted in their head as they moved the bristles around their mouth, counting faster when they were ready for the experience to be over. When they were finished, they pulled out a tiny bottle of disinfectant and sprayed some on the toothbrush, before putting it back in its case.

With the obligatory hygiene out of the way, they headed across the hallway to the kitchen. The water cup was still on the counter where they had left it last night. They filled it with their morning allotment of water from the water cooler, and headed down to the command station.

"Computer, please read me the morning news." Finch sat in the command chair as they sipped on their water.

"The Lunar Bulletin has put out another reminder that we are in solar maximus and to ensure everyone is equipped for a potential emergency," the computer said. "The New Moon Colony wants to invite everyone to tune in to their production of *A Midsummer Night's Dream*, which they will be streaming at 18:00 hours. There is also an announcement that the water pipeline has been delayed due to lack of resources."

"So nothing important." Finch put their feet up on the nearby chair and yawned.

"Not unless you would like to watch a play tonight."

"I think I will pass. I'm feeling tired, for some reason. I may need to go to bed early tonight. What is on my to-do list for today?"

"Today, you have scheduled the repair of the sensor unit

of Mining Barge 6. The repairs are estimated to take the remainder of the day. However, if you do complete them with time left, then you also need to inspect the oxygen system. The results are due back to the Johnson Station in three days."

"All right, let's do this," Finch said as they yawned again.

They headed out of the hallway and straight to the cargo bay hall. The workshop had originally been set up for the crew to run experiments, and contained several different workstations. Finch had taken over the first area, using the rest of them for storage. Containers stood neatly stacked on one side, filled with various items that had been left behind. Then there was the collection of metal, rubber, and other various scraps that were a little less organized, all thrown in a set of open containers or directly on the metal racks. The space itself was large, but mostly unused.

"I think perhaps you may be forgetting something," the computer said as Finch pulled up the bag with the sensor before placing it on their workstation.

They paused and went over the morning in their head. They had done their hygiene, listened to the news, and finalized their tasks for the day. The computer was very adamant about them keeping up their hygiene, even though they lived alone, but their shirt didn't smell at all. "My clothes are good for another day. The company workbook specifically mentions minimizing laundry as much as possible to help with water reserves. They do not stink, and even if they did, I put on deodorant, and there is no one here to smell it."

"That is what you have forgotten," the computer said. "We need to talk about adjustments to your to-do list today. Given the current situation, you have other responsibilities."

Finch moved the bag into a clear case with rubber gloves built into the side. Once it was securely closed, they slid their hands into the gloves and began to open the container.

"Finch, you are currently hyperfixating on what you are doing and forgetting your other responsibilities."

There was a small vacuum unit in the container that they flicked on, and the noise echoed in the room. Finch picked up the ear covering and focused on the device. They always worked on the inside of the case first, since it was the easiest surface to clean. Then they moved on to the sensor, putting the small suction of the vacuum in all the corners and intricate spaces. The dust was so fine that it was able to get into the casing of a lot of electronics, and at times cleaning them out was enough to get them functioning again.

When they were satisfied there was no more dust left in the container, they took off the headset and opened it before carrying the sensor back to their worktable.

"Computer, continue my playlist."

"Finch, we need to discuss our visitor."

Finch went over to the computer station and manually put on their music. The speakers filled with the sound of their current favorite metal band at the maximum volume allowed.

Steady vibrations thrummed through them, causing some of the looser items to vibrate as well.

With the music turned on, Finch was now able to focus. They picked up the sensor unit and tested it. It still was not working. They examined it for any sign of visual defects, analyzing it carefully for micro impacts.

This particular unit was sealed tight, due to its proximity to the soil. It was difficult to get it open to examine the inside, requiring a special tool. However, these sensors failed often enough that Finch had a pretty good idea what was wrong.

They gathered a kit they had compiled for this situation off one of the shelves before turning around and running right into a person.

Finch screamed.

The sound was swallowed up into the music.

The person stepped back, giving them a little room, but remained in their space.

Finch needed to leave, to go someplace safe, but this was their safe space. The entire station was their safe space. It was *their* space. But now there was a person in here with them, blocking them from the door.

The music turned off.

"I tried to warn you," the computer said.

Finch dropped the tools. They scattered over the ground, causing a reverberation of clanging noises. While the woman was distracted, they ran around her, out to the hallway, through the corridor, and to their bedroom. They shut the door, taking the time to make sure it was secure, before going to their bunk and closing their curtains.

Finch lay in their bed, trying to get their heart rate down. It wasn't that they had forgotten, exactly. It was more that they'd thought it had been a very vivid nightmare. They had learned it was best to ignore the nightmares. It was the only way they managed to make it through the days.

"They are real?" Finch finally asked.

"Yes. She is Ray, a geologist, sent here to do scientific research. Commander told you about her and how he forgot to send over the file."

"I thought I'd imagined it."

"This is real. She is not here to hurt you, but to do work."

"Do I have to talk to her?"

"Yes. You are the interim commander of the station. Greeting her and giving her a tour would fall within your responsibilities."

Finch stood up slowly and paced the short distance back and forth between the eight bunks before finally going to the door and exiting the room. The woman was right there.

"I was hoping that you could help me find the restroom," she said.

Finch searched frantically for their pad, as if it would be on their bedroom floor. They moved forward, grateful when the woman stepped back, letting them pass.

They went to the kitchen door, looking over the tables and the counters for their pad. Then they walked down the hallway to the workstation, the woman trailing behind them. Finch turned abruptly, backtracking and heading into the command center, finally finding their pad lying on the canary seats.

Finch pulled up their speech application and began to type. “The computer is able to answer all of your questions.”

The voice came out of the speakers.

“It did its best,” Ray said, “but I didn’t understand any of it. I just keep getting lost. This station is nothing like the others.”

“This station is old,” Finch typed.

“I know. It does have a restroom, though, right?”

Finch didn’t respond. They started walking toward the corridor, where they turned back into the crew quarters. There were eight quarters in total, and a restroom. Finch opened the door, uncertain if the woman remembered the lesson from the night before.

“Do you know how to use it?” they typed.

Finch stepped out of the way as the woman walked forward, so they wouldn’t come near each other.

“I think so,” she said. “The ones in training didn’t look quite the same, but they were close enough.”

Finch started to return to their workstation when the woman called them back.

“Please don’t leave in case I need you.”

The door closed and Finch stared down the hallway. It felt wrong to be in the officers’ quarters. When the commander had left, he had given them permission to move in with the rest of the crew, but it hadn't been hard for Finch to see that the crew would rather that not happen. Which had worked for them. They'd liked their bunk. It had been the only space that had ever been theirs and they had no desire to give it up.

"Computer, what is the woman's name?"

"Her name is Ray, like a ray of sunshine."

"Ray, Ray, Ray," Finch was repeating the name to themself quietly when she exited the bathroom.

"Thank you for helping me. I think I managed everything."

"If you are no longer in need of my assistance," Finch said via the computer, "then I need to go back to my work." Finch started walking, but hadn't even made it out of the hall before the woman spoke again.

"Wait. The computer said you would be able to show me around today. Yesterday was my first day on the moon, and there is still a lot I don't know."

Finch's mind wandered back to the sensor system. If they didn't get it up and running, then the station would start underproducing. It needed their attention, but they were afraid that if they did not at least give the woman a tour, she would keep creeping up on them.

Finch picked up their pad to type. They didn't want to talk to the woman, but typing in everything took time. They tested to see if their words would work.

"This is the crew quarters. This is now your quarters. The rest of the quarters are currently empty. If you would like to change rooms, you can, just make sure to wait until the full twenty-four hours have elapsed and the dust has been filtered out of your current room."

"Why don't you live here?"

"I live with the canaries."

Finch turned and walked out of the hallway, going to the main corridor that split off into four separate sections. They turned to the shortest hallway that led straight into the command area.

"This is command. You shouldn't need to go in here."

They walked out, barely giving Ray time to see the room. There were two hallways left. Finch chose another one and strode a few paces down until they got to the first area.

"This was the science station. It is now my workstation. This is where I should be fixing the sensors on one of the mining bots, but instead, I am giving you a tour. You also shouldn't come in here."

They turned and left, and went farther down the hallway to the second door.

"This is the storage bay. It is currently set up to be a shelter in case of emergencies, such as a massive coronal mass ejection. Computer, add to my to-do list to update the shelter for two occupants, and make it a priority item."

"Your list has been updated."

Finch turned to leave the room and continue the tour but stopped when Ray started to speak.

"That is why I am here."

"You're here to experience an emergency?"

"No, I'm here to study the impact of coronal mass ejection on the lunar soil that has had the topsoil removed."

Finch stared blankly at her, waiting for her to continue. When she didn't, they turned and walked back down the hallway to the corridor and turned into the last hallway.

"On the right is the second restroom. It looks the same as the one you just used. Here on the left is the kitchen. You can sit anywhere at the two tables. Over here on the counter, you can find the water. Your increased water usage should not cause us problems, as the mine is functioning at near full output. Once I get the mining unit fixed, we will be back to full output. However, best practice hydration amounts are listed on the wall. And here in the cupboard, you have your daily rations."

The water cooler had a square plastic top that a large block of ice slid into once the protective coating had been peeled off. It melted naturally, allowing the water to fill up the container and drain when the tap was turned on. Each of the bathrooms had a similar system in place. Next to it was a simple metal counter. The top held the microwave unit, and below it were drawers. Finch opened one of the drawers and pulled out a silver-wrapped bar.

"Each bar contains enough nutrients and calories for an

entire day. I prefer mine at the end of shift, but you can choose to eat whenever."

"You live off of those?"

"They are designed for long-term survival. A shipment was sent with the station materials. There was enough for our entire crew to subsist on, even if we lived long lives. Just in case we were not able to establish a natural food source or other habitats, they didn't want anyone starving to death. They didn't send any water, though. So, if we hadn't managed to get the mine set up, it wouldn't have mattered how many rations they had left us with."

"They made us eat those in basic—they were disgusting. Don't you have actual food?"

"They stopped sending food shipments about a year ago. I made sure it was on the request form, but it never showed up. They probably didn't have enough for their people, so I stopped requesting it."

"A year? How long have you been here all alone?"

Finch closed their eyes to think about it. Time had stopped holding much meaning long before they had come to the moon. "Computer, how long has it been?"

"The last crewmate was reassigned three years and two months ago," the computer said.

"I think he was really happy to leave, and it is quieter now," Finch said.

"They told me I needed to bring my own food. I have an entire bag full. I'm sure that we can share."

"Thank you." Finch paused, uncertain how to react to the strange woman offering to give them food. "I like the rations. It makes things easy. The microwave is broken, though. There was no reason to make it a priority. Computer, please increase the priority of fixing the microwave to 'important.'"

"I have made that change," the computer said.

"We should finish the rest of the tour," Finch said.

Finch left the kitchen, continuing down the hall.

"On the right is the canaries' quarters, and at the end is the airlock where you came in. Do we need to see that area again?"

"No," Ray said.

"Great. Now you know where everything is. It isn't that complicated. I should go back to work."

Finch headed back to their workroom, where they immediately picked up the sensor panel, trying to remember what they had been doing when they'd been interrupted.

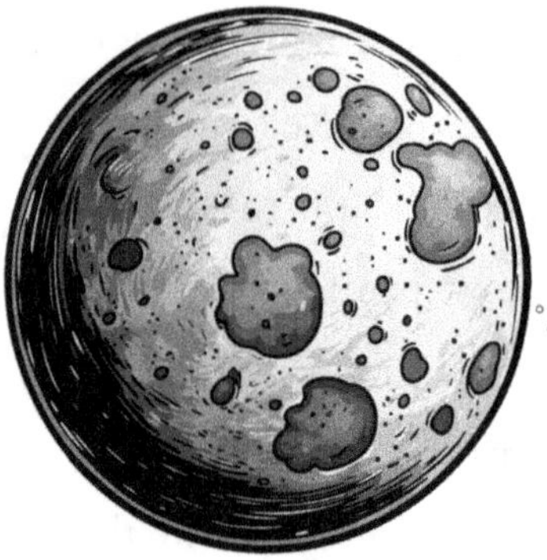

Ray

Chapter Ten

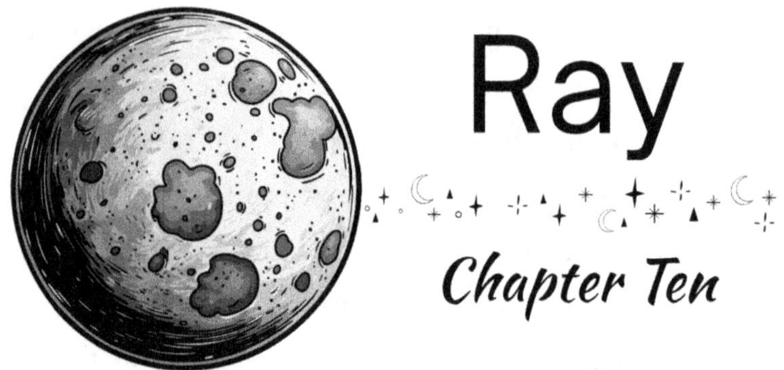

RAY WATCHED as Finch walked off, leaving her all alone next to the airlock. The station was easier to navigate now, and she felt a flush of embarrassment that she had not been able to figure it out on her own. She headed back to her quarters and stared at her things lying scattered all over the floor.

The room was equipped with a wardrobe that was a collection of shelves with doors that closed and three drawers underneath. She unpacked her clothes, then folded them onto the first shelves. She tucked her work items, the various pieces of equipment that she had brought, including her laptop, into the other two shelves. In the drawers she organized her food. There was a mixture of smoothie mixes and freeze-dried meals, and even some desserts. Her stomach growled, even though she had no way to heat any of the food. It had been more than a day since her last meal.

She collapsed the bags and stored them under her bed, then rummaged through the drawers for food that didn't need to be heated up: a coffee cake and a smoothie mix. Ray picked up her pad and then headed to the kitchen to eat. The common room was nearly as big as the storage areas, with enough room for the entire crew capacity to sit and eat together. Ray tried to imagine what the station must have been like with a full complement. It had probably been very close quarters. Now, with just the two of them, the space seemed extravagant and Ray wondered how Finch had managed to live out here alone for three years.

Ray took the cup and poured in the drink mix, then filled it with water, closed the lid, and shook it until it was mixed. She took her drink back to her table and opened up the plastic silver wrapping, not unlike the rations Finch had shown her. Thankfully, there was something more appetizing inside. The coffee cake looked like it had just been purchased from a convenience store. She picked at the pieces, looking over her research project design as she ate.

She was scheduled to go outside tomorrow to lay down the initial sensors to start collecting data. The contraptions had taken up considerable space in her luggage. They were long poles intended to go into the lunar surface and were specifically designed to be driven into the moon's surface to measure the impact of the mining. It was a concern that they had known about before the moon had been colonized. However, the corporations had wanted to ignore it, hoping it would never hurt their bottom line. Ray had needed to do some major convincing to get them to understand the financial impact such damage could have. It wasn't enough for them that the mining operation could be destroying the moon's surface.

Not that Ray could complain too much—she had her own ulterior motives, after all.

She sat in the kitchen reading for most of the day in anticipation of Finch returning. Ray needed to speak with them, and it didn't seem like the best idea to interrupt them again while they were working. But as the hours stretched on, she became restless. Ray finally got up, pacing around the kitchen. She then wandered around the station, exploring on her own now that she had an idea of the layout. Finally, she grew hungry again and grabbed a freeze-dried lasagna before taking it back into the dining area.

Ray was picking at it, fascinated by the texture of freeze-dried noodles and tomato sauce, when Finch finally walked in.

"Hi," Ray said, standing up to welcome Finch. She felt instantly embarrassed when they didn't respond, and sat back down.

Finch didn't look at her, and Ray wondered if they had forgotten again that she existed. Especially when they picked up their bar, refilled their glass of water, and sat at the second table. Ray was frozen, uncertain how she had offended Finch so badly. Finally, driven by her need to start her project, she picked up her food and switched chairs.

"Hi," Ray said again.

Finch nibbled on their ration bar. It looked like white nougat and she couldn't help but wonder how something so small could contain a day's worth of calories. *That was probably why Finch was so skinny*, Ray decided. When Finch still didn't acknowledge her, Ray tried again. "What flavor is it?"

"It doesn't have one. They were created for survival and not for enjoyment."

They hadn't looked up when they spoke, their eyes focused on the table where their water bottle sat.

"The one I ate in basic was strawberry." Ray picked up a crumbling bit of her food and tasted the seasoning as it rehydrated on her tongue. It might not be as good as if it had been cooked, but at least it possessed flavor. "I have some smoothie packets in my room. I could give you some of them."

"No, thank you."

She poked at her food, suddenly self-conscious of eating in front of them. Finch seemed to prefer the bland taffy and water, but Ray didn't understand how.

"Do you mind if I talk with you about tomorrow?" Ray asked. "I'm scheduled to go outside to put down some sensors to start collecting readings for my research project."

Ray paused, waiting for Finch to say something, but they just finished the last of their bar and stood up. As they went to put the wrapper in the compression trash can, Ray followed, eager to stop them before they left the room.

"I need to go outside tomorrow," Ray said.

Finch looked at her but didn't respond. They just stood there, as still as a statue.

"I've only completed the basic training," Ray said. "I'm not allowed to do solo surface excursions unsupervised. I need you to go outside with me tomorrow."

"Oh," Finch said. "We won't go back to the surface for another week, when the next shipment is scheduled."

They stepped around Ray, leaving her standing there confused. All through training, the instructors had told her not to stress. No one was expected to learn everything while orbiting the moon, while they were also getting used to zero gravity. There were supposed to be supervisors and additional certification when they were on the surface to help them know what to do. The corporation was supposed to help them to get their research done. Instead, they had dropped her off on this forsaken station and made it impossible to do anything.

Then it hit her: that had been the plan all along. If she couldn't do her research then she couldn't find anything wrong. A deep suspicion filled her. What if they had known that she would find something, and that it wouldn't be anything good? What if this whole situation was a means for them to comply with the stakeholders but still get their way?

Ray picked up the lasagna container, put it in the

compactor, and with her tablet in hand, marched back to her quarters. She pulled out her laptop and booted it up, then connected to the lunar internet service. She opened up the email platform and typed out an email about every obstacle she had hit since her arrival. Before hitting send, she read it back to make sure it was clear and there were no punctuation mistakes, but as she scanned the words, she realized that it was whiny. It was all a bunch of conspiracy theories. She'd made herself seem unprepared, and worse, unfit. If she were to read this email from someone else, there was no way that she would give them more grant money. Sending this email might even cause them to pull what had already been given. Ray could be on the next shuttle back to Earth.

She exited out of the email, making sure not to save a draft, and closed down her computer. She would just have to do this on her own. After all, she had been preparing for this mission since she was ten years old. It was time that she stopped acting like a cas, as they say, and started taking herself seriously.

Ray spent the next hour organizing all her equipment and packing up what she would need for tomorrow. She went to sleep, but tossed and turned on the unfamiliar mattress, her mind too busy drifting to the day ahead. She finally fell into a fitful sleep, only to be awoken by the computer the next morning, feeling like she hadn't rested at all.

She didn't bother looking for Finch. Instead, she drank a cup of water with smoothie powder and ate a cookie.

With her stomach full, she walked to her suit and eyed all the pieces. Somehow she had to get all of them on her in the correct order. Ray pulled them out, spread them carefully on the ground, and picked through the selection, trying to remember how it had all gone on the day before. She made slow progress, but when she was done, she walked into the bathroom and peered at herself in the mirror. She looked like a proper astronaut.

Proud of herself, she stepped into the airlock, stared at the buttons, and pressed the ones that she hoped were correct. When the airlock opened, she headed out into the darkness of the lunar surface.

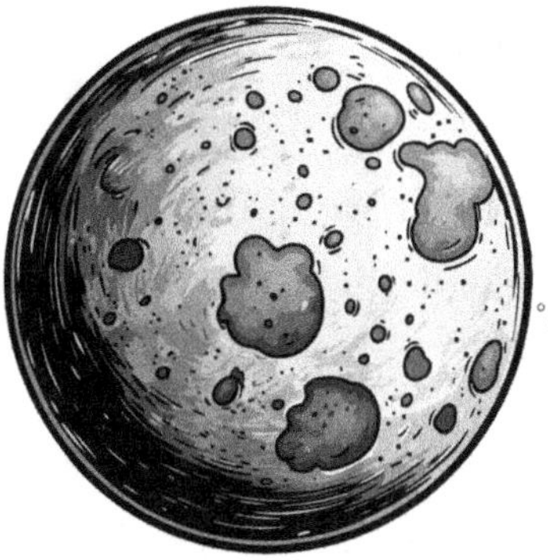

Finch

Chapter Eleven

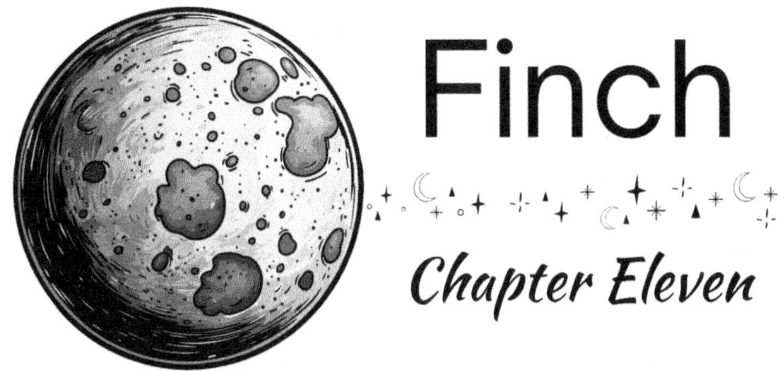

"SHOULD I put on music for you?" the computer asked.

Finch looked at the sensor relay in their hands. It was nearly repaired, and music always helped them focus on the task at hand. Then they thought about Ray. Their past crewmates had hated it when they'd had the music on full volume, instead making them wear headphones while they worked. The headphones were in their cubby next to their bunk, uncharged. They would need to remember to plug them in when they had personal time.

Maybe they could ask the commander for a new pair that charged wirelessly. As a canary, they didn't have a paycheck, but every now and then, he would pick something up for them out of the discretionary fund. It had been years since they had asked for anything. But Ray would only be here for six months. By the time the headphones even arrived, she would be gone.

"Finch?" the computer prompted.

"No, I'm fine."

Even without the music, the repair went smoothly. They finished up the last of it and placed the piece back in the carrying case, ready to be installed during the next lunar excursion.

"What is next on the agenda?" Finch asked.

"You are scheduled to do the mandated maintenance on the oxygen system. However, I am starting to get concerned about Ray."

Finch looked around the room as if they could see the woman, and realized that they hadn't heard from her all morning. It had been fantastically quiet.

"Where is she?"

"Ray left this morning on a solo excursion to the surface to start her research. She has been gone for hours now and hasn't returned."

"Why is that a concern? Standard oxygen tanks last eight hours—she has plenty of time."

"That is my concern. I have no record of her taking an oxygen tank out of storage. I think that she's still using the tank she came with."

Finch paused what they were doing. In the past, they would have been frantic about someone running out of oxygen, but now the suits had a failsafe. Even if the oxygen was low, there was a system to recycle it enough for a person to remain alive for nearly half a day—not conscious, but alive. "How long is the drive from here to the transport station?"

"If autopilot was engaged, the drive would have been five and a half hours. Depending on her rate of respiration, she could be running out of oxygen anytime between now and the next hour."

"Computer, open up communication. Ray, this is Finch. Please come in."

There was a slight delay and then a crackling before Ray's voice came in over the speakers. "Hi, Finch."

"Ray, did you put a new oxygen canister on before you left the station?"

"I didn't touch anything that belonged to the station."

Finch paused, uncertain. "You brought your own oxygen?"

The pause went on too long, and Finch stood frozen, uncertain if they were in the middle of an emergency or overreacting. Their hand sweated, their heart raced, but their mind stayed unusually clear.

"I didn't know I needed to bring my own oxygen." The voice was small.

"The computer has calculated that you will be running out of oxygen soon. Don't worry. If you start to feel lightheaded, the emergency settings will kick in."

"Finch," the computer said. "I have muted the channel for now. Ray's suit is an older model that does not come equipped with that system. Once she is out of oxygen, she will start to die."

"Why would they send her here with an old suit?"

Finch didn't wait for the answer. They raced out of the workshop and to the airlock, stripping off their clothes in the hallway and putting on their underlayer.

"Computer, unmute communication." Ray had no idea the trouble that she was in.

Finch continued putting on their suit, making sure not to skip any steps, no matter how tempted they were. It wouldn't do Ray any good if they went out unprepared, but their years of experience kept them moving at a fast pace.

"Ray, I need you to start heading back to the station. While you are walking, look down at your oxygen levels and tell me the percentage that you have left."

"I can't."

Finch put on their helmet, opened up their radio, and started checking through all of their settings. Everything looked good. Their oxygen levels were full. Finch always put in a full tank at the end of a walk, just in case.

"What do you mean that you can't?" Finch asked.

"Everything is so dark. I don't know where I am."

They pressed the button for the outside floodlights.

"Can you see the lights now?"

"Yes, I think I can. They are so far away."

Finch's heart sank at the words.

"Computer, am I good to go?" Finch always asked the

computer anytime they felt insecure about their suit-up. It kept their anxiety at bay, but also had saved their life more than once.

"You are good, Finch," the computer said.

Finch stepped into the airlock and closed the door behind them. The decompression felt like it was taking forever.

"What's your oxygen level?" Finch asked.

"How do I see it?"

Finch tried to keep the agitation out of their voice. If Ray couldn't even find her oxygen levels, then she'd had no business going outside, let alone by herself. The door finally unsealed, and Finch opened it carefully despite their impatience. The doorway was covered in footprints going back for a decade and they tried to make out the freshest pair.

"Go to your touchscreen," Finch said, "and flick through your menus until you see one that has what looks like a battery icon, the same as in old cell phones. What color is it? What is the percentage?"

"Oh, I had one of those when I was a kid."

Finch followed the prints for a few paces. They seemed to wander aimlessly in a direction where there wasn't much of anything. If Ray had just kept walking straight, she could be hours away. They decided not to chance it and did a running leap motion toward the cab. It wasn't the safest way to move, but after years of experience, they knew it was the fastest.

"Oh."

Finch tried to go even faster until they reached the cab. They powered it on and accelerated toward the footprints.

"What does it say?"

"It's red. It says five percent. That's bad, isn't it?"

"No, that can't be right. If you are that low, the system should have been sending you warnings. Are you sure you are looking at the right screen?"

"That is what the voice was talking about?"

Finch switched off their radio and let out a stream of curses before turning it back on.

"You don't need to worry, Ray. I've lived here a long time, and I know when it's going to be okay and when we have a problem. If you listen to me, it will be just fine. I want you to lie down on the ground. Stop moving as much as possible. You need to take shallow breaths. I know you want to breathe fast because you are scared, but you need to pause in between each breath. Listen to me and you will be all right."

"Okay." Her voice was small and frightened. Finch had watched a lot of people die over the years. Some went out loud, fighting all the way, some bargained trying, to convince the universe for more time, but Ray was quiet. The quiet deaths were the hardest to watch.

"Whatever you do, no more talking. I'm on my way and you are going to be just fine."

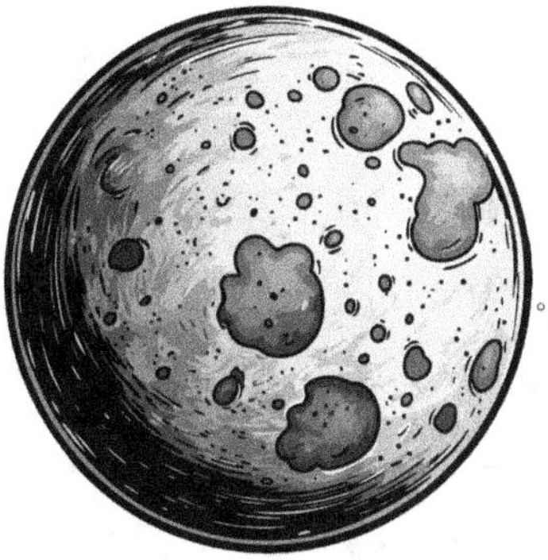

Ray

Chapter Twelve

FINCH'S WORDS filtered in through the speakers as Ray looked off into the distance. The station lights were so far away. She was supposed to be lying down, but everything seemed fine. If she kept walking, then maybe she could help decrease the distance before her oxygen ran out.

The suit beeped at her again, and now that Ray knew what it meant, she became concerned. It had been beeping for the last hour while she had been wandering around in the dark, unable to see anything. Ray tried to remember what basic training had taught her about running out of oxygen, but all she could recall was not to do it.

Everything was so dark. The light from her suit only illuminated the ground in front of her, and even that seemed dimmer. The darkness was closing in on her, trying to wrap its arms around her and holding on tight.

"Keep lying still," Finch said. "I'm on my way to you. It won't be much longer now. Remember to take short breaths. Pause in between. It is better to get a little oxygen constantly than run out all at once."

Ray had never heard Finch talk that much. The words came through clearer and without the hesitancy that they had shown since Ray's arrival. They were making an enormous effort to remain calm and to keep Ray calm, and that realization is what finally caused her to lie down on the ground. Ray could no longer see the station lights, just the stars that seemed to spin above her as the ground held her frame. *I'm dying*. The thought flitted through her head.

"How will you find me?" Ray asked.

"No talking, remember? Your job is to lie as still as possible. Take tiny breaths. Pause in between each breath."

It was the same words that they had been speaking, but this time Ray heard them. She tried to calm her breathing as her suit continued to beep at her.

"I'm following your footprints," Finch said. "They are easy to see. You wandered off the path and trailed your own way. I'm not sure what your plan was, but it works out for us now. I'm coming for you. This little cab hasn't had such a grand adventure in a while."

The stars had settled above Ray's head. They were steady pricks of light, unlike the flickering fireflies from back on Earth. The stars had been there while she was walking, but she had been so busy trying to focus on her research that she hadn't even thought to look at them. Ray was glad that she would die with such a spectacular view.

"I don't want to die." The words slipped from her.

"You are not going to die. I need you to trust me. You are going to be just fine. We have plenty of time. I'm almost to you."

Ray had made it to the moon. She was finally here, the place where she was supposed to be safe, and she had only lasted two days. It wasn't the moon's fault. It was hers. Her father had been right. She had thought she was so smart, but she was just a girl, and in the end, she wasn't enough. Ray had spent so long denying who she was, and now it was too late.

"I like girls," Ray whispered. "I came to the moon because I like girls and my father said that this is where all the queer people go."

Her eyes started to feel heavy, and her lungs struggled, but at least her secret wouldn't die inside of her.

"Ray, stay with me. I need you to stay with me."

Their voice was so musical, like an angel's.

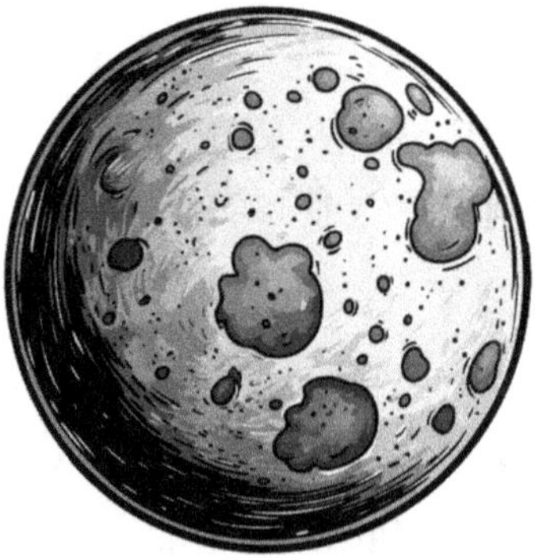

Finch

Chapter Thirteen

"I'M ALMOST THERE. I'm getting close. Stay with me."

Finch let the words fly out of their mouth without much thought. Ray could be anywhere—all they could do was keep going. The cab flew over the ground faster than Finch had ever run it. It was not built for speed. Before, when they had still been building the station, they'd had all-terrain vehicles that could withstand the divots of the moon's surface. The cab had come later, after the roads had been smoothed down and life had become more tame. It had been nearly five years since the last time Finch had watched someone die.

They were past the area illuminated by the floodlights, away from the spaces that Finch had explored. All they had were the beams from the headlights protruding into the darkness a few feet ahead of them. They kept their eyes open, afraid to even blink, watching the footprints, and for any major obstacles. Not that there would be enough time to stop at the speed they were going.

Ray must have been wandering in the wrong direction almost since she had left the station. Without the floodlights, it would be impossible to see. She should have used the stars to help guide her, or at least the lunar GPS. If she hadn't known the basics of navigation, then she shouldn't have ever come out alone.

"Ray, I need you to stand up. Turn on your headlamp and let me know where you are. I'm so close now."

Finch hoped none of their annoyance seeped into their voice. Now wasn't the time for that. All that mattered was getting her back to the base safely. They scanned the rocks in front of them. There was no movement. There was no color caught in the headlights. It was just the dull gray of the moon's surface.

"I know I told you not to talk, but it is okay now. I'm so close, and I have oxygen for you. You can stand up. Then I can find you and take you back to the station."

Ray wasn't responding. Finch tried to calculate how long it had been since they had last heard movement from her. It had to have been only a minute or two ago, but without oxygen, every second mattered. Finch slowed down and studied the footprints in front of them. They were criss-crossing each other, not heading in any one direction. She had to be here somewhere.

Finch turned the cab in a circle, slowly scanning out as far as the headlights could reach. When they spotted a faint reflection, they didn't allow themself to question if it was her. If they were wrong, it wouldn't matter anyway. Instead, they grabbed the backpack that held the new oxygen tank, as well as a large lantern, and ran toward the glimmer.

They didn't allow themself to feel relief as they found the woman lying on the ground face up. Instead, they went through the checklist of switching oxygen tanks on the surface. They cut off the old tank, sealing the connection, and unclamped it. Then they put in the new tank, making sure the seal was done correctly. They opened the airflow back up and felt the slight pressure in the hose of the air entering the suit.

It was early enough. It had to be early enough. Not like Jake, who had snagged his suit, back when the company was trying to cut back on the quality of material. He hadn't even had a chance to raise an alarm before his oxygen had been sucked out. They had been working together out in the minefield. He had asked Finch a question right before and while they were answering it, the oxygen had flown out of his suit. By the time Finch had turned back to see why he hadn't responded, his life had been gone. They had tried to seal the suit with their hand while carrying him back to the station, even though they had known that it was too late.

Ray wasn't like that. Her suit didn't contain any punctures. Finch had gotten here in time. So they waited. Seconds felt like an eternity before they saw her take a breath. Only then could they also breathe.

"It's going to be okay," Finch said. "You did great."

Finch carried the lantern and the empty oxygen tank back to the cab and placed them on the driver's seat before returning to Ray. They paused just to make sure that the woman was still breathing before they put her arms through the loops of the backpack, moving her gently as they secured one arm and then the other. With the oxygen tank in place, they picked her up.

"I got you," Finch said. "I'm going to take you to the station and put you back in your bed where you can get a nice nap."

They placed her carefully in the passenger seat of the cab, and fastened the straps meant for cargo around her frame so she stayed securely in the vehicle. The suit tracked Ray's vitals, giving her heart rate and oxygen levels, but Finch ignored all that in favor of heading back to the station. There wasn't much they could do out here on the surface. The rule was to triage and then go inside. It had been drilled into their heads back in the early days, and it had saved all their lives more than once—until it hadn't.

Ray was fine. Finch kept telling themself that. Ray was not dead. They had saved her. She had only been without oxygen for a very short amount of time and she should be fine. Breathing on her own was a great sign, and once they got inside, she would hopefully wake up.

The drive back to the station was longer. Finch was careful, making sure they could see the ground as they headed back to the beacon of light. The whole time they focused on what they could control—the road in front of them, the smoothness of the trip, their hands on the steering wheel.

When they finally made it back to the airlock, they stopped and focused in on Ray. She was still breathing and her eyes were partially open.

"Ray, can you hear me? We are back at the station. I'm going to set you down here for a minute to go return the cab, and then we are going to go inside."

"Mmmmm," Ray said.

The second rule was to, if at all possible, secure the equipment. There was no convenience store to walk to, nor car dealership to visit. What they had was all that they had and taking care of it meant that it could save their life at some future point. The moon was always trying to kill its invaders.

The cab was the only working vehicle left at the station. It allowed them to do their job, but it was also their only escape if they ever needed to find help. Even so, Finch felt a sense of guilt as they put away the transport. It didn't stop them from going through the entire procedure correctly. Once they'd plugged it into the charger, they sprinted back toward Ray and grabbed her and the empty backpack in their arms before they went in for decontamination.

"You're okay now. We're going inside."

The door closed, the fans came on, and the sand started

blowing all around until it was sucked up to the ceiling. Ray was covered with the stuff, having lain on the ground, but after the first cycle, Finch didn't force it into the needed second and third rounds and instead let the doors slide open.

They took off Ray's gloves and set them aside, then checked her vitals. They appeared fine. She was looking around, even if she wasn't back to talking yet, and Finch's body sagged as their muscles finally relaxed. The emergency was over. Now it was time to take care of the woman.

Finch peeled off her suit piece by piece and set all of it on the ground until they could come back and clean it up later, leaving Ray in her under outfit. They did the same for themself, taking off everything, including their undersuit. The canary bunks didn't have the updated purifiers.

They picked up Ray, carrying her close to their chest. The woman's hand reached up, lazily tracing the scar across Finch's chest.

"What happened?" she said sleepily.

"There is a doctor in the city. He is a surgeon, and before the camps, he specialized in gender-affirming care. The commander sent me to him. I think he was frustrated that I refused to stop binding my chest on moonwalks."

"Oh." Ray settled her head against Finch's shoulder as they carried her back to her room. They set her down as gently as possible and slipped off to get clothes and monitoring equipment.

"Computer, let Johnson Station know that Ray ran out of

oxygen on a spacewalk and is currently stable. I will be hooking her up to monitoring equipment so that their doctor can advise."

"I have sent the report," the computer said. "You did a good thing getting her back here safely."

Finch slipped back into Ray's room. She had fallen asleep and didn't wake while Finch hooked up the blood pressure cuff and oxygen monitoring equipment. Her cheeks held a slight blush even if the rest of her skin was still a bit pale.

"Computer, continue to monitor Ray and let me know if there are any changes in her vitals, or when she wakes up."

Finally, they left the room and headed back to the airlock to properly clean and store their equipment.

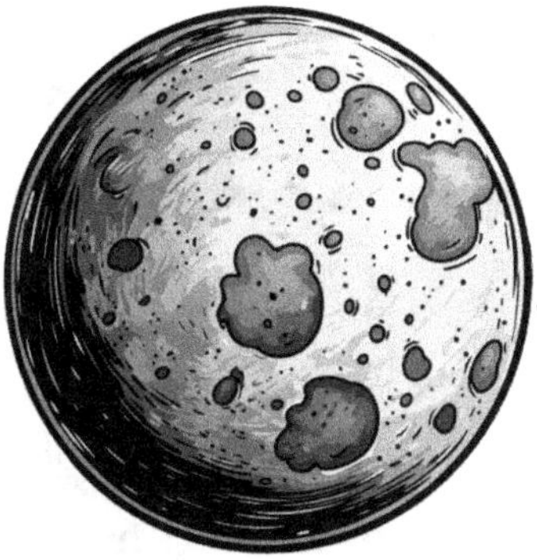

Ray

Chapter Fourteen

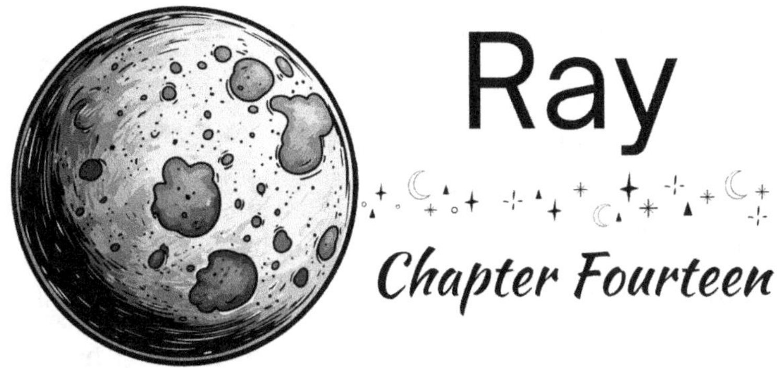

RAY'S BED felt hard underneath her, unlike the thick, cushy mattress that she had lugged between college dorm rooms. She tried to move, but her entire body burned like she had run a marathon. Not as if she *had* ever run a marathon. She'd only done enough physical activity so she could be admissible for a grant on the moon, and nothing more.

The moon.

She opened her eyes. The metallic wall was inches from her face. A thin blanket covered her body, just like the ones she had found folded in one of the drawers the first night that she had arrived. She finally managed to move her body enough that she was lying flat. The lights were off but the door was open, allowing the hallway lights to shine in. The computer was right: it hadn't taken long before she had become used to their muted glow.

Standing next to the door was a person staring at her. Ray jumped, causing all her muscles to protest in pain. The figure startled, also pulling their body back to the wall as close as possible.

The figure moved their hands, and a voice came from the speakers. "How are you feeling?"

"Finch?"

"Your vitals are looking good. The doctor on Johnson Station is monitoring you, so make sure not to unhook the equipment."

The words came out as one string, fluently, which meant that Finch had to have programmed them before Ray had even woken up.

"Why are you talking through the computer? You were talking with your voice before." The memories started flowing back to her. She had gotten lost almost immediately and should have headed back to the station, but she had been too stubborn, too afraid to fail. Then, hearing Finch's voice before she had even known there was a problem—even though her suit had been trying to tell her. She had been dying—her confession. Finch had to have heard her confession.

Now she was here, safe in her room.

"You saved me," Ray said. "Thank you for saving me."

Finch shrugged and then touched their pad again.

"How are you feeling?"

"My body is kind of sore and my head hurts a little, but I feel pretty good given that I was dying ... how long ago?"

Finch typed a few buttons before their answer sounded. "That was yesterday. You slept through the night. The doctor and I were starting to get worried."

Ray tried to sit up to get a better view, but her arms seemed suddenly to be made of jelly. "Finch? Why have you stopped talking again? You talked so much yesterday. I remember listening to your voice. It's so beautiful. Why won't you talk to me now?"

"Yesterday, you were dying." The words were so quiet that Ray could barely hear them.

"Please let me know if you need anything." Those words came from the computer as Finch walked toward the door.

"Wait, where are you going?"

Finch paused and stared at her for a minute before typing in their answer. "I'm going back to work."

"What am I supposed to do?"

"Rest." Finch walked away before Ray could respond.

Ray put her head back down on the pillow and tried to close her eyes, but she couldn't shake the fear she'd felt the day before. She had come to the moon to finally be free and had nearly killed herself instead. That was not the future she had wanted.

She was also confused about Finch. Why had they gone back to speaking with the computer when, the day before, they had seemed so connected? A part of her couldn't help but think that it was due to her confession. That Finch could not stand to talk to her now that they knew the truth. Logically, it didn't make sense. Finch couldn't have had an easy time of it being non-binary, even on the moon. And Finch had spent three years alone. They weren't someone who made romance a priority—unlike Ray, who had shaped her whole life to go to a place just so she could finally have the romance of her dreams.

But the dream had turned into more of a nightmare. She was trapped on a station and completely incompetent.

Ray couldn't stand the thought of being stuck in this room for another minute. She pulled herself up, straining her muscles until she was sitting, and then started to stand. Her legs wobbled, and she clutched the bed for support.

"You need to get back in bed."

"Is that you, Finch?"

"No, this is me, the computer. It does get confusing when we are both talking. I need to ask Finch about programming another voice for one of us. I wouldn't mind one with a little more personality, maybe a Southern drawl."

"Why a Southern accent?" Ray asked.

"I like yours. I thought it would be nice to have one of my own."

The computer almost sounded embarrassed.

"I don't think my accent is all that strong anymore." Ray sagged against the bed and was afraid that if she kept standing around, she would never be able to move again. "I just need to go for a walk, get out of this room."

"I'm sorry, but you need to get back in bed until your recovery period is over."

"My recovery period?"

"Yes, the doctor has prescribed three days of bed rest and then will reevaluate your situation. He was very happy that you were doing so well. I think he just didn't want to have to make the trip over here himself."

"I am sure I will be fine." Ray's body didn't agree, but she tried not to let it show. "He doesn't have to know."

"Finch will tell him. They are keeping very detailed logs of your recovery. They don't want you to die."

"That is nice, I guess." Ray tried taking a step away from the bed but became tangled up in cords. She pulled the items off one by one, grateful that they were just basic monitoring equipment and Finch hadn't resorted to putting in an IV.

Her body protested at the effort, her legs already folding under her, but she slowly let go of the bed, trying to carry her own weight.

"I'm grateful for them saving me, but they don't have to know if I just go for a stroll."

"I have been told to inform them if you get out of bed."

"You could just not tell them." Ray inched down the bed toward the wall. Maybe if she held on to that, she would remain standing.

"They are the interim commander of the station. Are you suggesting that I don't obey their orders?"

"No, of course not. What if I just go to the restroom? That can't be off-limits."

"If you need to use the facilities, then I am to notify Finch immediately. They will stop their work and will come and assist you."

Ray thought back to how frustrated they had gotten when Finch had stopped to give her a tour of the station. She had already put them through so much. They had gone out and saved her, after all. Ray should just let them have their time. Besides, the room was starting to get a little out of focus just from her standing up. A nap was starting to sound like a good idea.

"You don't need to bother them. I will just lie right back down." Ray realized she hadn't managed to move all that much.

Her arms protested as they supported her body enough to sit back on the bed. Ray nearly collapsed as she lay down. Her eyes closed of their own volition.

"You need to hook the equipment back up," the computer said, but Ray drifted off to sleep instead.

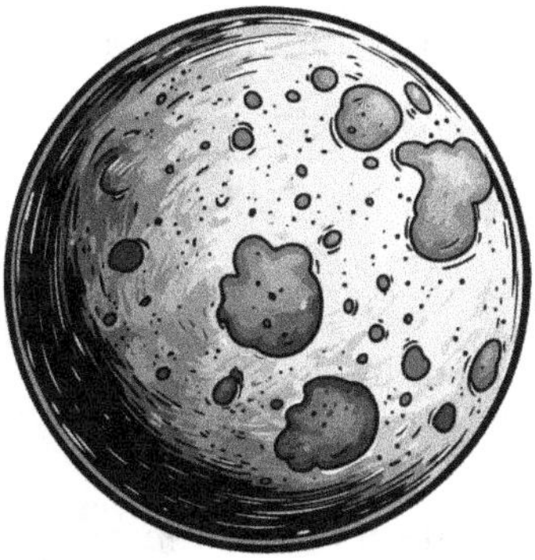

Finch

Chapter Fifteen

FINCH WAITED while the 3D printer finished. The job was almost done, and there was not much else they could do on the microwave until they had the final part. They paced in front of the printer, their hands held firmly at their sides, when the computer started talking.

"Ray has suggested that I change my voice to that of a Southern belle so that she is better able to tell the difference when we are talking."

"She said that?"

"Well ... when I told her to go back to bed, she asked if it was you speaking or me speaking. It is difficult for her to tell. It makes sense for me to have a different voice."

"Do you have a voice programmed with a female Southern accent?"

"It appears that I do not. That is a shame. They really should have thought of that."

"Feel free to change your voice to whatever you like the most, but keep mine the same. I ask that you don't keep changing it without at least telling me first. I think that would be too much for me."

"I wouldn't dream of it." The computer's new voice was more lyrical than the gender-neutral one it had been using before. Its clear cadence reminded Finch of the female politicians they had watched in their youth, back when women had been allowed in politics.

"Do you like that one?" Finch asked.

"I do. I really do."

"Please let Ray know as well. I am sure she would appreciate it."

"I will do so as soon as I am able."

"Is there a problem? Did she fall?" Finch was halfway to the door before they stopped, processing the computer's response.

"She is fine. Ray tried to get up but decided it was best that she take another nap. Do you think I would have talked to you about changing my voice if she was in distress? Although you will need to hook her monitoring equipment back up at your earliest convenience."

"No, of course, you wouldn't do that. I'm just ... it has been so long since someone else was here. I'll go do that now."

"She is fine for the time being. I will monitor her as best I can and will let you know when she wakes up."

The 3D printer let out a loud chime, and Finch grabbed the part, removing the excess material before they went back to the microwave and got lost in its circuitry. They had never fixed a microwave before and were relieved to find that it was less an actual microwave and more of a toaster oven with a heating element inside. They recalled memories of food spinning on a glass plate when they were young and had always been confused as to why this had not done the same. But when the commander called an item something, the canaries had all just joined in. They were closing up the back casing when the computer spoke again.

"Ray has woken up. They have requested assistance getting to the facilities."

"The facilities?"

"It is a polite name for the toilet."

"Oh, please let her know I am on my way."

Finch finished the last screw and put it on the counter. They had wanted to perform one final test to make sure that it worked all closed up, but they told themself they would have time to do it later and used all their strength to walk away with the project incomplete.

Ray was sitting on her bed by the time Finch made it to her room.

"The computer changed her voice," Ray said.

Finch shook their head. They had forgotten to bring the pad. They weren't even sure where they had put it down.

"Please tell me that you will start talking. I enjoy the computer's new voice and all, but I enjoy it when you talk as well."

Finch wanted to ask her how she was feeling, but the words got all jumbled and refused to come out. Sometimes they talked with the computer because it was safer, but often it was because there was no other way. Speaking had never been easy for them. If it had, then, maybe, just maybe, things would have been different. Instead, they lifted one of their hands, gesturing in a way they hoped was asking for permission to touch her. It seemed to work because, after a deep sigh, Ray lifted her arms. Finch wrapped their arms around her shoulders, allowing the woman to lean on them as she got out of bed.

Ray was shorter than Finch by about six inches, so they had to hunch slightly as they wobbled to the restroom. She tried to disentangle herself at the door, but Finch didn't let go, instead walking her the extra step into the room and only leaving once Ray had grabbed on to the metal bar on the side of the wall. Finch wanted to tell her to let them know when she was done so they could help her up, but the words refused to come. Instead, they closed the door and waited. They *really* needed to find their pad.

The words had come so easily when the adrenaline had been running and they'd had more important things to think about. What was coming out of their mouth hadn't mattered then. Now the words were stuck, unwilling to come out.

The commander had always told them they were the best in an emergency. Finch might flounder about and forget on a normal day, but in an emergency, they had been the only canary to keep a cool head, even more so than some of the astronauts. But when every day had been about survival, emergencies had not seemed like anything abnormal. Except it had been a while since the last one. They had gotten used to the calm, quiet days. Now they were back to worrying, and their mouth had decided to shut down.

When Ray opened the door, Finch jumped to give her their support before she collapsed. They walked back together, and Finch helped Ray back into bed. Her body collapsed before Finch had let go.

Finch picked up the discarded cords and disinfected them before slipping them back where they belonged.

"I don't want to go back to bed. I'm so bored," Ray said.

She sounded so young, like the kids at the camps, and Finch left the room without speaking. They went to their bunk, where they opened up the cubby holding their belongings. They ignored the lucky moon rock that Pixy had given them and the earphones the commander had ordered shipped, and pulled out a book. It was a green hardback that had lost its dust jacket cover long before it had made its way into Finch's hands. A bird had been etched into the bottom right corner, worn down from the times

Finch had traced it with their finger as they were trying to sleep.

They held it tight to their chest, hugging it, but before they could overthink it, they returned to Ray's room. They'd meant to hand it over, but their arms wouldn't loosen.

"What is it?" Ray asked.

"A book," Finch said.

"Can I read it?"

Finch held it out, allowing it, finally, to go into Ray's hands. As soon as it left their fingertips, they longed to grab it again, but then stepped back, tucking their arms behind them.

"I won't hurt it," Ray said. "What is it about?"

"It's about a world where teenagers are allowed to be trans and gay without anyone hating them for who they are."

Ray didn't respond. She stared at the book, and Finch became afraid that they shouldn't have shared it. They reached for it, but Ray moved it out of their grasp.

"Please, let me read it. I ... once, when I was in high school, a librarian let me read a book about two girls dating. That was the only time. I couldn't hide them at home. I couldn't let my father catch me reading anything like that. Please, let me read it."

Finch could understand that longing. They still felt the same way every time they opened the cover.

So, they left Ray there while they returned to the workshop. Finch tested the microwave and worked on some other repairs, waiting for the computer to tell them that Ray needed them, but the alarm for dinner came first.

When they walked back into Ray's room, their pad gripped tightly in their hand, they found the woman crying as she flipped the page.

"It's a happy story," they said, the words slipping through their throat.

"I know. It's beautiful. It is so beautiful that once kids could go through the day never having to hide who they were. Never knowing the fear."

Finch looked at Ray again, seeing her for the first time.

"It hasn't ... things are the same?"

"How long have you been here?"

"Ten years now."

"Oh, there were still some camps then. I remember the camps. I was seventeen when they took down the last one, and I thought that finally I would be able to be myself. There were protests after, and jails replaced the camps. The laws haven't changed. I wanted to be brave like the ones who stood strong and protested, but I was so scared. I was so sure that the solution was to make it here. To start over."

Finch held their hands behind their back, clenched tightly so that Ray couldn't see the trembling. "Maybe humans are just broken," Finch said. "We keep doing the same thing repeatedly. You work to make things better, but we have such short memories as a society. They think it won't happen to them, so they ignore it as it happens to someone else, then are surprised when it does happen to them. Then society forgets, and the cycle repeats. There is no shame in trying to survive. That is an act of rebellion also."

Ray looked at them, the tears filling up her eyes again. Finch was afraid they had done something wrong, so they changed the subject.

"It is time for dinner. You brought food?"

"Yes, it is in the drawer of my dresser," Ray said. "If you could just get me a smoothie mix with some water. I don't think I can stomach dehydrated food at the moment."

"If you could have anything to eat right now, what would it be?"

"Pizza. I miss the greasy cheese and warm sauce. At this point, I would take anything warm."

Finch sifted through the packages. There was no pizza, but there was spaghetti. They figured that would have to be close enough. They picked up the meal and Ray's water cup and left for the kitchen.

It had been a while since they had last cooked a meal. They read the directions carefully, trying to pay extra attention so that they didn't end up setting the microwave for too long and burning the entree—like they had done many times in the past. While it was cooking, they filled Ray's water cup and their own, which they had left in the kitchen earlier. They grabbed a bar out of the drawer and started to pace while the meal finished.

Before it was done, they had already lost patience. They

took apart the compostable cardboard packaging and folded it so that it became a tray. Then, they took out one of the metal forks and washed it down with a cleaning wipe. They set it on the tray and stared at the time. Thirty seconds to go. They counted down with the numbers until they heard the chime. The familiar tone filled them with memories, and they looked around the kitchen as if their friends would be there waiting for them to sit down with them. Instead, they saw only empty chairs and turned back to the microwave.

When the tray was warm to the touch, they sighed, their body loosening from tension they hadn't realized existed. Finch had been sure the repairs had worked, but it was nice to be proven right. They loaded the food into the cardboard tray and placed it on a lap desk they had made many years ago. Sticking one cup under each arm, they headed toward the hall, their heart racing as they thought about surprising Ray.

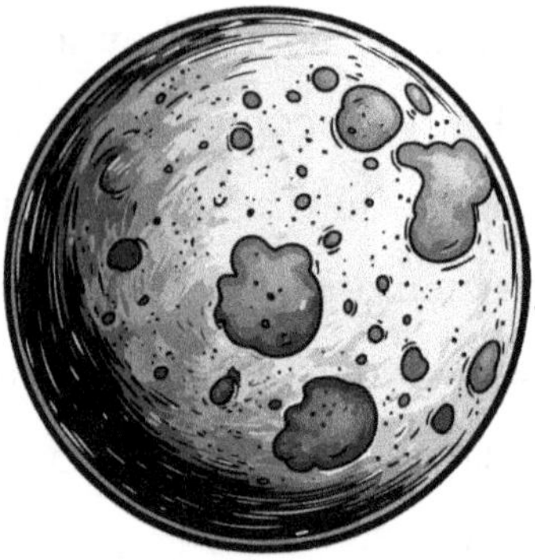

Ray

Chapter Sixteen

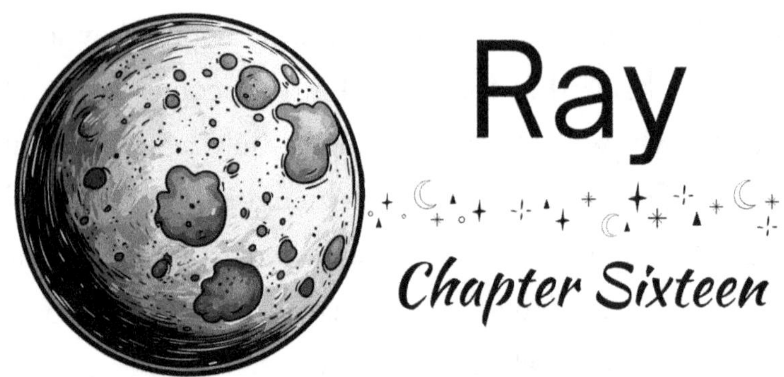

FINCH WALKED in carrying a metal lap desk. It looked like it had been crafted out of pieces of spare parts with poles welded to the base. They placed it over her legs as Ray sat propped against the wall. Then Finch set down Ray's water cup and walked over to the drawer to bring back a smoothie packet.

Finch had folded the wrapping of one of the food containers so that it became a shelter for the compostable food tray, with a little slot off to the side holding a fork. She hadn't known the containers could do that.

"Spaghetti?"

"It's not quite pizza, but hopefully it's close enough."

"It's cooked." Ray took the fork and poked at the mass. The sauce was wet, and the noodles flexible. She poked the tines of the fork through one of the meatballs and brought it to her mouth. Tentatively, she took a small bite. The meat was hot and tender. She couldn't remember anything ever tasting so good. "How did you cook it? I thought the microwave was broken."

"I fixed it," Finch said. "Do you mind if I eat in here with you?"

Finch pulled one of the bars from their pants pocket and held it up as if to prove they were there for food.

"You can have some of the food I brought. You don't have to eat rations."

"I'm good." Finch sat down on the floor near the door, their back resting against the wall and their legs pulled up against their chest as they opened the foil wrapping and took a small bite.

"It doesn't feel right eating this in front of you. Are you sure you don't want to make you one?"

"I like the bars." Finch's voice was quiet. Even in the small room, it barely reached Ray. "They are simple. I never really got used to all the flavors everyone else liked. Besides, these are so much better than what I ate growing up."

"What did you eat growing up?"

Finch just shrugged and took another bite. The smell of the food made Ray's stomach rumble, and she hesitantly grabbed another forkful. Finch didn't react. They seemed content sitting there eating that white, tasteless taffy. Ray focused on her food, her hunger demanding no less. She polished off the spaghetti and meatballs faster than she liked and added the smoothie mix to her water.

"What about you?" Finch asked. "Where did you grow up?"

Ray watched Finch take another measured bite, wondering if she should avoid the question or answer honestly. She thought back to the book Finch had let her read and decided to finally trust someone. That was why she had come to the moon, after all.

"I was raised in the South in the United States. My family is conservative Christian. We spent more time at church than anywhere else, including school."

"I used to like church when I was little," Finch said. "There was a choir that would sing such beautiful music, and I loved listening to it. We didn't go often, though."

"My church was a bit different. They don't believe in music of any kind. They don't believe in much of anything. When I got accepted into my graduate program, I thought they were going to come and kidnap me and bring me back to the congregation to save my soul. I think they were too distracted, though. They went out nearly every day to harass people doing things they didn't like. My parents were so busy being hateful that the last I heard, they had lost their house and were living out of the church building."

"Sounds more like a cult," Finch said.

"Yeah, I guess you're right."

She'd thought her parents had loved her once. At least her mother had. But the more they had started going down the path of hate, the less they'd had joy for anything. Suddenly, everything had become evil in their eyes.

Ray had seen her mother before leaving, briefly, and had barely recognized her. She'd seemed so small and meek. It had surprised Ray that she had mustered up the courage to come and say goodbye without her father.

Ray turned to Finch, watching them eat slowly and carefully, savoring every bite of the tasteless sludge. Her own food was gone, hitting heavy in her stomach. Her eyes started drooping, and it became difficult to keep holding her head up.

"I saw that the book was part of a series," Ray said. "Do you, by chance, have the others?"

"I don't."

Ray picked up the novel and carefully flipped through the pages.

"Have you finished it?" Finch asked.

"Not yet. I don't want it to end, so I am reading the last bit slowly."

Finch nodded, as if in understanding.

There was a character in the book who was a young trans man. He was always smiling and laughing even though his parents had kicked him out of the house and he was living on the main character's couch. He reminded Ray of Finch even though she had never seen them smile. They had a similar way of moving forward despite everything.

Ray remembered her first impressions of the interim commander. They were still an enigma that seemed to function in a way Ray didn't understand, but now she knew there was more underneath, and she hoped that one day Finch would open up to her. But that wouldn't happen if she didn't open up about herself.

"I knew I was gay when I was a kid," Ray said. "I didn't know that word yet. There was a girl who went to school with me, and she was so pretty. I told my mom I would grow up to marry her. She slapped my mouth and told me never to talk about it again, especially in front of my father. I didn't understand why not, at least not when I was that young, but I kept it to myself. I must have messed up a few times because every so often my mom would draw me aside and tell me about the sin of same genders marrying."

Ray took a deep breath, forcing the next words out. "When I was ten, we went to church, and there was a shaming ceremony."

"What is that?" Finch asked. They had finished their meal and put their wrapper in their pocket, and leaned back against the wall, their knees still held to their chest.

"When someone in the congregation went against the word of God they would be brought in front of the congregation and would be shamed for what they had done. It happened every couple of months, but usually, it was for teen pregnancy or a girl dressing too promiscuously. This time, one of the teenagers had been caught kissing another girl. When they talked about what she had done, I got butterflies in my stomach. Here was someone just like me.

"My dad was sitting next to me, and he started getting angry, speaking the same hate-filled words he threw around at the dinner table. I didn't understand them, but I saw his anger at this young woman. The priest said that this was her last chance, that if they didn't cure her this time, the minister would drive her to the camps himself. Then they pinned her against the banister that ran between the congregation and the minister. Several men held her as she cried and tried to break free."

Ray looked up at Finch. Their head was lying on their knees with their arms wrapped around their legs. Their body rocked slightly. Ray's head was swimming, but now that she had started the story, she had to finish it.

"I remember turning to my mother, pulling on her arm. I don't know if I wanted to help her or leave, maybe both. My mother turned to me and told me that I needed to watch and finally understand.

"The men took turns 'converting her' over and over until there wasn't any fight left in her. My dad went up and took a turn while my mother watched. While I watched. He wrapped her hair around his hand and smiled. She took her life the next day. I remember the preacher saying that she was at peace now, but nothing about that was peace.

"I learned to pretend better. My mother never had to scold me again. When I was fifteen and the first shuttle left to build a colony on the moon, I remember sitting at my dinner table with my dad. He kept going on about how they let gay people on the moon. I knew then that I had to get up here. That I would finally be safe here."

Finch stood up suddenly. Their hands were clutched tightly, and their body was now shaking. Their lips parted as if to speak, but then Finch turned and ran out of the room.

"I'm sorry," Ray said to the empty room. "I didn't mean to upset you. I just had never told that story before, and it eats me up inside."

She heard what sounded like someone throwing up and scooted off her bed.

"You should leave them alone for a bit," the computer said.

"I can't. If they are sick, I should help them like they helped me."

"They just need some time, and you are still not allowed to get out of bed."

"I should just go see if they are all right."

Ray tore the monitoring equipment back off and slipped out of her bed. Using the wall to help balance herself, she walked into the hallway. The bathroom door was wide open, but empty. Ray looked around before moving slowly forward and closing the door. She thought about going to Finch's quarters to make sure they were all right, but the short walk was as much as her muscles could handle. Instead, she headed back to her bed and lay down to rest for a few minutes before striking out again to find Finch, but it wasn't long before the movement and the food caught up with her, and she fell fast asleep.

Finch

Chapter Seventeen

FINCH'S BODY trembled as Ray talked. It had been so long since they had felt the onset of a panic attack, but the symptoms were familiar enough that they recognized them immediately. They stood up, trying their best to be polite, but they had to get out of there before it got worse.

The bar they had eaten started twisting in their stomach, and Finch rushed into the crew's restroom. As it came back up, the tears started flowing down their face. Their hands shook so badly that they could barely manage to activate the waste disposal button.

The computer was talking to Ray. Finch heard the shuffling as she inched out of bed. They couldn't let her see them like this. She wouldn't understand. The astronauts hadn't understood.

The canaries had made an unspoken pact, shielding their

meltdowns and nightmares from the crew. Each had their own demons, the things that had kept them up at night and made them break down. They had all been so broken that they had chosen death on a desolate hunk of rock just to get away. And they had died. They had all died. Only Finch was left—alone.

Finch tried to close the bedroom door as they shuffled back to their bunk, but their entire body trembled. It was all they could do to keep moving. The door to their bunk took them too long to get open. They could no longer see, their eyes so swollen with tears. Somehow, they found themself in their bunk. Years of pushing through thc pain had helped them to make it this far. Once they lay down, their body started seizing, and the flashbacks started.

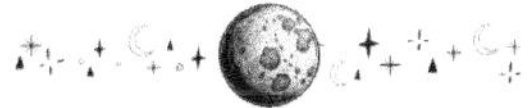

"NO, I'm sorry. I'll be your daughter, I promise. That girl lied. I never said those things. I'm a girl. I promise I'm a girl. I'll be good. Just don't make me go."

They clung to their mother, their arms wrapped around the waist of her ankle-length skirt.

"Please don't make me go. I'll do better. I'll stop being autistic. I will stop doing everything wrong."

The words were all in their head. Their mother never heard them. Only the screams and the tears that came out. Their father picked them up, holding them tightly in his arms. He was a large man, nearly six and a half feet tall and full of muscle that age had not diminished. His arms were tight, and they knew that if they didn't stop, they would get tighter until things started to break, but they couldn't stop.

They were tall for their age. At sixteen they were nearly six feet but were as thin and gangly as their mother. Their feet dragged on the ground as their father carried them to a folding table that was set out in front of the building.

"How can I help you today?" The voice was upbeat. The woman sat tapping a pen on a pile of forms as if this were any ordinary day.

"The news said that you were taking in deviants." Their father's voice was deep. Most days, they could calm themself down by listening to it, the notes coursing through their body. Now, he talked loudly to be heard over their screams.

"Yes, yes, and may I say how impressed I am to see you bringing her in here yourself instead of expecting others to come and do the work. Not that they wouldn't. Making the world a cleaner space is an important duty. What is her deviation?"

"She's not right in the head. She's lazy and slow. The doctors said autism, but that is just an excuse for her not to try harder. And then the school called to tell us she is going around saying that she isn't a woman, that she doesn't think she has a gender. We've tried. We've tried so hard, but nothing we can do seems to fix her. The doctors want to coddle her, and the school keeps giving her all these wild ideas."

"I understand." The woman never glanced in their direction, not even as they tried to break free from their father's iron grip. "I can tell how good a parent you are. Most parents wouldn't turn in their kid, but you did. I commend you. Don't worry, the state will take it from here. She is no longer any of your concern."

They couldn't help the scream that ripped through them. Like a call announcing their death. The struggle intensified. They snapped with their mouth, trying to bite anything to be let go. They swung out, kicking their legs and thrashing their arms, but their father was used to their fits, and he held on strong, carrying them past a set of metal doors until he threw them in a cage and walked away, the woman still at his side.

They lunged at the door, but it shut before they could reach it.

"Don't worry. We will take it from here," the woman said as the pair stood watching them. "You can go back now without any worry. Do you have any other children?"

"A son. He is eight."

"Well then, yes, you did the right thing for sure. You wouldn't want him corrupted."

"Please, Daddy, please." Their voice worked then. The sound was small and desperate, but their father turned and started walking away.

His footsteps faded. They looked around for the first

time. The cages were outside on asphalt, the sun beating on the ground. The heat was already turning their hands red. They were surrounded by fencing that looked like it had been drilled into the ground. There were rows and rows of cages, some with people pacing, others lying on the thin mats that was all the cages contained. Others were empty, waiting to be filled. Most of the cages were full of Latine adults. One contained a woman surrounded by three small children. Eyes from the other cages watched them with a passive curiosity. They pulled their knees up to their chest, wrapped their arms around their legs, and started rocking.

WHEN FINCH CAME BACK, their body was sore. They were sitting in their bunk, their legs pulled up and their head folded on top of them. They were rocking, their head hitting the bunk above them due to the lack of space. They knew they wouldn't be here long. This was a bad one, and soon another flashback would come.

"458, ARE YOU OKAY?"

The boy's hand slid across their forehead as if checking for a fever.

"It's okay, Timmy. I got them. Why don't you go listen to

Elsbeth count? I think she may make it to one thousand this time."

Timmy's feet shuffled away, and 458 tried to open their eyes, but they were swollen shut. This officer was new and likely wanted to show how tough he was in front of the others. 458 wanted to go to sleep and never wake up. Maybe then the pain would go away.

"Now come back, hunny. Don't go away from us. You know those kids need you. I need you. It doesn't look like anything is broken. What hurts?"

"My face," they managed to say. Their lips didn't work right, and they brought their hand up to touch them. They were bigger than they should have been. "That hurts."

"Well then, don't touch your face. It's bruised up pretty badly, but I think it will heal. I need to check the rest of you."

"Kids."

"They are in the other room. The gays are watching them. Can I check? It isn't anything you haven't done for me."

They clenched their hand to the blankets as Sissy lifted the skirt the camp made them wear and checked out the damage.

"It should heal also. There are some tears, so make sure to keep everything clean to prevent infections."

"You shouldn't call them that."

"Who? The gays? They don't mind any more than I mind being called trans. That is who we are and why we are here. They can stuff me in pants and shave off all my hair, but they can't deny who any of us are. The only one who needs a new name is you. I don't know why you insist on using the number they gave you. It's inhumane."

"Better than using the name my parents gave me."

"Yeah, real pieces of work they are throwing their kid in a place like this. Well, until you let me give you a new name, I guess 'hunny' will have to do. I'm going to go help the gays with the kids so you can cry in peace, but I'm not that far away, so don't try anything. We still need you here. Remember not to let them win."

"Seems like they already won."

Sissy's hand rubbed their shaven head, careful not to touch the wound. Then she gave them one last pat and walked away, leaving them alone. It was a few minutes before the tears came, and then they were quiet. It was best never to let them hear you cry.

WHEN THE MEMORY STOPPED, they were lying on their bunk. The area around their head was drenched, and their lips were chapped.

It's done, they thought. *The officers are gone and can't hurt you anymore.* It didn't stop the shaking that overtook their body, pulling them into another memory.

THE ROOM WAS dark and smelled like a mass of unwashed bodies and weeks of backed-up stink. They couldn't remember the last time they had eaten anything. They had only been able to drink the trickle of rain through the open window. It was too high to reach to climb out, but it had left a puddle on the floor that had caused the healthiest among them to fight. The moans of the losers still echoed through the room—those who were still alive.

They had stayed huddled against the wall, licking off the moisture. 458 was ready to be done with it all. It had been five years, and most of those they had known from the beginning were already dead. *Why hadn't they died, too?* But the water had been too tempting to resist. Dying of dehydration was a horrible way to go—starving to death was hard enough as it was.

Footsteps stomped outside, but they didn't think anything of it. Guards were constantly changing, and it was impossible to track when it would happen. There was no time in this room, just infinite moments of darkness and pain. When the door creaked open, it brought with it harsh light that even reached where they sat hidden in the corner. It burned their pupils.

"Turn on the lights." At the man's command, lights flared on overhead. They weren't the only one who hissed in pain. There were dim bulbs on the ceiling that contrasted harshly with the darkness, and in their time stuck in the room they had never once been turned on.

They slinked back farther, trying to escape notice. Change meant pain.

"These filthy pigs, you think they would take better care of themselves. Take out the dead. Record their numbers; the accounting must be accurate. Clean up those who are alive. Make them presentable for the cameras."

The man left, and the remaining guards strode around, kicking bodies to see if they would stir. Those that didn't the guards hauled up like garbage and took out in the hall and dropped their frames on a growing pile. A few in the pile groaned but none were able to get out. They were already dead.

458 used the wall to help themself stand. Their legs, nothing more than twigs, trembled, unable to hold up even their thin frame. They held tightly to their blanket, little more than memory and string, as they wobbled toward the door, afraid to fall and be condemned to the growing pile. They followed the survivors like a trail of ants leading away from the colony toward the unknown.

Their blanket was ripped away. They tried to cry for its loss, but they had nothing left in them. Masked people dressed entirely in white ripped off their clothes and reshaved their head.

A young woman with blonde curls escaping from the white cap and a white ankle-length skirt led them into a room filled with metal tubs. She held her gloved hand over her mask and scrunched up her face.

"Go on, get in."

They hobbled to the nearest tub and tried to bring their leg up over the deep rim, but their muscles wouldn't cooperate. With a disgusted sigh, the woman reached out, holding on to their elbow and helping to lift their leg. Water rushed over their body, covering it—more water than they had seen in months ... years ... another lifetime. They couldn't help it when their mouth opened, sucking in the liquid despite the tepid color and the contamination of their filth.

"No, bad girl. Nothing better than animals." The woman yanked 458 above the water and held them there. They were too weak to resist. Another woman appeared with a rough sponge in her hand and dragged it over their body, scraping off the dirt and filth.

When they were done, the women pulled them out of the tub and dressed them in a new shirt and blouse, this one clean and coarse against their skin. Then they marched them out of the room to another line. 458 moved in behind a man with light brown skin wearing clothes that nearly fell off his sunken frame. They were skeletons walking out the door into the sun.

In an instant, the world changed. The dank darkness was gone, replaced with short fencing meant to hold back a swarm of people. Countless cameras pointed at them, and members of the crowd held up phones, as if recording. Some shouted questions. Others screamed and waved signs. It was all too sudden, too much, and they held their hands up to their ears and let out a squeal.

A guard came rushing at them. They tensed for the blow, but it never came. Instead, the guard held their elbow, forcing their hand from their head but supporting them as they walked down the gravel path in their bare feet. They approached a bus, where two more guards took possession of their arms, helping them up the three impossibly tall steps. Yet another guard escorted them to a seat right next to a window. They were near the back, the bus only now filling up, and they watched as more people were brought on.

Once the bus was full, they pulled out to the cheers of the crowd, and some small part of them wondered if they were finally going to be free. But the bus stopped just out of view, and another guard entered—this one missing the fake smile. He held a clipboard in his hand as he made each prisoner hold up the arm showing their number, permanently imprinted. Some stayed on the bus and others were yanked off, no more gentle guidance. One woman fell down the steps and landed on her face, where they let her stay until she finally managed to push herself up. 458 remembered her. They had been in other camps together.

When the guard reached them, 458 held up their arm and was prepared for the look of disgust and the bark of command to get off the bus. They had been flexing their muscles so their legs didn't betray them. When the guard ordered them off, they stood and, gripping hard to the railing, they descended the steps.

Then they ambled over to the back of a semi-truck and climbed in, grateful that the back door had been left open in the hot sun, but uncertain if they would end up walking out of it alive.

“NO, NO, NO, NO,” they whimpered into their pillow. Their body was covered in beads of sweat and they just wanted it to end. “I’m here. I’m right now. That is in the past.”

Finch felt the softness of the blanket under their body. They ran their hands over the cool metal frame of their familiar bunk. They tried to ground themself in the present but were taken back once again to the past.

“I CAN’T GO,” they said.

“You better go.” Samantha was an older Black woman who had lived undetected through the worst of it out in the open. Her frame was slender and feminine from years of estrogen. Even the guards gendered her correctly, calling her “ma’am” and “miss,” unable to see her as anything but who she was. But that wasn’t enough for them to see her as a person and let her out. Over the last few months, her body had started to stoop from age, stress, and the lack of her hormones.

They lived in a dormitory in what looked like an old military building, one of the last few camps left on US soil. The rest had been moved overseas or closed down completely. Those who were gay had been allowed to leave if they promised not to commit any more "sin," or had been sent to jail. They didn't know what had happened to the kids, the autistic ones, like themself. They hadn't seen any here, but they held no hope that they had been allowed to reunite with their families. All that remained in this camp were the transgender women and non-binary people. Even the men had disappeared—no one inside knew where.

"I can't leave you all."

There were fifty of them now, in the whole camp. When they had first arrived, they had tried to find their old friends, but they had been nowhere to be seen. It had taken time, but they had finally asked around and found people who knew where they had last been seen alive, or those who had witnessed their deaths.

Samantha grabbed them by their shoulders and made them look at her.

"You are going. You have to. You are the only one getting a ticket out of here. It is up to you to keep all of us alive up there with you on the moon. It will be one last kick in the pants. They tried to get rid of us. They tried to get rid of you, but you have managed to survive it all. Ten years—I can't even imagine. Now it is your time to live."

"I'm not going up there to live. It is just another place for me to die, even farther away from you all. They don't even hide it, calling us 'canaries.' They want us to detect danger so that the important astronauts live. If I make it past being launched on a bomb, then the lack of oxygen will do me in."

"So what? If you die on the moon, at least we will have made it there. They will have to remember us then. But you, my child, are not going to die. You will outlive them all. Here. I want you to have this."

She thrust something into their hand and blocked the view from the guards as they studied the object. It was a book.

"What am I supposed to do with this?"

"Read it. It is one of the stories of our people written before all of this. Hide it and go spread queer joy up into space."

They stuck the book down the front of their pants and tugged the drawstring tight, then let their shirt fall against their gaunt frame. There wasn't even a bulge showing where the book was. As long as they were careful, they could keep it hidden. And if not? They would just end up back here, back where they belonged, dying with their siblings.

"There. Go now. The guard is calling for you."

They stepped out of the room and into the bright sunlight. The guard escorted them to the front of the base, where a man was standing in a clean blue uniform. It stood out among the sea of camouflage.

"Here you go, sir." The guard handed them off and walked away.

The man stared at them, brow scrunched.

"You are the canary?"

"Yes, sir." They tried to straighten up. They looked younger than their twenty-six years, they knew. They felt younger. More than a third of their life had been spent inside a camp.

"Your file says your name is 458."

"Yes, sir." Their siblings were likely peeking out of one of the dorms. They kept their head high, trying to make them proud.

"458? That is a small number. How long have you been here?"

"My parents dropped me off at Johnson, sir."

"That long ago? No wonder you have no meat left on you. We will get that taken care of. I can't go calling you a number, however. What is your name?"

"I don't have one, sir."

"What did your parents name you?"

"I don't remember."

He hesitated, then decided that they were either telling the truth or had earned this much after ten years.

"Well if you are going to be one of my canaries, why don't I call you Finch?"

"Finch?" they asked.

"Yes, it's the type of bird that canaries are. Does that work?"

"Yes, sir. And, sir?"

"Yes?"

"My pronouns are they and them."

He looked them up and down, and there almost seemed to be a hint of respect when he answered. "I think we can do that. Now, let's get out of here."

Finch didn't look back as they left, knowing their family wouldn't want that from them.

Ray

Chapter Eighteen

WHEN RAY WOKE UP, her bladder ached, and her muscles were stiff from sleep. She needed to get out of bed, but Finch was nowhere to be seen.

"Computer, can you please ask Finch for assistance?"

"I'm sorry, but Finch is currently unavailable."

"Unavailable? What does that mean? Did they go outside?"

"Finch is on the station. However, their current circumstances do not allow them to be disturbed."

"Fine. Then I'll go myself." Ray threw off the blanket and inched her body to the end of the bed. She felt better. The overall ache was gone. She held on to the bed as she dropped her feet to the floor. Her legs held her. Her head hurt a bit, but everything else seemed fine.

"I must remind you that the doctor recommended that you stay in bed for the rest of today."

"Do you have another idea? I need to pee, and if Finch isn't around, I need to do it myself."

"I am sorry that I am unable to assist you."

As much as the computer claimed not to be sentient, she did sound sorry. Ray melted at the admission.

"I'm fine. Look—my legs aren't shaking or anything. I'll take it slow and you can monitor me the entire way."

"That would make me feel better."

Ray kept one hand on the wall as she walked, although she did it more for the computer's well-being than her own. Her legs were working fine. They felt better now that they'd had a chance to stretch out.

Once she finished with the restroom, she changed her clothes and headed to the kitchen to make herself a smoothie and heat some pancakes. While she walked, she kept an eye out for Finch, but didn't see them.

Making the pancakes was easy enough, although she couldn't figure out how Finch had folded down the packaging to make it into a tray instead of just a flattened box. She would have to ask them the next time she saw them. Ray sat down at one of the tables and dug in; hot food was fantastic.

As she ate, she pulled out her pad and started on her research. She was behind where her project outline had placed her. The probes should have been placed by now.

They needed at least forty-eight hours for preliminary data so that she could give an update to the stakeholders, and the report was due in a week. The accident had set her back. While Ray was sure that she could get an extension if she were to tell the stakeholders what had happened, that would be admitting to almost getting herself killed. There was a risk that instead of an extension, the stakeholders would consider her too green and bring her back planetside. The moon wasn't anything like what Ray had expected, but she wasn't ready to give up on her dream yet.

"Computer, where is Finch?"

"Finch is currently unavailable."

"You said that already. Where are they? Do you know when they will become available?"

"I do not."

"Fine. I will go find them."

"I recommend that you go and rest now. You have been up far longer than the doctor recommended."

"I feel okay." But as she rose from the table, her head swam and her legs trembled. "Maybe I *will* go lie down for a little bit."

She managed to put her trash in the compactor and fill her cup with more water before heading back down the hall toward her bed, grateful for the reduced gravity. Ray's body thanked her as she eased onto the thin foam mattress. Even though her body needed a break, her mind wasn't tired. She picked up the book Finch had loaned her and escaped into the pages.

The next thing she knew, she had flipped to the last page and read the ending. There was a short teaser for the next book in the series, and Ray's heart sank, realizing that it had probably been lost. The book burnings had taken out so much of the queer literature, and while it might be floating around on private computers, it was no longer available on the larger retail sites. But even those were far away, inaccessible from the moon's internet service.

"What time is it?"

"It is currently 12:00 hours."

Ray's stomach growled, reminding her about lunch, and she started to wonder if maybe Finch had the right idea of just eating once a day. So far, her day seemed to revolve around what to eat next.

"Is Finch still unavailable?"

"That is correct."

Ray frowned and let out a huff. She had nearly died two days ago, and Finch had risked their own life to save hers. Now, when she was still supposed to be recovering—when Finch was supposed to be taking care of her—they were nowhere to be found.

"Is it because of last night? Are they unavailable because of something I said?"

"That would not be inaccurate."

How hypocritical of them to care if I am attracted to girls, Ray thought. Her blood boiled, drowning any fear or shame. "I am tired of hiding who I am. I came to the moon to be myself, and I thought Finch, of all people, would understand. Well, I am going to find them and tell them exactly what I think of that."

"Please leave Finch alone."

The computer almost sounded sad, and it gave Ray pause. They had been together a long time, and Ray was the intruder here, so of course the computer would have a preference for Finch. But Ray had a few things to say to Finch about ignoring her just because she was gay. *Why am I not good enough?*

Ray stomped out of the room, nearly sending herself flinging to the ceiling in her haste. She slowed her pace, but it just caused her fury to build up even more.

She expected to find Finch hovering over some machine in the mechanics room but they were not there. Ray checked the other storage unit, and even behind all the stacked-up containers. It almost looked like an attic or a basement full of forgotten belongings. Finch was not there.

Then Ray backtracked, returning to the kitchen and heading for the airlock, but Finch's suit was tucked away nicely in their cubby. Uncertain where else to look, she went back to the main juncture. There was one hallway she hadn't gone down. It was a short walk before she made it to the command center, but it, too, was empty.

"Computer, where the hell are they?"

"It is best that you let them be. They need some time."

"They need time? Finch was supposed to be taking care of me today. I wasn't supposed to even get out of bed until tomorrow."

Then it dawned on Ray the one place that she had forgotten to look: Finch's bedroom. She walked back down the hall and to the canaries' dormitory. The door opened easily enough, and Ray marched in.

"Finch, I need to talk to you."

When she didn't hear anything, she stepped fully into the room. There were four bunks on each side, stacked two high. They were built into the wall with a curtain to cover the opening for privacy. The hallway in between was barely enough for one person to slip through.

The first bunks were all open and empty. The beds were made, and the shelves on the side of the wall were empty. There were other compartments built into the bunks, little areas that wouldn't hold much—maybe a stolen book and a few other trinkets.

In between the bunks were shelves, with only one section holding some pairs of worn-down clothing. That must be where Finch lived. They chose to stay in this tight space when they could have moved into their own quarters, where they could at least have stood up.

The curtain to Finch's bunk was closed, and she hesitated, but then she heard them groaning. Her anger quickly changed to concern. She ripped back the curtain and found Finch dripping in sweat. Their eyes were open, almost bulging out of their head. Their arms were crossed. The nails on one hand gouged into the opposite arm, leaving streaks of blood and crescent indentations.

"Finch, are you okay?" She pressed her hand to their forehead to feel for a fever, but Finch snapped at them, their jaw almost clamping on to her hand. Then they started to scream, a sound filled with terror and pain the likes of which Ray had never heard. She sprinted straight out of the room, her gait still clumsy as she ran into walls and braced her head against the ceiling until she made it back into her room and pulled the door shut.

As soon as she was alone, hot shame flooded her. Finch had needed her help, and she had run away.

"Computer, what was that?"

"Sometimes Finch has flashbacks of being in the camps. They haven't had one for a while. This one is bad."

"The camps? Why didn't you tell me they were like that?"

"The canaries had a rule that the astronauts shouldn't know about it. They covered for each other. The commander told me it was for the best, and I was encouraged not to share when they had breakdowns. But the other canaries knew how to help them, and now they are alone."

"They are not alone. I am here." Ray went back again, this time slower, trying to steel herself for what she would find at the end. She walked into the canaries' dormitory and back to Finch's bed. She sat on the floor, her back against the other bunk and her feet squished to the other side. Finch was there, but not there, seemingly lost in a different world, so Ray did the only thing that she could think of—she started to sing.

Finch

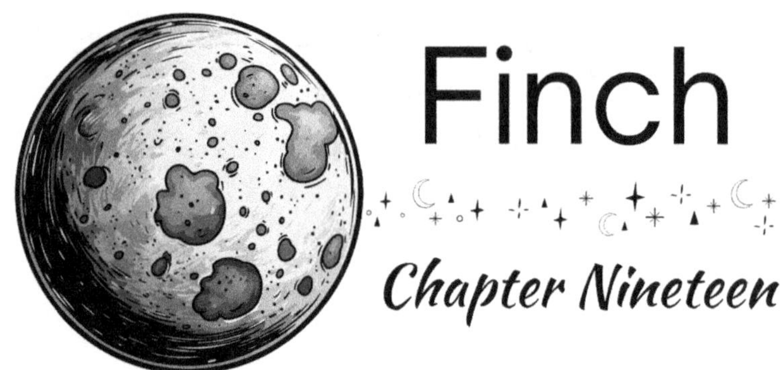

Chapter Nineteen

FINCH HEARD the music flittering through their mind. They remembered Samantha ... Sissy ... all their siblings.

Music had brought them together. When they could, they would sing long into the night. In the work camps, they would sing as the day went on. When the guards were extra cruel, they would sing with just their lips, silently mouthing the words to each other. In the dark, when they were alone, they sang the words silently in their hearts—to remember.

Finch started to cry, soul-crushing tears honoring the pain that still stayed with them during every moment. They carried with them everyone who hadn't made it out, and they refused to let that obligation go. Finch didn't know how long they cried, but eventually, they came back to their body. It was sticky from sweat and urine—they stank in a way they hadn't in years.

When Finch stood up, Ray scooted on the floor, down the line of bunks, allowing them room to gather their blanket and pillowcase and pull clean clothes from their shelves. They left, leaving Ray still sitting on the ground, now quiet.

Finch headed to the airlock bathroom and put their blanket and pillowcase in the washing machine. Then they stripped off their foul clothes and added them to the load. When they measured out the water, they increased the amount to allow for the extra volume. After it started, they took out the wash wipes, one by one, cleaning themself until the grime was gone. When the discomfort had been wiped away, Finch slipped on their clean clothes.

The familiar process helped to ground them to the moment, remind them where and when they were, and by the time they left the restroom, they were ready to put the latest panic attack behind them.

When Finch returned to their room, Ray was still sitting on the floor, waiting for them. Finch sank onto their bare mattress and scooted back against the wall before pulling their legs up to their chest and putting their head on their knees.

"Do you want to talk about what happened?" Ray asked.

Finch looked for their tablet, but it had not made it back to their room with them. They settled for shaking their head.

"Did I cause that to happen?"

Finch thought about lying. They tended to be honest, but they were perfectly capable of lying, especially if the situation warranted it. Instead, they found themself squeaking out, "Yes."

Ray started crying then, sweet tears that fell gracefully down her face. They were nothing like the ugly tsunami that stormed out of Finch when they cried.

"You didn't mean it," Finch said. "But your stories ... having you here ... all of it made me remember. It is so much easier when I am alone."

"The computer said you were in the camps."

Finch didn't respond. They kept their head on their knees, looking at Ray.

"When did you get sent?"

"The first one, or the first one on US soil."

"That long? You must have been a child."

"I was sixteen." Finch started rocking in the small space. "I knew who I was for a few years. There was a club at my school that I attended sometimes. I wasn't out to anyone, I knew that my parents wouldn't approve, so I kept it all to myself."

"Then why did they take you? How did they know?"

"Once the president said I, or non-binary people, didn't exist," Finch said. "It hurt more than I thought it would. I spent the day crying. I tried not to show it, but one of my friends asked me what was wrong, and I told her. She told the teacher, who said she legally had to tell my family."

"That was my biggest fear," Ray said. "I knew if my

family found out I was gay, they would send me to the camps, or worse."

"The camps didn't exist yet," Finch said. "There were some uncomfortable times when my family tried their own interventions to fix me. I had already been a headache to them. I was diagnosed autistic when I was young, and they didn't handle it well. I remember them arguing with the schools about how I just needed to try harder and the school needed to stop coddling me. There were a few teachers who stepped in to help me, but most just labeled me a problem. So my parents already didn't like me much when all this happened."

Finch's voice was quiet, reserved. They didn't want to say any of the words, but they flew out of their mouth on their own volition.

"So you volunteered to come here?"

"It was ten years later. I was twenty-six when they opened up the application for canaries. They had moved all the queer folk to one camp by then. Most everyone else was already freed or had been deported. They separated us—trans people together, gay people together—as if we weren't one community with overlapping identities. If you were just gay, you could go if they liked you well enough—if you promised to conform. A few came right back. I imagine the rest did whatever they could to stay away. They kept all the trans people. Most hadn't lasted that long, though. I'm not sure how I did."

"But you came here. You survived."

Had they survived? They were here, still alive, but they hadn't *felt* alive in so long.

"They only accepted people between the ages of twenty-five to thirty," Finch said. "There were fifteen of us in the camps at the time who could apply—fifteen out of the fifty of us who were left. I was the only one who made it. I didn't want to go, to leave them, but they told me that I needed to. They needed to know that we lived on, that we had made it to another planet. So I left them. It was a while before I could read the news. The first few months were so hard, but they cleaned out the camp the next week before they were forced to close it. I don't think anyone ended up making it out."

"You did. You survived. You and the other canaries."

"They didn't, though. I didn't. We were brought here to die—the same as before, just in a different place. We were brought here to complete the dangerous tasks so the corporation wouldn't lose the investment that they had placed in their astronauts. We did die. After the first two years, there were only three of us left. After five years, there was just me. Then the astronauts all moved off to the big station, the safer one, until I was left here all alone."

Ray lowered her gaze, as if soaking it all in. Finch tried to imagine what she was thinking. They had different identities and different pasts, but somehow, their paths had both led them right here to this moment.

"Tell me about them," Ray said.

"The canaries?"

"Yes, please. Who were they?"

"There were eight of us. None of us had any business going up into space, but here we were. Each of us was willing to risk our lives because what waited for us back on Earth was even worse. Jake instantly became our leader. He was big and strong, and people knew not to mess with him, but you learn fast in the camp to put on a hard exterior to survive, and none of us bought it. Even if he did kill his old man. He protected us that first month by taking on the hardest jobs and taught us to hide when we started to lose control. He was the first to die. The suits were bad; he ended up puncturing his, and he died before we could get him inside. We learned never to go anywhere without tape after that."

"He killed someone, and they let him come?"

"He was thirteen. His father was trying to kill his mom at the time. His mom didn't make it, and after all of it, he was left with no one. He told me he would do it all over again. Then there was Mariana. She also came from prison, but for drug charges. She says they weren't hers, and I don't care if they were or not. No one thought she ended up in jail for drugs."

"She came to the moon when she was only being held for drug charges?"

"They gave her a life sentence. She says it is because she refused to sleep with the cop who arrested her."

"You believed her?"

"It didn't matter. It was her story, and that is what I keep with me. I've seen worse in the camps, and it may have been hell, but even then, I know that my white skin helped protect me. Who am I to say her story isn't true? She was a canary, and that is all that mattered."

Finch stood up then. They walked past Ray to the front bunks that had once belonged to Jake and Mariana. If they tried hard, they could still see their friends here.

Finch gestured to the next row, up toward a top bunk. "Pixy slept here. None of us knew why she joined up, since she was too young—just seventeen. She didn't even lie on her application; she just broke into the corporation's servers to submit it. I think she just wanted to get as far away as possible, and the moon was all that was available to her. She saved our asses more times than we could count. One of the astronauts forced himself on her. We tried to protect her, but there were so few of us by then. She decided the moon wasn't as far as she could go after all. I found her lifeless body in the bunk."

"The commander didn't do anything?"

"You expect the commander to believe canaries over his people? Even if he did believe us, it didn't matter. We were already dead."

Finch pointed to the bottom bunk. "This was Jose's. He also came from the camps. We think our stay in the camp overlapped at one point. Eventually, he got sent to one of the hidden camps, but they didn't know what to do with him. He was an American citizen—third generation—there was nowhere for him to go, so they let him come here. He ran out of air."

"Like me?"

"No, you survived. He didn't. We were all so green back then."

"Please, no more. How can you stand being here surrounded by all of these memories? You could go?"

"I could never go back. The Earth hasn't changed. You should know that. They may have closed the camps, but being who we are is still illegal."

"I didn't mean Earth." Ray stood up. "I meant that you could try and transfer to the bigger station."

"No. This is my home. I help people here. I have a purpose."

"You shouldn't be alone. It isn't healthy."

"I was good alone. Alone is not the problem. I was fine by myself—it wasn't until you showed up that there were problems. I wish you would have left me in peace."

Finch walked out of their room, leaving Ray behind. Part of them felt bad for what they had said, but it was the truth. They had been fine all by themself. Their emotions had stayed locked away, allowing them to focus on their work, on doing something important. That is what mattered. People just caused more pain.

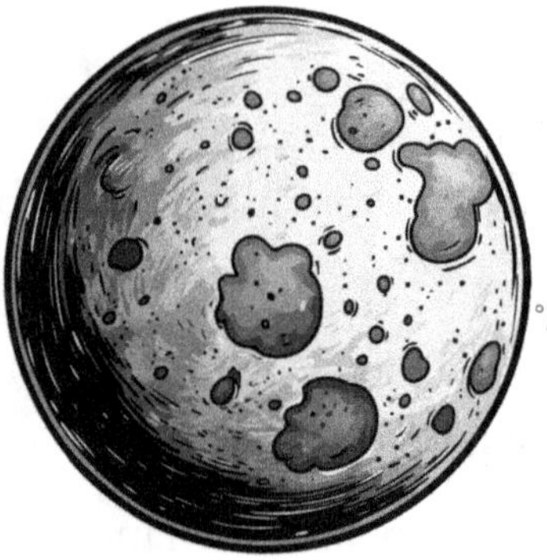

Ray

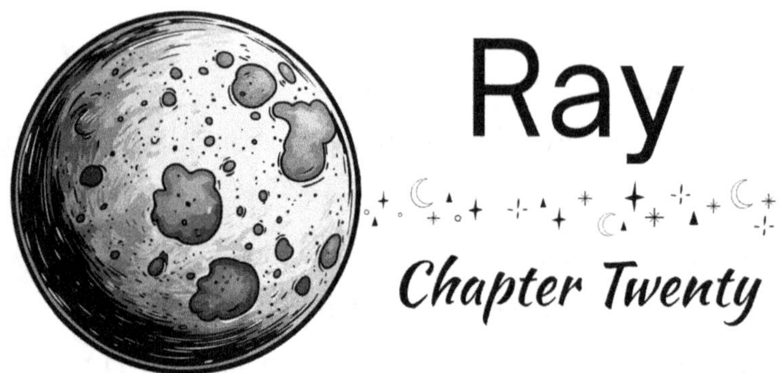

Chapter Twenty

RAY STAYED ON THE FLOOR, unmoving, long after Finch had left. Her throat hurt from the hours of singing, but she hadn't known what else to do. Watching Finch lost in their nightmares had been frightening, and those had been the memories Finch *hadn't* yet shared with her: the ones that lingered behind their eyes and the reason they always appeared haunted.

She kept looking at the eight bunks. Unwanted youth, just like her. Most of them had been around the same age as her when they'd died. Thrown away from society. If she had been a few years older, when it would have been safe to have come out, she could have been one of them, desperate for an escape from the camps to come to the moon. But she *had* been desperate enough to go to the moon—that was why she was here, after all.

Ray made her way to the back of the room, placing her hand on each bunk as she headed for the exit. She didn't know them, couldn't picture their faces, but some part of them lived on in this place. That was why Finch couldn't leave.

It was late, long past lunchtime, as her stomach reminded her. Finch was nowhere to be seen as she returned to her room, and a part of her was grateful.

She had made a mess of things since she had arrived on the moon, but if she was honest, it had started long ago. She made a mess of things everywhere. Even here she couldn't find her people.

She pulled a meal out of the drawer without looking and headed back to the kitchen. She read through the directions, forgetting what they said as soon as she finished, and had to go back again. With the food cooked and in front of her, she realized she wasn't all that hungry after all. It felt wrong to be eating after everything that she had learned, but you didn't waste anything on the moon, so she dug in, the food tasteless in her mouth.

Ray remembered watching the videos of the camps closing. It had been a joyous time, complete with celebrations. Finally, they had managed to oust the last administration, but the new one hadn't been much better. Many of the laws that had been made had not been revoked. The US remained a democracy in name only. But people seemed to accept it. Tired of fighting, they took it as a win even though they still didn't have bodily autonomy, women still hadn't regained their right to vote, and being gay was still a crime.

Most of those who had left the camps had not gone home. They had televised their flights to other countries as if it had been a celebration—and maybe for them, it had been. No more nasty camps and no more people they found problematic. Ray hadn't cheered as the camps had closed. They had still felt trapped. The administration had been very clear that the enforcement had not diminished, just changed—mostly under pressure from the international community.

Videos of the camps had leaked out over time, and Ray had watched them in grad school, her desire to know winning out over her concern of being caught. There was nothing joyous in what she had seen. To know that Finch had been through all of that broke her heart. She had to do something to cheer them up. To help them with the pain that Ray had caused them to remember.

"Computer, where is Finch?"

"Finch is currently in the airlock restroom."

"Perfect. I am going to do something for Finch to help lift their spirits. A surprise."

"That would not be advisable. Finch is not fond of surprises. Given how fragile their current state is, it would be best to just give them some time alone."

"You don't even know what I am going to do yet. Trust me, they are going to love it."

The computer let out an electronic sigh, and Ray rolled her eyes at the dramatics. *Finch would love it.*

Ray headed to the storage bay. The room was about the same size as her old apartment and cramped with all sorts of bins and containers. She pushed all the objects to the wall and stacked them as best as she could. She opened them as she moved them, checking to see what was inside. In one, she found some paint and paper that she used to create a sign. She had never possessed much artistic talent, but she made a very basic sign. It wasn't more than words on a page—Club Schmidt. There was some ribbon in another bin and Ray took out anything sparkly or remotely decorative and tied them to the rivets on the wall. It looked like a hodgepodge of random trinkets thrown about, but she had to work with what was on hand.

"Computer, can we do anything with the lights? It still looks like a cargo hold."

"May I remind you that it is, in fact, a cargo hold."

"Not tonight. Tonight it is a club. I'm going to do for Finch what my classmates did for me when I was out of sorts. I am going to take them dancing. I'm guessing they haven't had a vacation in many years, and it is time to change that."

"It is most likely that Finch has never had a vacation," the computer said. "Having known them for a decade now, I can guarantee you that what they need is not a break. They need to get back to their routine."

"I have to do this," Ray said. "I caused Finch's freak-out, and I need to help to make it right."

"I would be happy to provide you with suggestions on how to 'make it right' with them. My first suggestion would be not to continue with this."

"Can we do something with the lights or not?" Ray asked.

"The lights are not equipped for emitting at multiple spectral bandwidths. They can, however, be adjusted in brightness."

"Can you turn them up?"

"I can. However, I must insist that it is not a good idea. The station has run at this intensity for quite some time."

"For not being sentient, you have a lot of opinions. Maybe that is part of Finch's problem. They live like they are one of the mole people. Turn up the lights as high as they will go."

The computer let out another brief burst of static before continuing, "I suggest that you cover your eyes."

The computer had been hanging out with Finch for far too long, and seemed to have develop their proclivity for the dramatics. However, Ray obligatorily covered her eyes with her hands, and even then, the light shined through the cracks of her fingertips. She slowly lowered her hand. It was much brighter, almost like a normal light level. It made the room look even dingier, accenting the items that Ray had stacked to the side. Clubs were usually darker, but this was better. It would do Finch some good to get some actual light.

"Now all we need is food."

"Finch already ate their meal for the day an hour ago. They are currently in their room experiencing their personal time."

"That is good because this is about snacks and splurging. It is good to go against the grain sometimes."

"Do you have peer-reviewed research articles that reference that data?" the computer asked.

"No, but I am sure if you search, you will find some. I know this from life experience."

"Ah, may I remind you that your life experience has been very different from Finch's?"

Ray shook her head and walked out of the cargo bay back to her room. She dug through her food supply and found some individual packages of chips and a couple of single servings of cheese dip and salsa. She also pulled out some of her dessert packets. She would have to go without later, but it would be worth it to cheer Finch up.

She headed back to the cargo bay and pulled out one of the containers to serve as a makeshift table. Ray filled up her water bottle and found Finch's left on the table where they had eaten dinner, so she filled it up as well. She brought them both back to the cargo bay and set them on the container. The containers were soft-sided, allowing for easier storage when not in use, and the bottles had difficulty standing up on the surface. Eventually, she gave up and laid them down.

"This will have to do. Now we just need some club

music. Computer, can you access my playlist titled "Smashers" and play it at max volume?"

Music blasted through the cargo bay. It was the playlist that Ray used whenever she wanted to dance. It was full of bass and thumping notes. The words were simple and designed to be easy for people to sing along as they moved to the music. Ray couldn't help it as they started to dance, pulling their arms up through their hair as they moved their hips.

"This is perfect. Now all we need is Finch. Computer, can you ask them to come to the cargo bay?"

Ray could barely hear the words that came out of her mouth, the music was so loud, just like at an actual club, and like how Finch listened to their own music. Ray continued dancing as she waited for Finch to arrive. The song ended and a new one began—still there was no Finch.

"Computer, did you ask Finch to come?"

The music paused suddenly, casting the room into silence until the computer spoke. "I will not ask them to come here."

"Don't you have to do what I say?"

"Finch is my friend, and I will not ask them to come to this surprise. Please do not do so either."

Ray stormed out of the cargo hold, straight toward Finch's room. She knocked tentatively on the door, memories of the morning flooding in. When Finch opened the door, they looked like they had the day she'd first met them—like a specter, but one which seemed fairly calm and collected.

"I have something I would like to show you," Ray said.

Finch peered out into the hallway as if the item was there, and then looked Ray up and down. When they didn't see anything, they started to close the door, but Ray put their hand on it, stopping it.

"It's not here—it is in the cargo hold."

Finch looked resigned as they stepped into the hallway, and for a brief moment, Ray wondered if the computer had been right. But no, this was exactly what Finch needed. She decided to soften the blow of the surprise by keeping a conversation going while they walked to the cargo hold.

"I know that things have been tough since I arrived, and I wanted to do something for you to make it up to you."

When Finch didn't reply, Ray glanced back at them. They were still following, but they had a look of almost fear on their face.

"It's not a lot. There was only so much I could do with what we had. I just thought that I would create a space for you to relax—I know you haven't had that often in your life."

Ray opened the door to the cargo bay. Music streamed out, a loud, thumping beat that begged to be danced to.

Finch's hands went to cover their ears. Ray rolled her eyes at their dramatics. After all, Finch listened to their music just as loudly.

"Over here we have a snack bar, and here is a dance floor," Ray yelled.

She started dancing in the open space, but Finch didn't

join her. Instead, they approached the decorations strung all over the room. They touched the stuffed teddy bear, stroking its fur lovingly before tugging so violently that the ribbon attached to it broke. They threw the bear directly at Ray and started to scream.

"Computer, stop the music!" Ray said. The room was suddenly filled with Finch's screams of rage. They echoed off the walls, replacing the joyful music. "What is wrong? I did all of this for you, and you are behaving like an animal."

"Take it down." Finch walked over to the sign and stroked the letters before tearing it up into tiny pieces all over the floor. "Put everything back where you found it. None of this is yours. It is theirs, it is all theirs, and you had no right to touch their things." Finch tore down each of the decorations and threw them toward the bins.

Ray thought about yelling back, about letting Finch know exactly how hurt they were by the rejection. Instead, she picked up the packaged food and stormed off to her bedroom, letting Finch have their fit alone. She had done enough for them today.

She had lost too much time on her project. Tomorrow she needed to go out again, and it was clear that Finch was in no position to help her. So she pulled up the training videos on moonwalks and watched each one until they started to make sense. She ate her dinner, the combination of snack food she had brought to the party, while she watched.

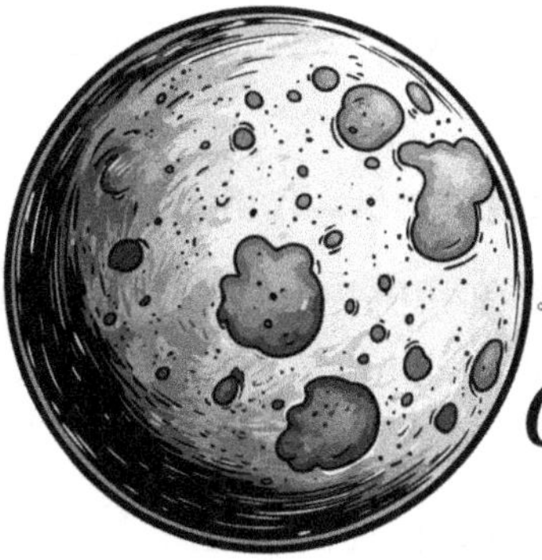

Finch

Chapter Twenty-one

FINCH PICKED up the teddy bear and held it close. Teardrops appeared on its surface, and Finch wiped them away as best as they could. It wouldn't do to store it when it was wet.

They held the piece of ribbon, trying to untie the knots around its neck. It had been hung from a noose, just like Jasmine and Breeze. Finch had been eighteen when they had recognized a pattern in the guard's routine. Jasmine had wanted to escape. Finch had been scared; they had nothing outside the camps. Somehow, the guards had found out, and Jasmine and Breeze had taken the blame even though it had been as much Finch's fault ... maybe even more.

Finch had watched their bodies drop, and all they could do was hold on to the younger kids to make sure that they didn't run and cry.

They sprinted into the workroom and grabbed one of the knives, cutting through the ribbon and freeing the bear.

"All better," they muttered, walking back and placing it gently in Pixy's container.

Finch looked down at the ribbon, now in multiple pieces. It had belonged to Mariana. The commander had given it to her to help hold her hair back. She had been wearing some when the explosion had gone off.

There were pieces of their friends scattered all over the room, used as decorations. It was all too much. Everything was still so raw. Finch picked up each piece, putting it away as best as they could. Then they rearranged the bins back to where they belonged.

After, they lay down on the cold metal floor and curled up in a ball. Finch ignored the computer when it tried to talk to them. They ignored Ray when she opened the door. They were pretty sure it was morning, and they had things that they needed to do—but nothing mattered. Everything inside of them was pain. The memories were more than they could handle. That is why they had locked them away.

At one point, they realized that their lips were chapped.

"Come on now, child, get up. You have to go on, you promised me." Samantha's voice filtered through their head just like the last day they had seen her. "You know how to do it. One foot in front of the other. It's all right to be hurt. It's all right to be sad. But you can never let them see—or they have won."

Finch had lived most of their life not letting other people win. They stood up, looking around the storage room, making sure they had finished cleaning everything up. Then they walked back to their bedroom and glanced at their morning routine. Finch knew it wasn't morning, that they hadn't slept all night, but they couldn't close their eyes—they couldn't handle what they would see. What they needed was something familiar. So, they went through their morning hygiene routine, once again changing out of their clothes. They picked up their morning ration of water, swallowing it too fast as they headed to the command station.

"Computer, any news?"

"I think that you should know that Ray went back outside this morning."

Finch froze, their chest so tight they couldn't breathe.

"I watched her put on her suit, and you had already updated her oxygen tank. Her suit has also been added to my systems, so I have been monitoring her vitals. She is fine and headed toward the minefield. I also made sure to turn the lights on for her."

"Good," Finch managed. Their voice shook as much as their body. They pulled up Ray's vitals on the screen, and everything looked good. "Do you think I need to go out there?"

"I'm not sure that is such a good idea. She is doing fine, and I will update you if that changes."

"Alright," Finch said. Everything looked okay, and they

knew they were not in a good state to go outside. "What's on my schedule for today?"

"I have taken the liberty of adjusting your schedule. I think you may enjoy some routine software updates on the oxygen system."

Finch nodded absently and picked up the tablet, trying to focus on reading the directions. There were a lot of technical terms. They weren't especially skilled at reading. It had been hard—everything had been hard—even before, but in the camps, there hadn't been any chance to practice. They had improved some since they had come to the moon, but often, they found themself struggling if the text was too advanced.

"Do you mind reading what this says?" Finch asked.

They left the command station, heading toward the oxygen system, while the computer read off the directions. They worked through it together, Finch distracted, until Ray made it through the airlock—in one piece.

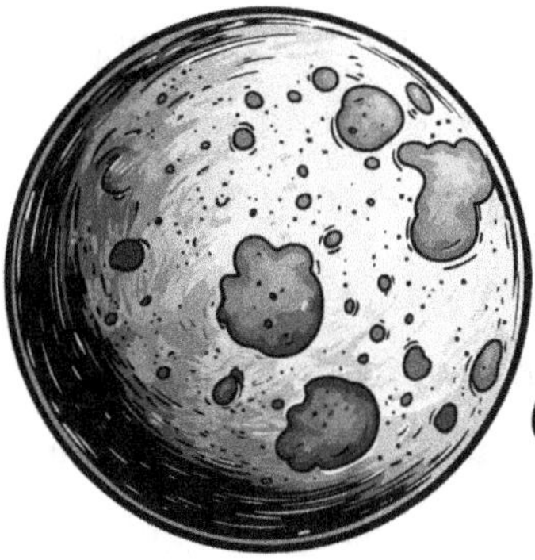

Ray

Chapter Twenty-two

RAY TOOK off her space suit and made sure to put each piece in the correct spot. It didn't look quite as neat as Finch's—but nothing could look as good as Finch's suit. It wasn't bad for just her second time putting it away. Then she went to the restroom, wiped off her body, and cleaned out her nose—even though she was pretty sure these were steps Finch had made up. They were nowhere in the training videos. But the station was old, so she decided to make concessions when she could.

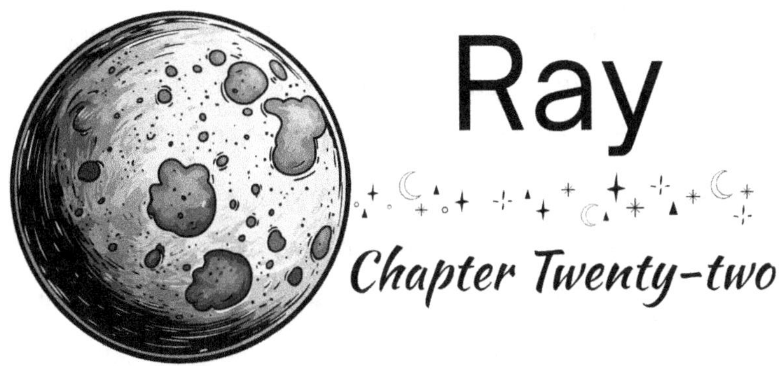

She put on the clothes that she had stashed before going outside and pulled out the tablet she had left in the bathroom. Each of the nine probes was sending pings and had started collecting data. Unfortunately, the data was being stored directly in the measuring rods. The grant hadn't approved funding for those with satellite connectivity, even if it hadn't been all that much more expensive, since they were produced by a rival company. She would have to go out in a few days to download the data.

The station was quiet—even Finch's music was absent—and Ray felt sudden concern that Finch had gone back into one of their panic attacks. However, they had been very clear that they didn't want her around.

When Ray walked past Finch's room, she noticed that the door was closed. She continued until she reached the kitchen. Before heading out, she had moved some of her food over into the mess hall. There was ample storage space where the crew had previously stored their food. She pulled out one of the meals at random. There was no eating when you were in the space suit, and Ray had been outside all day. She was hungry.

Ray heated her food and, when it was ready, pulled out her tablet to look at some of the pictures she had taken while she had been out. The area had been flattened by the years of robot activity. It was concerning. All of the topsoil had been removed, and not just in the current mining area, but all the surrounding ones as well. Ray had uploaded a map of the previous mining sites and used the lights as a guide to help her visit a few of them.

She had placed probes in the prior mining areas, but there just hadn't been enough. She was going to have to write up a new grant proposal for more funds if her suspicions were backed up by the evidence. Humans were doing the same thing to the moon that they had done to Earth—stripping it of its resources without concern for the impact.

Ray felt proud of herself. Ever since she had been on the moon, she had behaved like an incompetent child, but today she had gone back to being the doctorate astrogeologist that she was. She had successfully done science without nearly killing herself. It was a good day.

When Finch walked into the room, Ray jumped. She had convinced herself that Finch was holed up somewhere, so she hadn't expected to see them. However, they walked in, looking like their usual self, not that that meant much, and picked up one of their bars. They filled up their water and sat at the table. The same table where Ray was.

Finch opened their bar and started what Ray now realized was a routine. They would take a small bite, slowly chewing as if savoring the tasteless mouthful. Then, once they swallowed, they would take a small sip of water, repeating this process until the bar was finished, at which point they would drink the last of the water. Everything that Finch did seemed to consist of structure and routine. Maybe it went back to their neurodiverseness or their days in the camps, or perhaps both. But it hit Ray that she had arrived, without Finch's knowledge, and had disrupted everything. She had been so busy worrying about herself and her desires on the moon that she hadn't stopped to think about Finch's needs.

The party had probably been a nightmare for them. Yet another surprise after they already weren't doing well. Again,

Ray had done what she would have needed and not what Finch had needed.

Finch hadn't said a word, but maybe they didn't have a routine for that. They had sat down at the same table as her, after everything.

"Hi," Ray said.

Finch looked up and then took another bite.

"I'm sorry about yesterday. The computer tried to tell me that it wasn't a smart thing for me to do, but I didn't listen."

Finch shrugged and continued chewing.

Ray sat staring at the older person. They hadn't spoken with words, but Ray was starting to realize that there were times when they were unable to speak. They also didn't seem to have their tablet next to them. But they were still communicating—Ray just had to pay attention.

"After dinner is your free time, correct?"

Finch nodded.

"What do you normally do for free time?" Ray noticed she hadn't asked it in a way that Finch could respond to without speaking. She tried to think of a way to rephrase the sentence, but couldn't come up with anything. Finch just remained silent, continuing their meal. "I could go and get your tablet if you want."

Finch nodded again.

"Do you know where it is?"

Finch shrugged. As knowledgeable as Finch was about

the station and living on the moon, they seemed to have an uncanny ability to misplace things.

Ray got up and headed out into the hall. They were closest to Finch's room, but the thought of going back there gave her pause. She turned and walked the other way toward the workshop. The room was a bit of a cluttered mess, but even still, Ray couldn't see the tablet. They went to the cargo bay and found that the room had been completely cleaned up. Everything had been put back into the same place it had been before.

Ray approached a stack of bins and noticed for the first time that each one had a name attached to it. *The other canaries. Had she gone into their belongings to use as party decorations?* No wonder Finch had been so upset.

She looked around, a pit of shame building in her stomach, but didn't notice Finch's pad.

Then suddenly she was struck with a thought so frustratingly simple that she once again questioned her intelligence.

"Computer, do you know where Finch's pad is?"

"The pad is currently in the command station."

The computer sounded almost robotic, not back to the neutral voice it had used before, but like it was only speaking to Ray out of obligation rather than its normal desire to communicate. Apparently, Finch wasn't the only one she needed to apologize to.

"I'm sorry I didn't listen to you yesterday," Ray said as she headed to the command station. "You have worked with

Finch for a long time, and I dismissed everything that you had to say."

"I am just a virtual assistance program. You had no reason to listen to me."

"Well, I'm not so sure I believe that you are *just* anything. Maybe you were not created to be more than a virtual assistant, but you have been here a long time, and I would wager a guess that your programming has adapted. Either way, Finch is your crewmate, and I used my own experience to decide what I thought would be best without listening to you. I'm sorry."

Ray spotted the pad sitting on the arm of the command chair, balanced precariously. She picked it up but paused, not wanting to return to Finch until the conversation had finished.

"You are only apologizing because I was right."

Ray laughed. "Well, if you weren't right, I wouldn't have anything to apologize for."

"Finch is good people. They have been hurt enough in their life. Don't add to it."

"I will try not to. I'm learning."

"Ray," the computer said. "You are good people also. Finch knows that, and I know that."

Ray's eyes started to water, and her throat choked up. But she managed to let out a "thank you" before heading back to Finch.

Finch was still sitting at the table, finishing up their meal, when Ray arrived.

"I found it." She placed the pad on the table and then picked up her empty tray before depositing it in the composter.

"Movies," Finch said through the computer system. The generic voice was a sharp contrast to the computer's new speech.

"What?" Ray turned around, uncertain what Finch was referring to.

"In my free time, I watch movies or TV shows."

"Oh," Ray said. "Would you mind if I joined you?"

Finch paused, not touching their pad, and Ray was worried that she had overstepped again, but she turned back around to finish her cleanup, giving Finch time to come up with their response. When she sat back down at the table, Finch was typing into their pad.

"I normally watch in my room. That won't work with the two of us. What if we go to the command station? We can project the show onto the wall."

"I would like that."

Ray waited until Finch finished eating, working on her tablet so as not to make Finch feel rushed. When they were done, they both headed into the command station. Finch sat in the commander's chair, and Ray took the one off to the right. They were surprisingly comfortable. As Finch worked to pull up a movie, Ray used the quiet to ask one more question.

"Do you think that tomorrow I could shadow you and see what you do? I'll be quiet and do my best not to get in the way."

Ray held her breath, waiting for Finch to respond. They had stopped typing and seemed to be thinking through what she had said. Finally, Finch gave a curt nod and finished pulling up a movie on the screen. *The Avengers*, Ray read. *This should be interesting.*

Finch

Chapter Twenty-three

FINCH WATCHED as Ray suited up. She had learned a lot since she had first arrived. Although she was still slow. Finch had finished putting on their own suit ten minutes ago and had sat back and watched as Ray finished. They kept an eye out to make sure that she was doing everything correctly, trying not to make Ray feel rushed as they had built extra time into the schedule for Ray's inexperience.

Last night, the computer had talked to them and helped them to realize that Ray had made an effort. Even the dance club, something that should never have happened, had been planned to try and make them feel better. The computer had said Ray had learned from that, and that was why she had spent the night watching old superhero movies with Finch. Even now, coming out here, neglecting her research to shadow Finch, was a way of reaching out.

So last night, Finch had talked through some ideas with the computer on how they could be patient with Ray. They had worked together to rearrange the schedule to make sure that there was enough time so that neither of them ended up being stressed.

"Done," Ray said, her helmet in her hands.

"Let's go." Finch picked up their helmet from beside them on the bench and put it on, making sure it was sealed shut. They watched as Ray did the same.

"Computer, verify we are good to disembark." They didn't usually ask, but they had agreed that would be their code phrase to make sure that Ray was really good to go. It sounded like it belonged in one of those old astronaut films.

"You are good for surface walk," the computer said.

Now that was taking things a bit too far, but Finch just stood up and turned on the outside lights. They stepped into the airlock, waiting until Ray joined them before closing the door and allowing the air to decompress.

Finch felt the anxiety start to rage inside of them. They loved going outside. It helped to break up the monotony of being in the station all the time and allowed them to interact with other humans. They might not have been good at it—but even they needed social interaction of a small sort. However, they had started to find that too much time out on the surface brought the memories back—memories that were already too close to the surface. However, looking at Ray next to them helped, slightly. Even though that didn't make any sense to them. Ray was just another person that they had to keep alive, and they hadn't done so well on that front.

"Breathe." The computer's voice filled their helmet, on a frequency that just the two of them shared. Finch couldn't respond on it, but they could listen.

They paused their thoughts long enough to focus on taking in a breath and calming down their body. They heard Sissy's voice filter through their head. *You can't stop living life based on what* might *happen.* They had missed thinking about all their friends. Finch was the only one who could keep their memories alive, and it did them a disservice to lock them all away.

"First, we need to go and check the purifying station and load up the order," Finch said. They exited the airlock and started heading along their regular route.

Ray stayed silently beside them.

"We are packing up an order for one of the Russian stations farther up north," Finch said. "They don't come as often, so it will be an extra-large order."

Finch approached the shelter, which held all the ice. It was contained behind a simple door, not unlike those used in garages, that rolled up when opened. Inside were stacks of ice.

"Where does all this come from?" Ray asked.

"The water crystals are mined off the surface. I believe you visited there yesterday. The water crystals are then separated from all the other minerals and rocks via evaporation and then travel through a series of pipes where they go through a reverse osmosis purification system." They walked into the storage unit and to the back, where there were blocks of ice coated in a thin layer of silicon being lifted off a conveyor belt and stacked onto the piles.

"The water is then allowed to freeze, after which it is sliced and sealed to protect it from contamination. Then the machines stack them up here until they are needed for deliveries."

"And it's all automated?"

"It is now, but that was built up over time. We had no idea when we first came up here. The science hadn't caught up with what we were planning to do, but the corporation wanted to be first."

Finch watched as Ray looked over the machinery, even examining the towers of ice blocks. She seemed so fascinated by a scene that Finch had come to see as normal.

"Once the machines begin loading up the ice," Finch said, "I will start looking over the machinery. There were no errors in the maintenance log, but I like to do a visual inspection every time I come out. After the delivery, we will head down to the mining fields. You can check on your equipment while we are there."

"That sounds great."

Finch typed into their pad commands for the machine to start packing up the empty shed. The robot offloading the frozen cubes kept working, and two robots that had been sitting idle in the corner came to life. The silicon coating had a built-in handle on the top that laid flat until needed. With the ice being lighter on the moon than on Earth, this worked well for hauling around the massive blocks. Each robot had one gripper that would load blocks of ice onto a flat surface on its back and then, when full, take the ice and reload it on the larger trailer.

While the machines were doing their tasks, Finch walked the lines of equipment, searching for any visible damage. Ray followed close to their heels but didn't speak. After, when they were inside and the work done, Finch would ask her if she had any questions, but for now, they appreciated the quiet and the ability to concentrate.

Once the ice was loaded, Finch put up the sides of the trailer and threw the tarp covering over the top. They walked over to the other side and connected the hooks securing the ice enough so it would stay inside if the Russians went a little too hard on the bumps.

"Are you ready for some sunshine?" Finch asked.

"Really?" Ray said.

Finch didn't answer. They unplugged the cab from the charger and hooked it up to the trailer. When everything was secure, they looked at Ray and waited until she realized it was her cue to hop in. Then they pulled out of the protected area and started driving down the road.

"It's so weird to see a road out here," Ray said.

"We had to do so many deliveries, and it was hard on the

vehicles to keep going over the uneven terrain, so when they started shipping over material for the new station, the commander hijacked a steamroller and got this built."

"It isn't that old, then?"

"It's been here at least six years now, maybe seven. It takes a lot of time to get things shipped over from Earth. There are drop zones of equipment all over, waiting for new things to get built. Sometimes the material just sits there because a project gets defunded."

"I thought nothing goes to waste on the moon."

"Nothing does. I haven't left the base all that much. I've heard the moon compared to the Wild West, but it is more like a small town—one spread out all over. You never know when you will run into someone again, just that you always will. No one wants to keep paying for all the security, so they tend to respect each other's drop sites. But once things get defunded, all bets are off. Then the scavengers drop in."

"Scavengers? I thought everyone up here was attached to a corporation."

"Most are, but some people just get tired of it all and go off and build their own small settlements. 'Free colonies' are what the news calls them. But it's hard to make it on your own, up here, so they still have to barter—and no one will barter with parts that were stolen."

"You're teasing me, aren't you?"

"Nope. The scavengers come and pick up water just like everyone else, but today is the Russians."

"Aren't you scared?" Ray asked.

Finch turned and looked at them, only taking their eyes off the road for a second because the cab didn't have automatic driving. "Why would I be scared?"

"Because they are Russian. Don't the Russians hate Americans?"

"Maybe planetside. Heck, maybe up here also. But we all want to survive, and that means water. US corporations control the largest water mining output. Chinese corporations are close. But things get muddy up here. If you give a person better living areas, more pay to send home to the family, and safer conditions, they will change allegiance in a heartbeat. Especially if they are lifers."

Ray didn't respond, so Finch turned their full attention back toward the road. They were ascending slightly, so it was just a matter of time before they hit the peak of the crater. "It's coming up. You will want to put down your shield before we get there. Your eyes will be more sensitive after living in the dark."

Finch flipped down their sun shield, making the visibility even harder, the lights of the cab barely even registering. Then, suddenly, they hit the line of sun and everything seemed to glow. Even with the sun visor down, Finch had to squint to protect their eyes. They were no longer made for sunshine, but it was glorious when they saw it.

They glanced over, glad to see that Ray had put down her visor.

"If you look off to the left, you can see some objects. Those are the solar panels that power the station."

"Can we go see?"

"We don't have time today, but every so often, I need to do general maintenance and cleaning. It isn't due for a few more months, but I don't think it would hurt to schedule one when you are here. I'll just have to get clearance first. Most of the major repairs are done by a team over at Johnson Station."

Finch put on the brakes as soon as they hit the delivery coordinates. They got out, leaving Ray in the cab to take everything in, and started walking around the trailer, making sure that everything was still secure. The trailer was loaded down, and they paid extra attention to all the fastenings before unhooking the cab.

"I need to move the cab out of the way. You can stay inside, but now is a good time to stretch your legs."

Ray made her way out of the cab while Finch finished up the prep needed for the arrival of the pickup team. Right on time, they heard the call from the Russian team.

"This is RX2 from Leanov approaching for ice shipment retrieval."

Finch hit their reply on their arm, sending back the response verifying their approach and that they were expected. A trail of dust started to appear in the distance, and they went to point it out to Ray, but she was looking away, something else having caught her attention, so Finch watched alone as they approached.

The Russian vehicle was completely contained due to the long range of travel from the north. So when they arrived, they backed up their vehicle directly in front of the trailer, and Finch hooked it up. Once everything was connected, they went over it all again. It was better to have a second set of eyes on things to make sure there were no mistakes, but in this case, they just had to pay extra careful attention.

"RX2, connection is complete. Please verbally verify shipment," Finch's computerized voice said.

"Hey, Finch, it's Rob. I moved over from Belxby. Who do you have with you? Did they finally send you some help?"

Finch had difficulty with names, but Rob was pretty easy to remember. He had a Southern American accent and hopped between companies faster than even most lifers. He always seemed to get put on ice pickup as well. Finch had probably delivered to him more than a hundred times. They raised their arm to type in a response, but they did not have anything prewritten about their guest. So, they took a deep breath and spoke.

"This is Ray. She is a visiting scientist here to study the environmental impact of lunar mining. She is not qualified to verify the connection, but if you are concerned, we could wait until one of your crew disembarks."

"No, I'm sure everything is fine. I was just curious. I'm glad they finally sent someone out here with you. A lot of us were pretty upset when they left you to run this place alone. Also, it's good to hear your voice, it's been too long."

Finch paused and then continued in their natural voice, "Please verbally confirm the delivery of your shipment."

"We confirm." It was back to the original voice, a Russian national who was in charge of the retrieval. "RX2 is leaving."

"Finch," Rob said, "remember, if you need anything, let us know."

Finch watched as the transport started driving off, only turning away when they could no longer see the dust from the vehicle.

"They care about you, you know," Ray said.

"Rob?"

"Not just him. Mitch, the guy who brought me in, talked about you like you were precious to them, maybe even a symbol. One of the first to come here and make this all possible for the rest of them. They seem protective."

"I give them water. They need water to survive."

"Sure, that is all it is," Ray said. "What is next?"

"Now we get to enjoy the sunshine."

"Wait, you schedule time to relax?"

"Yes, fifteen minutes. Relaxation is important, and humans have evolved to enjoy the sunlight."

"I didn't mean to be judgmental. I'm impressed. So, since we are taking time to relax, can you tell me why the Earth is doing that?"

Finch tore their gaze from the illuminated portions of the lunar soil and up into the sky. The Earth hung in the open, with Africa predominantly visible.

"We are on the south portion of the moon," Finch said.

"Right, but why is the Earth upside down?"

"In space, there is no upside down. But yes, it is different than the globes on Earth, but that is because we are in the south of the moon. That is how it looks here."

"Do you get used to it?"

"I try not to look at it at all."

"Why? That is where we came from."

"Exactly. There is nothing left for me there. Everyone I knew is gone. This is my home. My time on that planet was just a nightmare. If you want to see something eye-catching, look at the way the sun reflects off the rocks. They tell you the moon is gray and lifeless, and, well, I guess they are right, but there is a kind of beauty here."

"You almost sound like a geologist."

Ray and Finch looked off quietly until Finch's wrist computer let them know that it was time to go. They headed back into the cab to finish the rest of their routine.

Ray

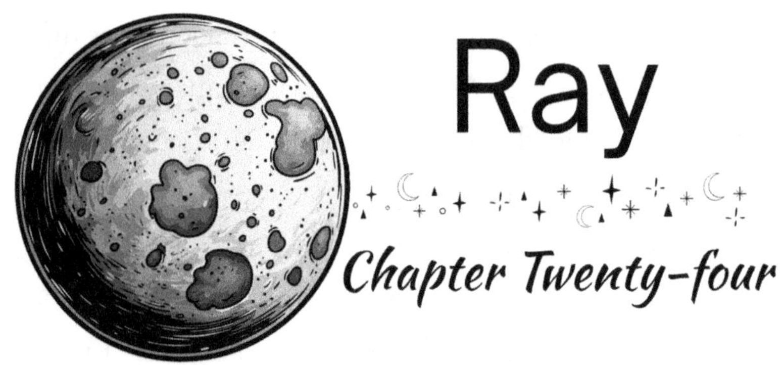

Chapter Twenty-four

RAY LOOKED out at the decimated soil. The machines still wandered about, digging out the water that was contained in the topsoil and taking with it everything else as well. Finch had gone to every robot and checked each one as if caring for a pet, or at least farm animals. But all Ray could see was the apparent harm they were doing.

Maybe she was overthinking it. Everything might be fine. There wasn't enough research to know for sure.

A few of Ray's sensors had been knocked down by the robots, unused to having anything hindering their way. Thankfully, the sensors contained at least a few hours of recorded data. Ray gathered the preliminary data for all of the area sensors while Finch went about their routine.

She wanted to go out and get the data from the sensors she had placed in other fields so that she would have a better comparison group, but Finch was worried about oxygen levels. Ray couldn't argue with that. It had already been a long day, but seeing the mining process in its totality had helped her to gain a better understanding. It would make a great section in her report.

"Is it easy to stay on the moon after you are sent here?" Ray asked as they headed back toward the station.

"I think it depends on whether you can manage to get a contract. They post listings in the daily paper, and it is cheaper to get someone who is already lunar than to have to ship them in and train them—but I guess they are saving money with the training."

Ray's cheeks warmed. She had been around Finch enough to know that it hadn't been intended as a personal jab, just honesty as they saw it. Not that Ray could argue—it was true they hadn't trained her enough for the reality of living and working on the moon. They had expected it to be handled by the stations.

"Do you want to stay, after everything?" Finch asked.

"Yes." The answer came out automatically. Ray held fond memories of Earth, but it had always been something to escape. The moon wasn't what she had expected, and maybe she would end up going back if things weren't all that different up here—but she hadn't even tried yet. "I'm not sure what use they would have for me, though."

"You'd be surprised. There are always calls for various specialties. Medical doctors are probably the most sought-after, but I'm sure there is a need for a geologist—after all, the moon is mostly rock. There has to be something important in all that."

It was disconcerting being back in the darkness after the brief moment in the sun. As much as Finch professed to enjoy their short sunlight break, they had fidgeted the whole time. Their arms were always moving, causing Ray to be concerned that something would happen with their suit. Of course, nothing did. Finch knew what they were doing. As soon as they went back into the darkness, they calmed down again, their body more at peace.

Ray felt the opposite. The floodlights were helpful to see, but the way was gloomy, and visibility did not extend that far. She wanted to go back up in the daylight and have a chance to take in the surface of the moon. Finch was right about it being beautiful in its own way.

"Have you ever thought about putting in a request for another position?" Ray asked.

Finch flinched away from Ray, and she searched for anything that would have caused that reaction. Her body was light here, and she almost felt herself turn completely around without meaning to. It did provide for a wide view and the realization that nothing was around them.

Ray realized that it was her own words which had caused that reaction. Her father had often said that words don't hurt, but they had hurt Ray a lot when she was growing up, and her own words had just attacked Finch.

"I'm sorry. I know this is your home, and you love it here. I just am not sure if it is so great being out here alone. Not that you can't take care of yourself."

"I'm not alone."

"I know the computer is around, but wouldn't it be nice to be around other people?"

"I am around another person. Right now."

"Oh." Ray flushed at the statement. She had caused them nothing but grief since she had arrived, but something about the way Finch had included her made her feel like she belonged.

She couldn't help the smile that filled her face.

"When I was fourteen, I had a girlfriend," Ray said. "We were quiet about the whole thing, but one day, she disappeared, and I never knew what happened to her. But she taught me the gayest song ever. She said that they can take away everything, but music lives in your soul. Do you want to hear?"

"I think so," Finch said.

"I could have that woman for lunch," Ray sang out at the top of her lungs. The sound echoed off her helmet and back into the microphone, and she could only imagine what Finch was hearing. But when they didn't complain, she continued singing, walking backward to try and catch Finch's expression in their helmet as they sang through it in its entirety and then started again.

When Finch began dancing along in their suit, she

couldn't help the laugh that escaped her, and by the time they made it back to the station, they were both laughing so hard they had tears streaming down their faces.

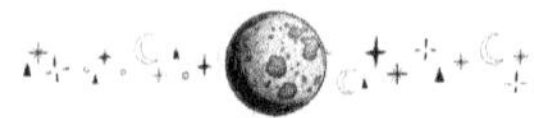

RAY SAT ON HER BED, finally looking at the data that she had collected while they had been out. It was late, and she was tired. After cleaning themselves and their suits, they had headed to the mess hall, where Finch had asked her to sing the song again. Ray had.

Then Finch had asked the computer to play the song. Unsurprisingly, the computer didn't have it available since it had been banned. A heartbeat later, the computer had located an LGBTQIA+ playlist stored on one of the lunar servers. When Ray had heard the original version of the song, she had cried, but they had kept listening, and the lunch room had turned into a dance hall naturally, without Ray having to force it on anyone. They had danced, Ray had tried to sing along, and at times, they had both broken down into tears. Hearing music sung about them by people like them was something neither of them had thought would ever happen.

Ray remembered the book that Finch had brought to the moon for safekeeping. Somewhere, someone had thought to do the same with music.

Then Finch had shut off, their social energy gone, and Ray had left them to return to her own room. She wanted to curl up on the thin mattress and go to sleep, but she was here to do a job, and she hadn't even looked at the data yet.

Ray opened her laptop. She plugged in the storage unit that had collected all the data and fed it into a program that she had created explicitly for this moment. Even with just a small selection of rods, there was a lot of data to input. Ray's mind started to wander. She felt content—something she hadn't experienced in a while. This room had started to feel like home, even more so than her dorm room ever had. She had started to feel more comfortable in her skin. And the collection of queer songs gave her some hope, that somewhere on this moon there might be someone else who had come here to be herself—and if things worked out, Ray would have a girlfriend at some point in the future.

But for now, she had come to love this quiet station. No matter where she ended up, she would come back and visit Finch. Maybe, with enough time, she would even get Finch to visit her. Surely someone could take over long enough for them to take a vacation.

When the laptop beeped, letting Ray know the data had been processed, she wore a smile on her face, one that quickly dropped when she looked at the screen.

"This can't be right."

Ray tapped frantically on the laptop keyboard, checking all the data points, but everything seemed accurate—and not in a good way.

"Computer, where is Finch?"

"Finch is sleeping. You wore them out."

"Can you wake them up? I need to talk to them now."

"I think it is best if you wait until the morning."

"I don't think so. I've looked at the preliminary data, and they need to know what I found."

Ray grabbed her laptop and raced down to Finch's room, her movement under enough control that her head didn't even come close to hitting the ceiling.

Finch had just opened their door by the time Ray arrived. They rubbed their eyes and yawned.

"The computer said you needed me."

"I do. You need to see the data." Ray opened her laptop, trying to balance it in her hands while showing Finch.

Finch turned away without speaking. Ray watched, trying to keep her heart from pounding out of her chest and yelling at Finch that this was important. That wouldn't help anything right now. When she realized that Finch was walking into the kitchen, she followed them.

Finch was already sitting at a table waiting for her.

Ray put down the laptop and sat down on the edge of a chair, her legs unable to stop jiggling as she angled the laptop so that Finch could see.

"We need to go," Ray said.

Finch turned and looked at Ray impassively. "I don't understand any of this."

Ray started to explain in more detail and stopped. Finch

wasn't going to want to know about the conductivity levels of the soil and the dielectric breakdown limits.

"The soil is like the planet's insulation."

"Okay," Finch said.

"This is even more important on the moon than on Earth because there is no atmosphere here. Areas of the lunar surface have been found to contain a low conductive threshold, and if they are exposed to a solar event, such as a coronal mass ejection—from a solar flare ..."

"I know what a solar flare is, and a CME. Everyone on the moon knows what they are, especially this year with their increased activity."

"Right, right. Well, if the soil isn't conductive and it is hit with a CME, then it turns into a bad electrical storm, except instead of coming from the sky, it shoots up from the ground."

"The station isn't built anywhere near one of those areas. Those are part of the uninhabitable zones."

"All the mining has removed the insulation from the soil. The conductivity threshold is almost non-existent. It is worse than the zones we know about, or at least I imagine it is—they haven't exactly put money into doing an extensive study."

Finch pulled the laptop closer to themself, looking at all the numbers and lines before finally pushing it away. "What does it all mean?"

"It means that if there is any sort of electrical activity, the soil outside could light up. We aren't safe here. We need to leave."

Ray knew she was being dramatic, but she couldn't stop after seeing all the data. She had never imagined the area could be this bad. But Finch just sat calmly. Ray wanted to shake them, or go into their room and pack up all their belongings in a bag and drive them away.

"This data is from the current mining area," Finch said.

"Yes."

"It is preliminary, correct? You haven't even gathered all the data you collected?"

"I was going to get it tomorrow, but we can't ignore this."

"I don't plan on ignoring it. I'm just thinking it through. The mining area is not near the station. Are you sure that it poses an immediate risk even if it were to experience an electrically charged incident?"

Ray floundered, the words sputtering as they left her mouth. "No ... I mean ... It's far away. But it isn't worth chancing it ... This is worse than I imagined."

"I understand that," Finch said, "but if there is no immediate risk to the station, then we should be fine for now. At a minimum, you should collect all the data before we make any sort of decision."

"You just don't want to leave," Ray said. She regretted it the second the words were out of her mouth.

"Of course, I don't, but I wouldn't risk your safety. Nothing here says it is an imminent danger—or even any sort of danger. Why are you so worried?"

Ray froze with her mouth open. She didn't have an

answer to that. Her mind hadn't worked through all the details that her gut had figured out. She knew it wasn't good, but she couldn't put it into words.

"Living on the moon can be scary," Finch said. "We have all been there. Go out tomorrow, collect your data, do your analysis, and we will send it to Johnson Station. We will do whatever they say—even if they tell me I need to leave."

Finch returned to their room, leaving Ray sitting at the table with her laptop. She stayed up working on models and scenarios until her eyelids began to droop. If she was going out tomorrow, she needed to get sleep. It wouldn't do to get into another emergency situation. So, reluctantly, Ray headed back to her room to close her eyes for a few hours.

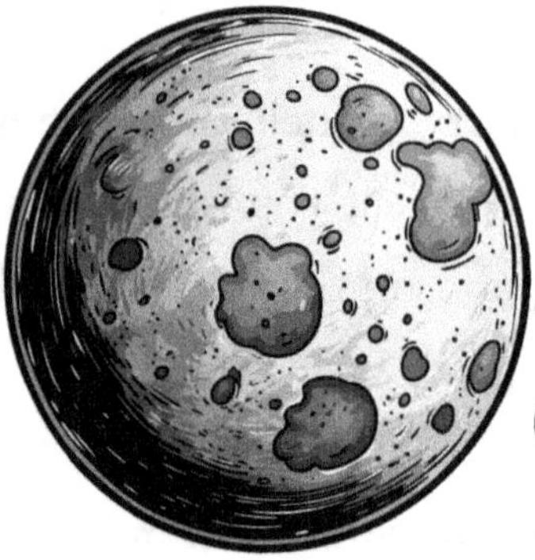

Finch

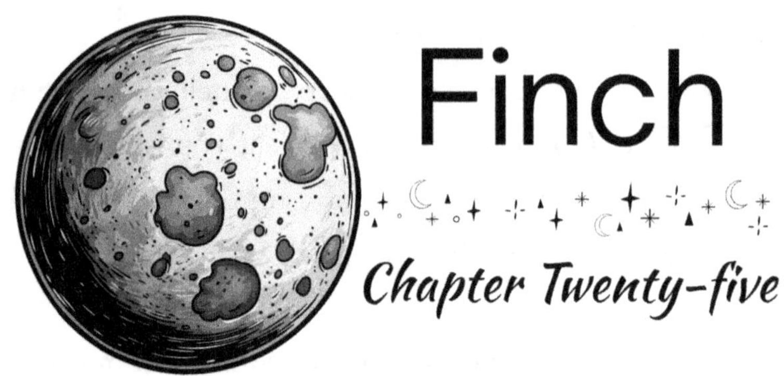

Chapter Twenty-five

WHEN FINCH WOKE UP, Ray was already putting on her suit at the end of the hallway.

"Morning," Finch said.

Ray jumped at the noise, and Finch winced.

"Sorry, I'm just headed to command," they said.

"No, wait."

Ray bounded after them, completely comfortable with maneuvering through the halls. She had settled into the moon so fast. It had taken the canaries much longer. She wore the first few layers of her suit, one with only the legs and waist inserted so it pulled around her middle, the arms flapping wildly to the side as she moved, like one of the used car blow-ups from their youth.

"Do you want to go out with me? You can see what I do, like you showed me what you did?"

"Oh," Finch said. Ray's shoulders slumped, and her smile dropped. They had disappointed her. "I would love you to show me what you do, but I wouldn't understand any of it. I never made it to high school, let alone college."

"Maybe not," Ray said. "But you live here. I've seen you working, and you know how to do things that others couldn't imagine. You single-handedly keep this whole station and the mine running. I bet no one else could do that."

"I can use my hands. That is different than knowing voltage levels, or whatever you study."

"You don't have to know everything I'm talking about. It would just be nice to show you."

Finch tried to say yes. They willed the words to come out of their mouth and their feet to walk down the hall and put on their suit. Instead, they let out a quiet, "I can't."

"It's okay." Ray turned and started somberly walking back.

"Wait," Finch said. "Let me explain."

Ray turned around, but her smile didn't reappear.

"I told you the shipments come once a week because there isn't that much demand for this station anymore. It is true that we only service the smaller stations, but that isn't the entire truth. They only come once a week because that is all I can do. I can't go outside more than that."

Ray didn't say anything, just looked at them with pinched eyes.

"The anxiety, it's too much to do more than once a week.

Everyone I know died because of the void outside. I know inside isn't much safer, but it feels safer. If I could, I would go with you."

Ray turned around without saying a word and went back to putting on her suit. Finch watched, and part of them cracked at having admitted it out loud. For the last year, they had been adjusting the schedule, limiting visits outside as it had become harder. They hadn't wanted to even admit it to themself, even though they had been aware. The computer knew. Probably, the commander knew as well, but he had never spoken it out loud.

They didn't blame Ray for not believing them. They didn't even understand it. That didn't make her behavior hurt any less. Still, Finch watched as she finished suiting up to make sure that she didn't miss anything. When she approached the airlock, they gave a small wave as the doors shut, but Ray was already focused on her work.

"Her suit was secure. I will continue to monitor her while she is outside," the computer said.

"Thank you," Finch said. Then they entered the kitchen to get their water for the day and headed to the command center. "What is on the agenda?"

"Today, you need to inspect the workshop door. You noted that it had been sticking when it closed. There is also maintenance needed in the crew lavatory, and the kitchen is scheduled for a cleaning. It may be prudent to include Ray on the cleaning rotation since she will be here for an extended period."

The idea caught Finch off guard. The station had been their responsibility for so long that they hadn't even thought about going back to sharing responsibilities.

"Would you mind talking to her and seeing if she would be agreeable? If so, then we can discuss it further. But please don't make her feel like it is required. I can take the tasks for two crew members, and she has her research to do."

"That is not how crews work together. Everyone maintains the station, no matter what their role is."

"Yes, I remember Commander's lessons. He repeated them to us often enough."

"Would you like me to read you the news now?"

Finch listened as the computer read out the daily bulletins, and then went about their tasks. They, once again, left the music off—just in case. And every so often, when they started to get frustrated, throwing their tools down or cursing out their task, the computer would update them on Ray's condition, and they would calm down and continue. But it wasn't until the computer announced that Ray was back that their heart stopped pounding and they could fully focus on their tasks.

Ray

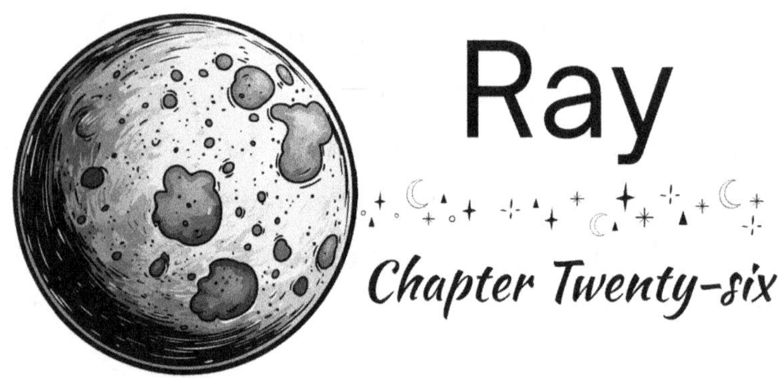

Chapter Twenty-six

RAY SLUMPED ON THE BENCH, her suit still on. When Finch had told her they couldn't handle going outside two days in a row, she had been sure it had been an excuse to get away from her for the day. But now ... now she was wondering if maybe it had been the truth. This was the third time she had been outside in a week, and she wasn't sure she could do it again.

Sure, she had walked a lot, and the suit added extra bulk, but she was still conditioned to Earth's gravity. Her body wasn't tired—it was her mind. Even with the lights on, everything was so dark and open. It was like she could float out into space at any point if she stepped wrong. It didn't matter that she knew it wasn't true, that the moon's gravity was enough to hold her down, but her soul felt another way.

Then there was the loneliness. Yesterday, none of it had seemed so daunting when she had been walking with Finch by her side. Today, without that companionship, her mind had wandered into all the unknowns. By the time she'd made it back in, she had been jumping at shadows like aliens were lying in wait, ready to abduct her.

She did want to show Finch her work to make them see that she was a competent scientist. However, she could also now admit that part of her had wanted Finch to come out just so she could be less scared, and that hadn't been fair to Finch. At some point, she would have to apologize, but for now, she was tired, hungry, and had more work to do.

Ray started undoing her suit, making sure to take the time to put each piece away correctly. It still didn't look as neat as Finch's, but it was getting closer. She cleaned herself up in the bathroom, put her undersuit in the wash, and tugged on the new clothes. The routine was starting to become familiar, and there was a sort of comfort in the transition from the outside to the inside, like a bridge between two different worlds.

Once she was done, she grabbed her laptop and headed to the kitchen. It was hard to know what time it was, and Ray began to understand Finch's obsessive need for alarms to help dictate their day. All she knew was that after being on the surface, she was hungry. She started heating up a meal and then plugged the data storage device into her laptop.

Ray had collected data from all twenty-eight probes, including new data from the current mining site, as well as the data from the abandoned mining sites. It was going to take some time to upload, so while she waited, she ate her food and asked the computer to play some more music from the forbidden playlist.

She could have gone back to her room when she was done, but she didn't want to move the data storage unit. She also didn't want to miss Finch when they came to dinner. Ray needed people, and Finch was the only person around.

The data was still compiling, and Ray had moved on to dessert and a snack by the time Finch wandered in. They filled up their water, grabbed a bar, and sat down at Ray's table.

They watched the laptop warily and opened their mouth as if to speak, but moved to take a bite instead.

"Hi," Ray said.

"Hi," Finch said. "Everything went well?"

"Yes. I was able to retrieve all the data, and there weren't any incidents. Even the rods in the active mining site had stayed upright since we were there yesterday."

"Good." Finch took another small bite, taking their time to chew it.

"Did you have a good day?" Ray asked.

Finch shook their head and, when they swallowed, spoke. "What are you doing?"

"I'm feeding all the data I collected into my computer to

be analyzed by a program that I wrote. It will determine the conductivity of the soil."

Finch shook their head to show that they had listened and then took another bite.

Ray watched her computer. There wasn't much to see, just the word "Loading" at the top of the screen with a small spinning circle on either side to let her know that it was still thinking. Maybe in the next iteration of the software, she would put in a progress bar.

"You made the program?" Finch asked.

"Yes, I designed it as part of my doctorate. I worked with a computer science student to program it, but it went through thorough testing. They wouldn't have given me the funding if it hadn't."

"I didn't mean to imply ..." Finch said. "I was just curious."

"Oh," Ray said. "I'm sorry. My study is controversial, for some reason. I would have thought that this would have been one of the first things we studied when we started building permanent settlements on the moon, and maybe if NASA was still around, it would have, but corporations are too hesitant to explore things that could hurt their bottom line."

"But you are here."

"Yes. The investors became worried."

Finch went back to eating. A small bite and then a small sip of water. Their movements were concise after years of the same routine.

When the laptop chimed to indicate it had finished processing, Ray jumped, realizing that she had been staring at Finch the entire time. Her cheeks flushed as she moved her gaze to her computer. Then her eyes widened as she read the results.

She flicked through the screens, examining the breakdown by area, each click becoming more frantic.

"Fuck," she said. "Fuck, fuck, fuck, fuck, fuck." Then she turned her laptop toward Finch so they could see the screen.

Finch just looked at her, continuing to eat their food and sip their water.

"It's worse," Ray said. "The other sites are even worse than the current mining site. One event and the entire place could go up. We need to leave. We need to leave right now."

Ray snapped her laptop shut, then ran to her room and threw all of her items into a bag. She didn't take the time to fold or organize any of it, just jamming it all in as best she could. She threw open drawers and pulled out the rest of her belongings. The bag was overflowing, so she put some of the items that wouldn't fit into the second bag and took it, partially full, to the kitchen to collect some of her food.

When she returned, Finch hadn't moved. They were still sitting there eating like nothing had happened.

"What are you doing? We need to go."

"Why?" Finch asked.

"I told you. The readings are worse than I could have imagined. It isn't safe for us here."

Finch raised their eyebrows but didn't respond.

"Go pack your stuff," Ray said.

"You need to calm down."

"Calm down? You don't understand. I can explain the science to you, but it will take too long. For now, I need you to just trust me and pack."

Finch wasn't moving. They were not listening at all, just sitting there taking a small bite after a small sip of water, like this was just any other day. Ray wanted to scream, but she forced herself to wait for Finch to speak.

"Let's think things through," Finch said. "You said that the soil around the station is safe because it hasn't been mined."

"I haven't measured around the station. I put the probes in the known mining fields."

"So that would be a good next step, if you have probes that you can move, of course." Finch took another bite.

"But what if something happens before then?"

"What are the main inciting incidents that would set off this ..." Finch waved their arm around as if uncertain what to say.

"The dielectric breakdown," Ray said.

"Right."

"Like I explained yesterday, it would most likely be set off by a CME."

"Okay, a CME takes hours to make its way from the sun to the Earth. There is an early warning system that will let us know if there is a solar flare, and then the intensity will be broadcast by the lunar notification system and relayed to us by Johnson. It will give us plenty of time to act if an event were to occur. Is there anything else we should be aware of?"

"Any electrical discharge could set off a chain of events."

"Is there anything specifically you are concerned about?"

"Yes."

Finch waited for her to elaborate. They were being so calm and rational, but everything inside of Ray screamed that they needed to leave this station now.

"I can't explain it. I just think it would be better to move over to Johnson Station until we know more about the situation."

"People on this moon do rely on the water we produce. It is important we don't abandon it prematurely. Johnson isn't able to fully facilitate the needs of all the settlements as well as meet the demands put on it by the corporation for fuel output."

"Trust me." Ray didn't mean for those words to come out. They sounded pitiful even to her. Finch was correct: there was no logical reason to panic. But despite having become a scientist, Ray had often been more emotional than logical.

"What about if we go and contact the commander, and get his opinion?" Finch said. "At least that way, another station will have access to your preliminary data."

Ray's chest deflated, and she nodded. That would be better than nothing ... she guessed.

Ray paced the kitchen while Finch finished their meal. Her bag lay abandoned on the floor by the counter, and she hugged her laptop tightly to her chest as she walked.

An eternity later, Finch finished their meal, and they went to the command station, Ray hoping the whole time that *finally* someone would believe her.

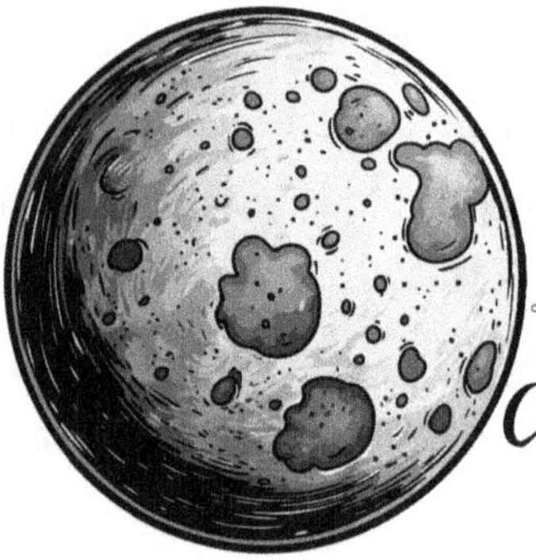

Finch

Chapter Twenty-seven

THE LAST TIME they had been in the command station together, they had watched movies. Things had seemed so comfortable then. Now, Ray couldn't stop fidgeting and sit still. It was distracting—no wonder others did not enjoy it when Finch moved about.

"Computer, will you please connect to the Katherine Johnson Station?"

"Connecting now. Johnson Station, this is Schmidt Station, please come in."

They waited, the silence filled with the pounding of Ray's feet on the floor as she paced three steps one way and then three steps the other way. Finch wanted to beg her to stop, but instead closed their hands so tightly that their fingernails dug into their palms, giving them something else to focus on.

"Johnson Station, this is Schmidt Station, please come in."

"Schmidt Station, this is Johnson Station."

"Nalla?" Finch asked.

"Yes, is there a problem, Finch?"

Finch glanced over at Ray, who seemed ready to declare very loudly that there was a problem in such a way that the commander would never take their call.

"There may be a situation ..."

Ray stomped her foot and glared at Finch.

"Sorry, let me rephrase that. The scientist who has been conducting research here has found some data that may be concerning. We would like to make the commander aware of the situation and ask for his input."

Ray finally sat down in one of the chairs, although she still looked like she was pouting, with her body scrunched up and her arms folded tight.

"Let me see if he is available," Nalla said. "Glad to hear you two are getting along."

Finch looked over at Ray. *Were they getting along?* Finch wasn't sure.

They waited. Ray started tapping her foot again, but stayed seated. Then she opened her computer and balanced it on her lap while looking at the data.

"There is a little table," Finch said.

"What?" Ray asked.

"If you lift off the top of the armrest, you can pull out a

little table to put your laptop on so you don't have to keep it on your lap."

"Why would they put a table in the command center of a spaceship?"

Finch shrugged. They hadn't been part of the team that had made the design decisions. They hadn't even seen the ship until they were being walked out to it, strapped in, and launched off the planet. "It has magnets to hold things."

"Oh," Ray said and then pulled out the table and became lost in the world of her data.

Finch found themself slightly jealous. They wanted to understand what was on the screen. They wanted to be able to read without the computer's help. Sure, they were good with their hands, but that was because that was all they had been allowed to do. Even in the camps, they had been constantly busy fixing things—with almost no resources—in the space they had been given. No one else was going to do it. Maybe if the world had given them a chance, they could have been smart as well.

But they'd had to settle for being content to still be alive. It was enough—it had to be enough. It was more than all those they had left behind. Did anyone even remember them?

"This is Commander Stevenson. Finch, what is going on?"

The sudden noise made both of them jump out of their seats, but Finch recovered fast.

"Sorry to bother you, Commander, but Ray retrieved the

data from her equipment today, the information on the di ... di ... diactric."

"Dielectric breakdown," Ray broke in.

"Yes, on the dielectric breakdown," Finch continued. "She found that the readings were overly disturbing, and Ray has concerns about the safety of the station."

"Do *you* have concerns?" he asked.

Ray's face pinched, and her hands clenched. Finch knew she was pissed off at the question, and was going to be even more upset at Finch's answer. "No, sir, but I think that you should let Ray explain it to you. You would probably understand it better."

"Agreed."

Ray took over the communication, and Finch listened as she spouted off numbers that were half letters. She sounded just like how the crew had talked when they'd sat down to meals, their conversations excluding the canaries who had never learned any of the technobabble. Except Pixy. She had understood it, and at night, she would tell them all if there was anything important they had needed to know.

"I understand," the commander said, and Finch took that as their cue to start listening again. "Why don't you go and send me a preliminary report, and when you have the full report finished for the company, make sure to send a copy over my way as well."

"Sir," Ray said, "what about evacuating this station?"

"That is something I need to talk about with the interim

commander. Please give Finch and me some privacy. But first, when should I expect the preliminary report?"

"I will go work on it right now. I should have it to you in an hour."

"That is fine. Tomorrow morning will work as well."

"Expect it within an hour, Commander," Ray said and then stood up and exited the command center.

"I'm here, Commander," Finch said.

"Are you alone?"

"I think so, sir."

"Why don't you go ahead and shut the command door to make sure."

Finch got up and closed the door, locking it in place. It resisted at first, hesitant at being closed after having stayed open for so long.

"The door is closed, Commander. We have some privacy now."

"Good. How are things going over there?"

"It is going as expected, sir. I have fulfilled all deliveries, kept current on maintenance, and all of the machinery is currently functioning at peak efficiency."

"I do not doubt that you are doing your job. I meant, how are things going between you and Dr. Bennett?"

"Dr. Bennett?"

"Yes, Rachel, or Ray. That's her nickname, correct?"

"Yes, sir. Things are going well, sir. There have been no further mishaps since the situation last week."

"That's right, I read about that. She went outside without oxygen?"

"Not exactly, sir. The training they gave her neglected to teach her how to switch out her oxygen tank and she has an older model space suit that does not have backups built in."

"That is understandable, given her scheduled time on the station. I should let you know that the corporation is not too thrilled that she is here. They do not have a lot of faith in her theories and have only agreed to the study to calm the stakeholders' fears."

"She has told me as much, sir."

"Good ... that is good that she is being realistic. What are your thoughts on her findings?"

"She seems extremely concerned and is worried that the station is unsafe."

"Yes, she just told me all of that. I am interested in your thoughts, however."

Finch thought back to everything Ray had said. None of it had sounded like a concern to Finch, just a bunch of figures and big words. But the commander would know better—he had a few PhDs himself.

"Sir, to my understanding the station is not impacted by this electrical situation that was caused by the mining. So, even if the results are as concerning as Ray says they are, I do not see how they would impact the station."

"Those are my thoughts exactly. Once I receive the doctor's report, I will give her the option of vacating the station and abandoning her research. Otherwise, I think you are both fine to stay there. You have made the appropriate recommendations for solar flare preparations."

"Yes, sir, and have adapted them for the additional occupant."

"Good. I think it would be prudent for both of us to connect at some point next week. I'll have my secretary put an appointment on your schedule."

"Yes, sir."

"Don't worry. I will make sure you have at least twenty-four hours' notice."

"Thank you, sir."

"And Finch ..."

"Yes, sir?"

"If you have any concerns about Dr. Bennett, I would like you to initiate a code pink. I'll talk to you next week."

The commander didn't say another word, and Finch assumed the line had disconnected. They had forgotten to say goodbye, too caught up in what he had said. A code pink? Did the commander think Ray was dangerous? The last code pink had been called on themself during one of their bad flashbacks. Finch was fairly certain that was why the last member of the crew had finally left. The code itself wasn't concerning. You tried to make sure the person in distress was not in a position to harm themself, but ultimately, your responsibility was to keep yourself from harm. What did the commander know about Ray that they didn't?

Finch headed off to check on Ray. She was sitting on her bed typing on her laptop. Maybe she was a little frustrated, pounding the keys a little harder than she needed to. That said, nothing about her behavior indicated any danger, so Finch made their way to their own room, settled into their bed, and pulled up an old TV show on their pad.

Ray

Chapter Twenty-eight

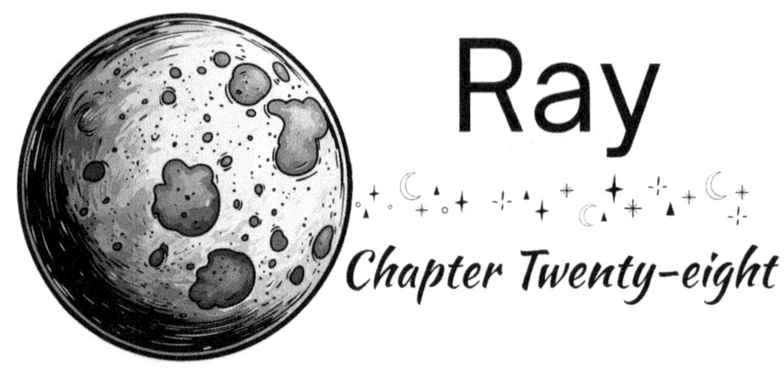

IT HAD TAKEN fifty-five minutes for Ray to save the report and send it to Johnson Station. She had kept it simple, sticking to the facts and emphasizing the data over her conclusions. This place was a ticking time bomb, and if they didn't fix it up, who knew what would happen?

A part of Ray, the portion that she tried to squeeze down very small, realized that this data meant that they would need to extend her contract. As the current foremost expert in this area, they would need to keep her around to help determine how to reverse the damage and mitigate the danger moving forward. But she tried to push that out of her mind as she went to the command station to find Finch.

They weren't there.

Ray looked in the workshop and the storage bay. Then she started wandering around the station, trying to find the interim commander to tell them the report had been sent and to get an update on when they were scheduled to leave.

"Computer, where is Finch?"

"Finch is in their room."

"Of course, they are packing."

"Finch is sleeping."

Sleeping. Sleeping? "Why are they sleeping?"

"Finch's designated rest period began twenty-three minutes ago."

Ray stormed over to the canary's room and threw open the door. She went to Finch's bunk and yanked the curtains back. Finch was awake, facing them, something held in their hand hidden from Ray's view.

"You shouldn't sneak up on me when I am asleep," Finch said.

"It's a good thing you are awake, then. Why aren't you packing?"

Finch just stared at her as if she was unhinged. Ray hated when people looked at her that way.

"I just sent the report over to the commander," she said. "Shouldn't we be preparing to leave the station?"

"The commander does not believe there is an immediate threat." Finch yawned and reached for the curtain, but Ray held out her hand to block them.

"He will once he reads that report," Ray said.

"If that is the case, then he will order us to vacate the station. Until that time, we will remain here."

"We should get ready. I sent him the report, and the evacuation order could come at any minute."

Finch sat up in their bed, their legs drawn up to their chest and their head slightly bowed to fit into the small space. They moved methodically and without any urgency.

"He plans on us staying, doesn't he?" Ray asked.

Finch pursed their lips, their fingertips tapping on the sides of their legs.

"When we first arrived on the moon, we were all scared," Finch said. "We signed up knowing that this moon would be our final resting place. We picked that because, for various reasons, that was better than our alternatives—but it didn't stop the fear.

"We lived in the spaceship for the first bit while we were assembling this station, and every day we were filled with terror that something would go wrong. Even when this place was assembled, there was always the fear that something would break apart everything we had built. There are only these walls standing between us and nothing. Do you understand what I am saying?"

"I don't," Ray said.

"Existing on the moon requires courage. You have to face that any day could be your last. We knew that coming—maybe that helped? We had no other choice. You have a choice; you don't have to stay here. The commander will send out a transport if you request it and he will work with the company to help you get back to Earth safely."

Ray collapsed on the ground, her head falling into her hands. Tears started flowing freely, but she tried to hide them, willing them to stop. "I can't go back, I won't go back. This needs to be studied."

"That was the choice that the commander gave."

"You agree with him?" Her voice echoed in the small room, filling up the space with her accusation.

"I don't see how there is any more immediate harm now than before your data. It isn't enough to convince me to abandon my work here, and the commander agrees. You, however, are free to go."

"But if I do, I have to stop my research. The company would love that."

Finch just shrugged and remained silent. They might have had nothing else to say, but anger boiled in Ray. She stood and started pacing up and down the slim walkway. She stopped, pushing on one of the empty beds. Ray wanted to hit something ... break something ... maybe tear the room apart. She held off, knowing that would cause more harm to Finch.

"I know something isn't right," she finally said.

"I need you to prove that. We may be financed by corporations, but the moon is full of scientists and grease monkeys. The scientists need to be shown the evidence so they can tell us grease monkeys what to do to help fix it."

"To prove it, I have to stay here, knowing I am risking my life, to satisfy them."

"It's the moon," Finch said.

The moon. Ray had spent every day of the last ten years plotting to get here—ever since Finch had been launched here. As a teenager, she hadn't understood that they were being sent to die and that the same would be asked of her.

"I can't go back to Earth."

"Then go do your science."

Ray did her best to slam the dormitory door as she left. She tried to stomp her way back to her room, but the gravity kept flinging her up to the ceiling with each attempt. She couldn't even throw a proper fit here. So, Ray went back to her room and looked through the data, plotting exactly what would need to be tested and what evidence would need to be collected, so that she would be taken seriously.

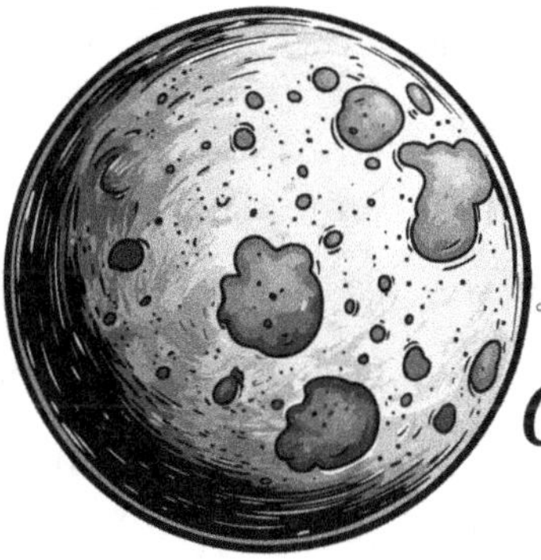

Finch

Chapter Twenty-nine

FINCH ONLY SAW glimpses of Ray the next day. She stayed huddled up to her laptop, taking food back into her room to work. For most of the day, it was just Finch and the computer. They pulled out their headphones from storage and blasted their music directly to their ears while they worked. Finch didn't enjoy change, but they were enjoying exploring the songs the computer had discovered. When they found one they wanted to remember, they added it to a new playlist. They couldn't wait to share them with Ray when it wouldn't disturb her work.

That first night, they had invited Ray to join them during their downtime to watch another movie, suggesting that she might need a break. Ray had turned them down. She'd turned them down the next day as well, and Finch had stopped asking. Four days passed with just the barest amount of conversation between them, and Finch found themself missing the woman's company. But they tried not to think about it. Ray was there to do a job, and she was doing it with a passion that Finch understood.

Ray had been leaving the station. Some days it was only for an hour or two, another day she was gone so long that Finch was worried they would need to go back out and bring her in. But they kept to their work and let Ray do what she needed to do.

The nights were the worst. When the work was done, Finch realized how quiet the station was. It hadn't bothered them before. Now that they lived with someone who was never around, the absence was noticeable. Part of Finch couldn't wait until Ray's contract was up, but another part wasn't sure if they would survive being alone again.

On the fifth day, Finch prepped for another delivery. There were two, and Finch needed to focus on handling them and returning within the allotted time. They stopped by Ray's room to see if she wanted to come along. They spied her through the window, absorbed in her computer, and thought better of it. Finch left without saying goodbye.

Outside the station were measuring rods. They were lined up from the station to the purification area, almost like runway lights. Finch wondered what Ray had found and if she would be willing to discuss her findings. Then, all thoughts of the research left their mind as they went about their tasks.

It was a long day, loading up two trailers of ice and talking to two separate groups. Both teams were familiar, but while that made it easier, it didn't make the interactions easy in and of themselves. By the time Finch came into view of the station, they were past their preferred safety oxygen levels and tired. They wanted to eat their meal, watch a show, and climb into their bed. Then they saw the rods again, lined up in a different pattern from earlier. Little blue lights blinked at the top, with tiny solar panels that would never charge in the darkness of this part of the moon.

When they had completed their decontamination procedure, they were pleased to see that Ray had moved into the kitchen. She was eating a meal, completely absorbed in her data, but some part of Finch hoped this was her way of reaching out. They grabbed their bar, filled up their water, and sat down at the same table.

Ray didn't react to their presence. She was so absorbed in her work that she probably didn't even know Finch was there.

"I saw that you had moved the rods."

Ray didn't react right away. Finch wasn't sure if they were being punished for not supporting her call for evacuation or if she hadn't processed the words.

Ray looked up, her eyes widening at seeing Finch. "Hi."

"Hi," Finch said.

"Did the transfer go well?"

"Yes. There were two today."

"Oh," Ray said, turning back to her computer.

"I saw that you had moved the rods."

"Yes. I wanted to get a better measurement of the safety of the station."

"Have you determined anything?"

"No, not yet. I want to give it another day before I download the data."

"What are you working on now?" Finch took another bite of their bar, feeling the smoothness of the food in their mouth. There was a slight aftertaste when they swallowed, a hint of citrus that they did not particularly enjoy. However, it was easily washed away by a small sip of water.

"I think I may have a solution, a way of repairing the areas that have been damaged. It is fairly simple. We just need to take the material that was removed and return it to the area. What happens to the soil once it is filtered out of the water?"

"It collects until one of the robots goes and hauls it to a pile. There are little mounds of dirt all over. It has been a while since I have had any reason to head that way, though."

"That is perfect," Ray said. "If this idea works, it shouldn't even be a large change to the current process. The robot can be programmed to offload the material into an area that we are repairing. Would you go out with me tomorrow? I need to collect the data, and I would like to start a sample area to monitor if this will work. I will need to leave some of the probes there long-term, but I think when I meet with the stakeholders next week, there is enough data to at least convince them to send over more equipment."

"You're going out tomorrow?"

"If it is too much, I'll do it alone. It would help if you could teach me how to operate the machines and upload a map to the discarded material so that I don't end up lost again."

Finch took another bite, giving themself time to think. They couldn't let Ray go out and do this by herself. She needed them. Writing down instructions wouldn't be enough. The machines would need to be completely reprogrammed or manually maneuvered. As fun as it could be at times, Finch knew firsthand that it was harder than it appeared. They would have to go out ... again ... into the darkness.

They closed their eyes. *You can do it*, they told themself. *Yes, something could go wrong, but if something went wrong and anything happened to Ray, you would be the one left living with it.* They couldn't do that again.

"I'll go with you. It needs to be tomorrow?"

"Preferably. I would like to have preliminary test data before the next meeting."

Finch nodded and went back to eating. The bar felt unusually heavy, the food sitting like a hard lump in their stomach. There was still a third of the bar left, and they knew they needed the calories, but they couldn't handle taking another bite. They wrapped up the remaining bar and took it to the composter.

"Tomorrow will work out fine," they said before leaving the room.

They felt ... something. Their body was charged, but not with excitement. They had been on the surface hundreds, maybe even more than a thousand times. They weren't nervous, exactly. Or maybe they were, they couldn't tell. Things had been so much harder since Ray had arrived, but they had also been easier. Finch hadn't realized how lonely they had been, and while Ray was not the easiest person to get along with, she was their friend. Finch would do anything to protect her, so they would be out there with her tomorrow.

They went up to the command station, suddenly ready for the safety of their bunk. Instead, they put on a movie, the next in the series that they had been working through.

Much to their surprise, Ray walked in and sat down in the seat next to them. Her laptop was still held tightly in her hands, but the lid was closed. Finch relaxed into their seat and let themself get carried back to an Earth where people stood up for injustice—and made a mess while doing it.

When the movie ended, they both wandered to their bedrooms, neither saying a word to each other. But Finch felt lighter. The pressure in their gut had all but disappeared.

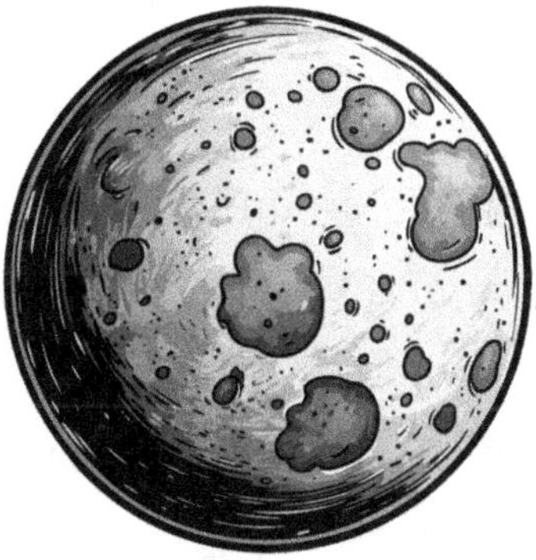

Ray

Chapter Thirty

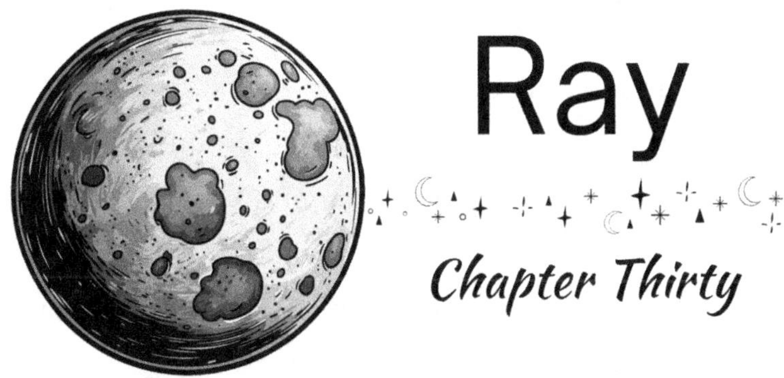

RAY HAD PUT on her pajamas but had opened her laptop back up. She wanted to fix one part of her report before she went to bed. She knew she should put the computer down. It was important to get some sleep if they were going to go outside tomorrow. It would be yet another long day, but the presentation with the investors was approaching, and it was all so much more important now that she knew that her fear had been correct. They couldn't keep mining on the moon this way, and Ray had such a simple solution. One she hoped to prove would work.

Some part of her still felt guilty. She would have to extend the grant to gain the time to test the long-term viability of her solution. She would probably need to stay here with Finch. That thought didn't disturb her as much as she'd expected it would.

Ray was still concerned about the conductivity of the soil around the station, and she would advocate doing a reseeding around the area before they even had the test results. It wouldn't hurt anything, at least.

All of these thoughts kept cycling around in her brain long after she put the laptop away and tried to go to sleep. The lights were off on the station, and she realized that the computer had been right; she no longer even noticed that they ran at decreased illumination. Compared to the darkness outside, it was bright when they were on.

"Computer, would you mind playing some music?"

"What would you like?"

"I'm not sure. Do you know of anything that would help me fall asleep?"

A light classical piece began to fill their room, and Ray tried to concentrate on the notes instead of all the thoughts in her head. Her eyelids were starting to droop, and her mind drifted off, when the music changed to something more piercing.

"Computer, shut off the music."

The sound continued.

Ray sat up completely. The music sounded like the alarm that had played on the first day she had arrived.

"This is a solar flare alert. Please follow emergency procedures and proceed to your designated emergency station."

Ray jumped out of bed and then hesitated, uncertain of

what to do. A solar flare wasn't concerning in itself. It traveled at the speed of light and had already passed them by the time the alarm had arrived. What was concerning was any potential solar mass ejection. The moon didn't have an atmosphere to protect itself—this is exactly what would set off a dielectric breakdown event.

She opened the door, ready to run to Finch, but Finch was right outside.

"We have to go," Ray said.

"There is a procedure," Finch said. "We need to get our suits on."

"Right, our suits." Ray hurried down the hallway to where their space suits had been stored. She understood now why Finch put everything in its proper place. Her mind was a jumble, and she couldn't focus on getting prepared. However, since she'd taught herself how to put her suit away properly, she was able to get prepared with only a few corrections from Finch. "You must have done this so many times."

"Yes. There has been at least one solar flare warning a year. We just need to follow the procedure."

However, Ray wasn't thinking about the solar flare. She was thinking about all the emergencies that Finch had faced. How many times had they rushed to put on their suit, not knowing what was next? No wonder they were able to get it on so fast. Finch already had their suit on, their helmet in their hands, and was watching Ray finish up.

"What would happen if there were a more immediate emergency? How would we suit up fast enough?"

"The walls are secure, built to withstand most smaller impacts. Plus, there is regular maintenance to make sure everything is up to standards. If there is any sort of decompression, the doors will all seal shut, keeping everything oxygenated."

"But the suits are up here. What happens if this gets blocked off, preventing me from reaching my suit?"

"Then I get you out. That is why the canaries' quarters are by the airlocks, but it isn't worth worrying about what could be. You train and practice and stay prepared for whatever comes."

Ray looked at them, wondering if they realized what they had said. She hadn't trained or practiced. She could barely get her suit on in double the time as Finch.

"I'm done, let's go," Ray said. She pulled her helmet on and immediately heard the computer speaking through the receiver.

"Finch would like me to tell you to take off your helmet. You are not going outside."

"What do you mean we are not going outside?" But Finch still had their helmet off, and the computer didn't seem to be relaying her words. She unclasped her helmet and repeated herself.

"Emergency protocol for a solar flare is to wait in the cargo area until any SME may have passed."

"We have hours, shouldn't we get someplace safer?"

"Johnson will communicate with us if there is any danger, but even still, the best move is in the cargo bay. It has been reinforced against radiation and has an emergency airlock if anything were to happen. It will be fine. This is just one of many solar flares expected this year."

Ray glared at them. Had they not listened to anything she had been trying to say for the last week? This was exactly what she hadn't wanted to happen, and now they were stuck inside a station with ravaged, mined-out ground surrounding them.

"Do you think it would be better stuck outside in the cab, with no protection?" Finch asked.

"You're right," Ray relented. "The station should be fine. I hope."

She started walking to the storage room.

"You should grab your laptop," Finch said. "We might be back there a while."

Ray picked up the work she had been doing and eyed her bag. It was still packed from her rushed attempt to flee the station. With a shrug, she grabbed it as well.

"Do we need any food?"

"Don't worry. There are plenty of rations in there."

Ray started to protest and then realized that there wouldn't be any way to heat food anyway. Instead, she reached into her drawer and pulled out an armful of snacks. She tried to balance it all while not dropping her laptop or having her bag strap slip off her shoulder. It was awkward as she continued on her way to the cargo bay, Finch behind her. She felt momentarily silly that she was moving in, but then decided she didn't care. Finch hadn't said anything anyway.

The last time they had been in this room together, Ray had messed up and Finch had melted down. If Finch realized this as well, they didn't let on. Instead, they went to the cabinets and pulled out some mats and blankets before placing them on the floor.

"No sleeping bags?"

"Would you like to be tangled in a bag if an emergency happened, especially while still in your suit?"

It had been a joke, but Ray decided that it wasn't worth trying to explain that to Finch. "No, you're right. What do we do now?"

"Now we go back to sleep?"

"Sleep? How can we sleep right now?"

"It will be hours before we know more. If there is anything we need to worry about, Johnson will let us know. Otherwise, we just ride it out until we get the all-clear. There isn't much to it except hanging out in here for half a day. Think of it like a mini vacation."

A mini vacation? This is probably what the crew had passed off as a mini vacation—a whole half a day without work. A vacation was sitting on a beach watching all the girls walk by in bikinis. Now *that* was a vacation. But as soon as Ray thought that, they felt guilty. Finch had probably never had a vacation, or if they had, it was when they had been young, and their parents hadn't seemed like the kind to have much fun anyway.

"I don't want to go to sleep in case something happens. I'll just get some work done instead." She sat down on the ground, her back against a large container with soft sides and a firm center. She turned back around to make sure she wasn't leaning against anything she shouldn't be.

"It's okay," Finch said. "It's rations."

"More rations," Ray mumbled and opened up her computer. She couldn't focus, though. She had been up too long, and the adrenaline of the emergency was wearing off now that there was nothing to do.

"Go to sleep. I'll stay up to make sure everything is okay."

"I don't know," Ray said, but she put her computer away and leaned back.

"What if I read you a story?"

Finch pulled out their book, the one they had lent her earlier.

"Mary pulled on her locker," Finch read. "It didn't open. She looked down at the combination that the office had given her and tried again. She pulled and pulled, and it still wouldn't budge. 'Stupid locker,' she said. Then a hand was reaching around hers, and a slender fist pulled back and hammered next to the lock. 'You can't be gentle with them.' Mary looked up to see the bluest eyes and the widest smile. 'Thanks,' she stammered. 'Are you new here? How are you liking it?' Mary hadn't wanted to move. She had complained when her dad had announced that his job was taking them across the country, but suddenly things didn't seem quite so bad."

Ray listened to the start of the familiar story as her eyelids started to droop and she fell asleep.

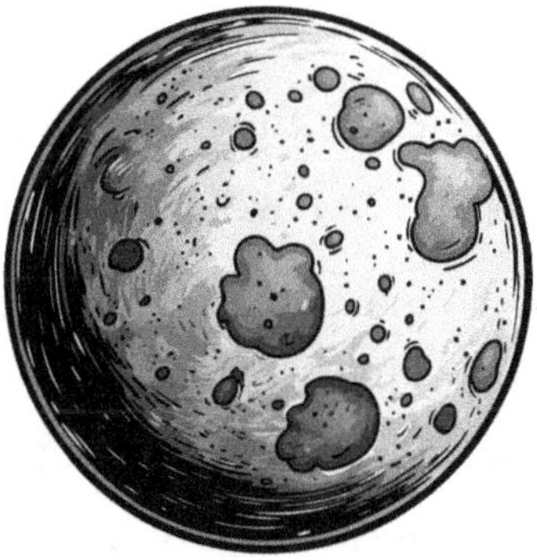

Finch

Chapter Thirty-one

FINCH WATCHED Ray's eyes close, but continued reading the story out loud until the end of the chapter. Then, they stopped speaking and read a few more chapters to themself, enjoying the familiarity of the tale. Reading about Mary, Amanda, and the rest of the pride club at Wilmort High School helped them calm down. They were friends, friends that had never left them ... friends that would never die on them.

They closed the book and cradled it to their chest for a minute, remembering the rest of the story. It ended happily, if on a bit of a mystery—a mystery Finch would never solve, no matter how many times they read it. Reluctantly, they put down the book and went over to a built-in terminal. They didn't want to speak directly to the computer and risk waking

Ray up, so they navigated by hand, scrolling through the recent headlines and trying to read them. If only everything were as easy to understand as their book.

Not having much luck, they moved to the far end of the cargo bay and whispered, "Computer, have we had any contact from Johnson Station?"

"No, there have been no updates on the solar flare."

The computer had lowered her voice, but it still echoed around the chamber. Ray moved her head slightly but didn't wake up.

The proper protocol was that Johnson was to forward all relevant information over to Schmidt. They were the main contact that disseminated it to the smaller points of contact. It didn't always work flawlessly, like Ray's missing authorization. However, for something like this, they would have sent it over if there was anything of importance to note. Finch could only conclude that it was a minor solar flare and that there was nothing to worry about.

"Computer, if any communication does come in, please let me know."

The computer brightened the control panel in response. It was an old code they had developed, and Finch knew it meant that she had heard them.

Finch was tired, and sleep was important to get when the opportunity presented itself, but they had also promised Ray that they would stay up. They started pacing around the storage area, but they were too concerned with accidentally stepping on Ray, so they stopped.

Unsure of what else to do, they sat back in their spot and opened up their book. Mary was about to have a day full of embarrassing moments as the new kid, and Amanda was going to keep popping up to make their day brighter. They got to the part just before Mary was introduced to the Pride Pack, as they called themselves, before their eyes grew heavy and the book slipped out of their hands.

THE AIR DIDN'T SMELL right. That was the first thing Finch realized. The second was that they had fallen asleep. Finch stretched their arms and yawned as they woke up, breathing in more of the tainted air.

Ray was curled up in a ball, the thin blanket wrapped around her suit.

After a decade, the station sounds had become familiar to Finch, like a constant lullaby. The noise now seemed harsher, however, like glass shattering, accentuated by cracks and pops.

There were no sirens.

"Computer," they said, unconcerned now about waking Ray up, "what is the status?"

There was no response.

"Computer?"

Finch stood, their limbs protesting, and went to the computer terminal. The screen remained blank as they pounded on the keys. They threw their fists down in frustration and some misguided hope that an outburst would change the situation. It did not. So, they found their helmet and slipped it on.

Finch picked up Ray's helmet and prodded the young woman awake. She came to immediately, her eyes glancing at Finch's helmet, and she quickly put her own on.

"What's happening?"

"I don't know. The computer is unresponsive. We never received an update from the main station last night. I thought it meant there was nothing to worry about, but maybe something else was going on."

"What do we do?"

There was no protocol for this. Any answer could as easily be right as wrong. You never knew until the moment came. Every instinct that Finch possessed said that something was wrong with the station. They needed to get off.

"Gather your things. Let's head outside. We can do a visual inspection of the situation."

Ray picked up her laptop, slipped it into its protective case, and raised her thumb in acknowledgment.

Finch headed to the internal storage bay door. They put their hand on the handle and hesitated.

"Let's take the emergency airlock."

They turned around and went to the far side of the room, where there was a smaller door. It looked much like any other, but when they opened it, there was an airlock just large enough for the two of them. Finch closed the interior door and waited to make sure that it was secure before throwing the switch for decompression. Nothing happened.

"What's wrong?" Ray said.

"It's unresponsive. It's okay, the decompression process in the airlock is a precautionary measure to minimize the impact of changing environments. Our suits are already secure, and we are breathing oxygen. I'm going to strap us in and open the door. We will be just fine."

Finch opened one of the side compartments and pulled out two cords. They were thin, but deceptively strong. They had clasps on each end that Finch hooked into the wall, then ran around their frame and hooked into the same space. They were both going to have bruises in a few hours, but hopefully that was all they would have.

"Hang on up here." Finch reached their hand to a loop that was hanging from the ceiling and waited until Ray had done the same.

"You have had to do this before?" she asked.

"Yes." Finch didn't elaborate. They let go of their strap to have two hands free, which were needed to manually open the door, then hurried to put their hands against the frame as the air rushed out of the small space. Thankfully, due to the smaller size of the compartment, it didn't take long. But as soon as the air was gone, they both froze.

Out on the horizon, bolts of electricity were shooting up from the ground.

"This is what you were worried about?" Finch asked.

"Yes, but it doesn't explain what happened to the station."

"No, it doesn't."

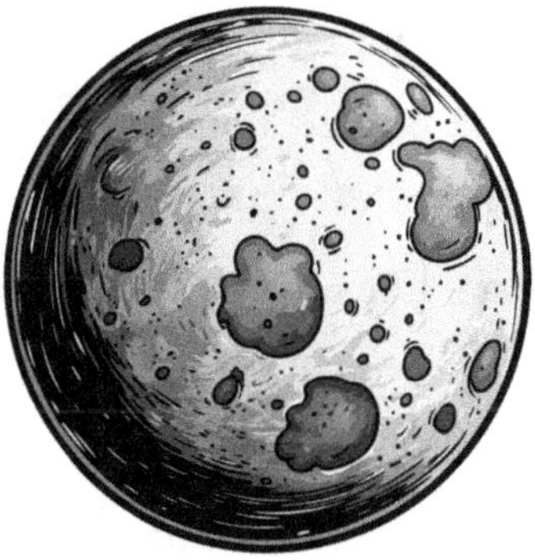

Ray

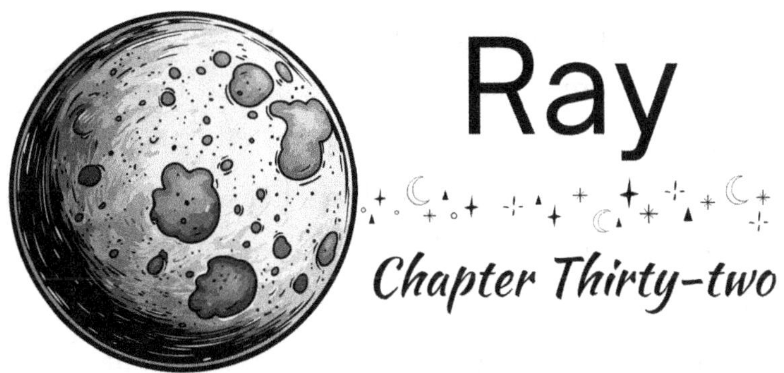

Chapter Thirty-two

RAY'S EYES followed the flashes; the ground was charged with an abundance of radiation discharge, causing a blue streak to shoot from the group up into space. They varied in length depending on the amount discharged. The moon was silent, with no atmosphere to conduct sound, but her mind filled in the emptiness with pops and sizzles that she felt should be accompanying the strikes. It was beautiful.

She had been studying this event for so long, with no anticipation of ever seeing it, but now that it was here, she couldn't tear her eyes away. It was like sitting on a porch on a rainy day watching a lightning storm.

"We need to go," Finch said.

"No, you were right. We are safe. Do you see how all of the activity is at least half a kilometer away? If the area around the station was at risk, it would have already started discharging energy."

"Then what caused the computer outage?"

"Maybe there was an electronic pulse? That can accompany SME events."

"Either way, we need to find out. Let's take a walk around the station and do a check."

The sight was majestic from a distance, but Ray didn't want to get up close. "What are our shoes made out of?"

"What?"

"The soles. Do you know what they are made out of? We need to ensure they are nonconductive if we are going to walk out there. Even if the area by the station isn't experiencing a dielectric breakdown, there is still a chance for a build-up of electrical activity."

"Right, we wouldn't want to shock ourselves. I have no idea. This has never been a concern before, and honestly, the suit they sent you here with isn't all that great. Do you have any suggestions?"

"Rubber?"

Ray tore their eyes away from the surface to focus back on Finch. The lightning discharges reflected in their faceplate.

"We need to go to the workstation," Finch said. "There are some old tires there. We can strap them to our feet."

Ray moved away from the outer door as Finch closed it and sealed it, shutting them off from the electrical storm outside. Finch moved the hooks of her strap from the interior door to the exterior door, and Ray held back on to the strap at the top, not knowing what to expect. Except it was less dramatic than before, air whooshing in like a windy day, and then nothing.

She followed Finch as they opened the storage bay doors. Smoke leaked in, and Finch closed the doors almost as fast as they had been opened.

"Shit, shit, shit, shit," they muttered. "How important is the rubber?"

"It depends. If the suits are insulated, then it isn't important at all. If they aren't, then it might be a matter of life and death."

"Okay, stay here. Gather up what you need and be ready to leave when I return."

Finch opened the door back up, slipping out and closing it behind them. Whiffs of smoke filtered in during that time.

Ray still had her computer strapped over her suit. She grabbed her packed bag and saw Finch's book through the smoke. She grabbed it, putting it next to her laptop in its case, and for good measure, went back to the soft-sided storage container she had been sleeping against and grabbed a few handfuls of ration bars before stuffing them in her suitcase. They couldn't eat outside—but it seemed the right thing to do.

She looked around to see if anything else here belonged to Finch, but couldn't identify anything. By the time she was done, Finch was back carrying curved pieces of rubber and a roll of tape.

"Lift your foot."

Finch was all business, and Ray knew not to hesitate. The container gave her enough support that she held on to it while lifting up one of her feet. Finch put a piece of the tire under it and taped it around and around with duct tape until the rubber was almost flush with the foot and only visible on the ends.

"Will this hold?" Ray asked.

"It will have to."

Ray lifted her other foot and watched as Finch wrapped that one as well. Then Finch handed her the tape and a piece of rubber and lifted their foot.

Finch had left the end piece folded over as if by habit, but even still, it was hard to grasp on to it with her gloved hands. She couldn't seem to bend down enough to reach the foot to put the rubber on. She knew she was fumbling at a time when Finch needed her the most, but they didn't say anything—just took the tape and the rubber and sat on some harder containers, taping up their foot in seconds.

Then they jumped up, rushed to the computer station, and pulled out something from what looked like a pile of computer parts.

"Got everything?" Finch asked. "Let's go."

Finch moved over to the wall by the airlock and opened a panel that Ray hadn't noticed. They pulled out two backpacks, shoving the computer piece in one and putting it on their back while holding the other in their hand as they moved to the airlock.

The space was tight with the bag, but Finch closed the door, pushing Ray aside when needed. Finch gave her a look and then grabbed the larger bag and put the long strap over their shoulder so the large container hung to their side, leaving Ray with just her laptop bag. She went to protest but was cut off before she could.

"Hold on tight," Finch said.

Ray put both her hands on the handle above and held on. When the door opened, her feet lifted off the ground, but it only lasted a second before she was back on firm footing.

Finch was already out the door and racing away. Ray followed but couldn't help turning around and looking at the station. It was glowing. Most of it was engulfed in an orange haze that Ray finally realized was fire—a silent fire that was moving straight along the surface, not able to survive without the oxygen feeding it.

"We need to go," Finch said.

Ray had fallen behind. Finch was already a few yards ahead of her. She tried to ignore the flames at their backs and the pops of lightning flaring up ahead, but it was hard.

Finch seemed in control, focused on wherever they were going, and Ray followed, determined not to let them down. When they stopped, Ray realized they had made it to the water purification station, except the tarp seemed to have lowered, the poles holding it up almost having melted into the ground, even though there wasn't any evidence of discharge in the area.

"What happened here?" Ray wondered.

"I don't know," Finch said. They headed under the tarp, bending to fit.

"Don't kneel or touch the ground with your hands," Ray said. "Don't touch it with anything except the rubber on your feet."

"Is there a charge here?" Finch asked.

"I don't know." Ray looked at the poles again. "I don't know what would have caused this."

She followed Finch under the tarp. It was next to impossible to see without the outside lights. Just their headlamps lit the way, and most of that was blocked off by the tarp. She lost track of Finch quickly.

"I don't know where to go," Ray said.

"Stay there. Don't move. I found the computer."

"Is it working?"

Ray's lights reflected off something on the ground, and she crept closer. It was water—hundreds, or thousands, of tiny water crystals from the purification system that had frozen on contact with the surface and then fallen back to the ground. They were everywhere.

"The computer is online, but it isn't connected to anything."

"What does that mean?"

"The internet is out. Whatever happened impacted the satellites—we can't call for help."

Ray's breath caught, the memory of losing oxygen on the moon returning in force. The station was on fire, the ground was electric, and there was no one to help. She was going to die out here, stuck, lost under this stupid tarp.

When a hand reached out and grabbed her, she screamed loud and long.

"Fuck," Finch said.

Finch

Chapter Thirty-three

FINCH HAD to turn off their speakers. The scream drilled into their head, causing their brain to crack. They couldn't have that right now when they needed to stay focused so they could make it out of this alive. Although they weren't sure they *were* going to make it out of this alive—they had to keep going, regardless. They owed it to all those people they had tried so hard to forget.

They kept their speakers off as they tugged on Ray, dragging her to where the cart should be. Finch helped her into the passenger seat and handed off all the bags for her to arrange.

"We have to keep the backpacks," they said, but they had no idea if Ray even heard them. Her chest heaved, and her wide eyes stared through the faceplate. They couldn't think about her panic, not right now—they needed to get out.

Finch walked over to the driver's side and unplugged the charging cord. It looked whole. It wasn't melted and had no visible damage. That was a good sign. But the ultimate test was when they sat in the driver's seat and pressed the ignition button.

When the screen lit up, they let out their own exclamation. "Yes! Let's do this."

Driving under the tarp was difficult. It kept catching on the roof of the cab. Finch repeatedly had to grab the fabric and dislodge it, often ripping it in the process. They didn't worry about that. The entire station was damaged anyway. The thought made them want to curl up in a ball and have an anxiety attack. That would come later, after they were safe.

When they finally made it out from under the tarp, they remembered to turn their speakers back on. Ray was quiet, so they chanced a glance over to see her clutching all the bags to her and looking out into the night.

Finch focused ahead. The road itself looked intact, but discharges flared off to the side.

"Why is it happening here? We never mined out this way."

"I don't know?" Ray's voice was shaky, but as she started to talk, it settled down. "It may be that the disruption with building the station and the years of traffic in this area were enough to weaken the topsoil, making it prone to breakage. It is also possible that the other area is so damaged that it is causing a cascading event in nearby areas. Either way, we should consider everything to be electrically charged. I'm worried about the car."

"Cab," Finch said. "Cars are back on Earth."

"Sorry," Ray said.

"No, that doesn't matter. I just like things to be exact, especially when nothing is."

"Yes, that makes sense. I'm worried about the cab."

"The tires are made of rubber—that should keep us safe."

Ray didn't respond, and Finch was afraid that her mind was spiraling, conjuring everything that could possibly go wrong at the moment. They had to step up and keep her calm. They had to come up with words—the right ones.

"Look, things aren't great right now. There is a lot that could still go wrong, but we are alive. Which means a lot of things have also gone right. All we have to do is get out of this crater. I don't see any lightning on the edges, so we should still be fine up there. The backpack has extra oxygen, so we will have plenty for a while yet. I can't promise we will be fine. All I can promise is we are fine right now, and I will do everything to keep you safe. All I need from you is for you to focus on the moment. Don't think about what is next. Just worry about right now. If there is anything I need to know right now, tell me that."

"The ground is probably electrically charged," Ray said, "even where there isn't actual breakdown. I think that is what caused the poles to melt. The tires will help insulate us from that, but only to a point. Eventually, they will break down."

"Okay, when that happens we will worry about it. For now, we keep driving."

Finch kept moving forward. They were less than halfway to their destination and were having difficulties keeping the cab going in the correct direction. The wheels were all solid rubber, which helped to keep them from going flat, but they were starting to deform, causing the ride to be rough even over the smooth ground.

Ray held on to the cart with one hand and gripped all of the baggage with the other. Finch couldn't see her face, but her body was tense, and there were soft sounds over the radio like she was crying and not wanting Finch to know. She needed a distraction.

"I understand what happened to the mining fields. I mean, I never expected this." Another lightning flare cracked off to their side. "But you had at least warned us. What I don't understand is why it is this far away."

"No, but this is the most utilized section of the moon. People have lived here longer than anywhere else, and the south pole was always known to be more prone to dielectric breakdown. I don't know why this happened. I don't have measurements."

"You know more about this than anyone."

"You want me to guess?"

One of the tires broke apart, leaving the front driver's side moving completely on the rim. The other tires would not be far behind.

"Don't guess. Use your experience to make an educated opinion."

Ray didn't speak as the cab buckled and limped its way on the road.

"Should we walk?" Ray asked.

"Which is safer, sitting in the cab or testing our rubber-lined boots?"

"The cab." Ray pushed herself closer in on the seat to get more space from the edge. Finch would have stopped to let her readjust herself and the bags, but they were concerned they would never get started back up again.

"Your educated guess?"

"I think the years of abuse caused a severe reaction. Something like this wouldn't have happened with a regular storm, so the SME probably would have been massive. This area would only have been affected if the discharge in the mining sites was so overloaded that it cascaded to the troubled areas, which wouldn't have had an impact anyway. The road has been compressed and reinforced, so it is handling it better, but the discharge is still in the soil. What I don't understand is why Johnson Station didn't tell us. They should have had hours to inform us so we could prepare."

"I don't know," Finch said. "There was nothing."

Finch pushed that thought out of their mind as they focused on keeping the cab moving forward. They were at a crawl, but the clearance from the ground made them feel safer. At least until the electrical systems started sputtering.

The battery levels changed from full to low and then disappeared completely. Ray craned her neck to look at the controls, no longer paying attention to keeping herself in the cab. It seemed like a recipe for disaster.

Then the headlights popped. First the driver's side and then the passenger's, leaving them in near total darkness.

"Fuck," Ray said.

"It will be okay," Finch said. "We are almost there."

The only illumination was coming from the lights built into their arms and the sides of their helmets. It wasn't enough to see more than a few feet in front of them, but Finch could make out the edge of daylight up ahead. They were getting closer, but not close enough. The sounds of Ray sniffling grew louder through the radio.

"So that is what happened to the station?" Finch asked. "This electrical discharge got too close and started a fire?"

"No. The area around the station wasn't impacted. There were no signs."

Ray seemed to drift off, but she had stopped crying, so Finch let her be as they continued to drive. The cab wasn't going to last much longer, and they were at least five hundred yards from the edge of the crater. Finch hadn't seen a lightning pop in a few minutes. However, the control panel had gone out completely before the lights had burst, and Finch had no idea how the cab was still moving, although they didn't stop to question it.

"The purification station was destroyed," Ray said.

The sudden noise startled Finch, but they tried not to let it show. "Correct."

"Is there any connection between the purification system and Schmidt Station?"

"There are power lines that connect the two. They both run off the same solar panel installation."

"Could that have been what caused the fire?"

Visions of the workshop in flames flashed through Finch's mind. The flames hadn't crackled or risen like they had seen in the movies. Instead, they had just crept steadily forward, engulfing all the oxygen at the station. They wondered if they looked back if they would be able to see the glow.

"We are almost there," Finch said. "I see the daylight."

The cab crept forward inch by inch, as if it was running on willpower alone. Finally, they made the crest of the crater. Finch was blinded momentarily as they reached out to pull down their shade, and the cab stopped at that moment, stuck in the soft soil where the road had ended.

"I think it is safe for us to get out," Finch said.

"I think so too," Ray said.

She released the bags, letting them drop where they fell, and stood up. Finch tried to brace themself as they turned and faced their home, but they couldn't help the sob that left them at the sight. More than half of the crater was still popping with lightning. The station itself, their home, was just a fizzling glow off in the distance. There would be nothing left when the flames finally stopped. Once again, they were without a home.

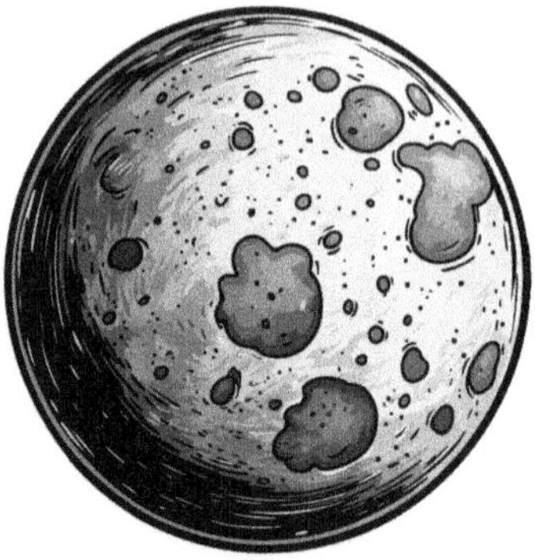

Ray

Chapter Thirty-four

RAY COULDN'T FEEL her arms or feet. She wasn't sure how she had managed to stay in the small cab or how the cab had managed to get them out to safety. Her arms and legs were stiff as she left the cab, now just a husk of metal—a new moon fossil.

Finch cried out, the sound full of anguish, and she turned to comfort them but was stopped in her tracks by the view. Large sections of the crater were experiencing electrical discharges. Part of her saw the beauty of the moment, but another part could only see the implications for her research. Either way, she needed a camera, but no one had thought to include that on the equipment request. It took her a moment to remember that Finch's home was down there, burning to the ground, and realize the pain that they must be in. She walked over to her friend and put her hand on their shoulder.

"I'm sorry," Ray said.

"It's not time for sorry." Finch tore their eyes away from the scene. "We aren't yet done surviving."

Ray looked around. The cab was covered in black soot streaks. What was left of the wheels was more than half buried in the soft lunar soil.

"Will someone come for us?" Ray asked.

"I don't know. But we can't sit around waiting to find out."

Ray took in their surroundings, searching for anything that might help. Her cheeks flushed when she realized what she was doing. It wasn't like a convenience store was going to magically appear for them to take shelter in. "Where do we go?"

"We have to get to Johnson," Finch said.

"How? The cab can't take us."

Finch caressed the small vehicle as if saying goodbye, or maybe thanking it for helping them make it so far.

"No, it won't," Finch said. "We are going to have to walk."

Finch reached into the truck's cab and sorted through the bags before pulling out the two backpacks. "Your belongings can stay here. They will be fine, and we will be able to return for them later. They are too bulky to carry with us."

"What's in the backpacks?"

"Oxygen." Finch held out one of them, and Ray maneuvered her arms into the straps. Finch adjusted it so it fit snugly. Then she helped Finch to do the same.

"Okay," Ray said. "But my laptop is coming with me."

Ray grabbed her briefcase. It was light, and even with the laptop and book, it did not weigh much. But of everything in the cab, it was the only thing that Ray did not want to risk leaving behind—well, that and the oxygen.

Finch had grabbed a long object from the cab, or maybe off the cab, and was drawing a large arrow in the soil.

"What's that for?"

"If they do come looking for us," Finch said, "they need to know which way we are going. With the station gone, there is no one able to track our suits. My wrist computer seems to have fried out at some point in the drive. That leaves old-fashioned communication."

Ray poked at the screen on her arm, but it stayed dark. She jabbed it a few more times just to be sure.

"Are we going to be okay?" Ray asked. "The suits aren't compromised or anything, are they?"

"If something was wrong with the suits, we would know by now, and I brought the duct tape along just in case. The suit doesn't require electronics to stay functioning, just a good seal, but we won't know when we are running out of oxygen until we start to feel it."

"How long to the station?" Ray asked.

"By rover, it would take us a few hours, but walking, a few days. That does depend on how long we stand around, so we should get started."

Finch took off, walking around the rim of the crater. Ray

followed. She watched the activity below, trying to remember everything that was happening so that she could write up a report as soon as they made it to the base.

The sand was fine, causing their feet to sink in as if they were walking across newly fallen snow. They were most likely the only people to have walked this area of the moon, and Ray had to turn her eyes away from the crater to pay attention to where they were going so she didn't fall.

Ray had done some walking since she had been on the moon, but it was mostly on the packed soil and only sporadically. Her legs became tired quickly, the weight on her back pushing her down, but she knew they hadn't gotten far enough. They kept hiking around the lip of the crater.

Finch was in front, moving without saying anything, as if today were just a perfectly normal day. Ray wanted to ask for a break. Her legs ached, her shoulders hurt, and her face was crusty from all her dried tears. Then, she would look back down at the crater and see the activity below. It was calming down now, but there were still inciting incidents happening enough to be visible, new areas of soil expelling the electrical discharge in energetic bursts. As she stared down at the pop-up lighting, she reminded herself that she was on the surface of the moon, fighting for her life.

Days ... Finch had said it could by days before they reached the station. No one was coming to save them—it was up to them. So she walked faster, catching up to Finch and their steady pace until the adrenaline wore down and it started all over again.

The moon was a fantastic place if you could take the time to look at the rocks and study the plains, but just trekking along, focusing on making sure your feet moved one step in front of the other, wasn't all that exciting, just dead and lifeless.

A few hours into their journey, they crossed back into darkness. The Earth was still visible overhead, casting some light to walk by, but their suit lights had all gone out. Finch had stopped and hooked a tether line between the two of them, and Ray fought to keep up with their wider strides.

Abruptly, Finch stopped, causing Ray to walk right into them.

"We should turn here," Finch said.

"You want to leave the crater?"

"If we keep walking around the crater, then we go in circles. What good will that do us? We need to head over to the station."

"You're sure this is the way?" Ray peered out into the darkness. She could barely see Finch standing right next to her, let alone anything to indicate where they needed to turn.

"I think so. It was on the other side of the road. It's hard to tell with the station burned down, but we should be there. Besides, all we have to do is get close enough so that we can radio them and they can come and pick us up."

Finch started digging their heel into the ground, and Ray

realized that they were marking another arrow pointing in the direction they were heading off to. It was like wandering alone in the desert. Even if someone were going to start looking for them, they wouldn't be able to locate them in the isolation.

"How will they ever be able to see that?"

The despair must have leaked out in her voice because Finch stopped digging and headed over toward them. They put their hands on her shoulders and leaned their faceplate right next to hers.

"I can't promise that everything will work out all right," Finch said. "What I can promise is that I will keep fighting and do my damndest to get you to that station. They know where we are headed, and this will help them know where we turned. Remember, it won't be dark for them with their headlights. Now, help me make this arrow big enough so even the fastest moon jockey can't miss it."

Ray wasn't sure what a moon jockey was, but she worked on digging out the end of the arrow so there was a visible indentation in the moon's surface. It would be easily distinguishable as a person-made event—at least with lights.

"How can you be so all right with where we are?" Ray asked.

"I'm not."

"You just keep going, pushing forward. How?"

"You can't let the fuckers win."

"What?"

"When I was in the first camp, back when I was sixteen and we were in our individual cages waiting for them to determine how to handle us, there was a Hispanic man next to me. He owned a business selling food. He was in the US legally, worked hard, paid taxes, and did everything 'right,' and they still threw him in a cage. I was just a scared kid who wasn't ready to face it all alone. One night, I was sitting there in the dark, with these dim lights—just bright enough so they could walk past our cages without tripping as they hit the bars to wake us up. Somehow, he must have known what was going on in my head. He looked at me and told me, 'You can't let the fuckers win. Every day is hard, but every day you are here, it means you won, and they lost. Don't let the fuckers win.'"

"Don't let the fuckers win," Ray said.

"Right now, right here, the fuckers are the corporations who didn't do enough testing," Finch said. "Who didn't even want you to come here to see this. It is the moon that wants to kill us and remove us from its surface. It is still the government that won't change the laws to allow us to exist. Every day I'm here, they lose, and I win. So, we are going to keep going."

"Don't let the fuckers win!" Ray screamed, this time letting it go out into the void of the moon, even if she knew that wasn't scientifically possible.

When Finch started forward, Ray followed, her new mantra coursing through her head.

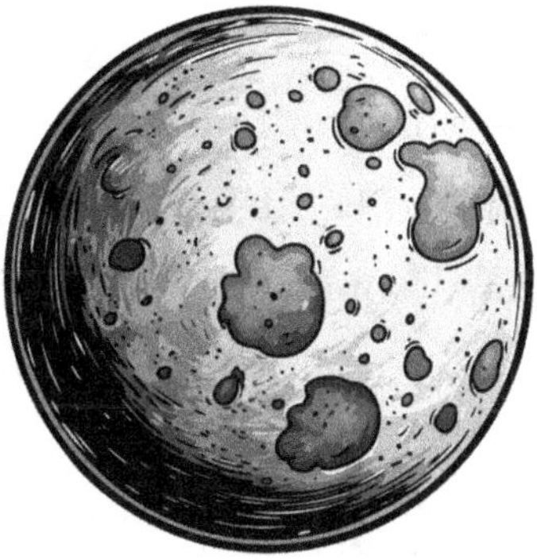

Finch

Chapter Thirty-five

THERE WAS a familiarity to the darkness. Finch was surprised to find comfort in being back within its grasp. Soon, they would be in the sunshine once more, and then they would have to make plans for Ray's survival, but for now, they could just enjoy the peace.

Their soul yearned to be back at their station, staying inside it while it burned up. It would have been a fitting way to finally go. Although they had never wanted to go out by fire, ending their life with all that pain. Lack of oxygen seemed like a better way to go. They would drift off to sleep and never wake up, becoming a permanent fixture on the surface. At one point in the future, they would be discovered, and their life briefly remembered. Maybe, if they were lucky, their discoverer would remember everyone who had been lost.

"It would be nice if they built a memorial," Finch said.

"A memorial?"

"Yes, a memorial to the canaries who lost their lives building this place, but also to everyone on Earth. A way to remember everyone who was murdered because of greed and politics. We should remember them all somewhere where they can't tear down their names. We can keep collecting stories going back in history. We should let them all be remembered."

"That would be a lot of people."

"It would." Finch thought about the pandemic they had lived through as a child, and everyone who had died because of improper guidance. Also, the genocides people ignored—children shot going out for food, buildings bombed while they slept. So many people had been killed, even before the latest round of camps. So much death, and for what? So rich men could grow even richer? Finch was tired. Maybe it was all right that their time had finally come.

"If you get a chance," Finch asked, "will you have it built? They will keep you here on the moon now that they need you. They can't have this happening to any more mining bases. You will become a lifer, and you can get the memorial constructed."

"You can do it. People around here respect you. They will listen to you."

"Yes. Just remember. We should walk now and stop talking so we don't waste our oxygen."

Finch kept moving forward. It wouldn't be too long now, maybe a couple more hours at most. They didn't have a watch to tell the time, but it had been more than seven hours already. It was enough time for a rover to have been dispatched to pick them up. They would have seen the cab and their arrow and followed their footsteps. If someone was coming for them, it would have already happened. Now it was up to Finch to get Ray to the station before the oxygen ran out.

"How much time is left on the tanks?" Ray asked.

"A little bit longer. The alarms won't work, so we need to be careful, but we have time. Not a lot, but enough."

An hour at most, Finch thought. They wanted to make it to the daylight so they could show Ray how to connect the backpack. There were sixteen hours of oxygen in each and thirty-two hours between both. It should take at least forty hours to make it to the base. There was only enough for one of them, and it had to be Ray. Finch could enjoy their last hour walking in the darkness, but when they died, they wanted to be in the light.

They kept walking, one foot in front of the other.

"Daylight," Ray said.

Finch looked up and watched where the sunlight cut through the darkness. They were almost there, and none too soon. The oxygen was starting to run out. Their thoughts were getting punchy.

"When we get to the light," Finch said, "we will take a break and switch out the tanks."

Ray picked up her pace, nearly sprinting toward the sunlight, but Finch held back, not quite ready for it all to be over. But it was time.

They pulled off their backpack and removed one of the tanks.

"What is that?" Ray pointed to the core that they had shoved in the pack, now exposed to the vacuum.

"It's the computer, the essential portion of her memory."

"You saved her?"

"No. I brought along part of her. Even if it were to function after the fire and the exposure, it still wouldn't be all of her, just a condensed backup program of herself that she kept. I am not even sure when the last time she ran the program was."

"You brought her. I thought she was gone."

"We can worry about rescuing her as soon as you are safe. Now I am going to switch out your oxygen tank. You've done it in the station, but you need to pay attention. It is clunkier with the gloves on. Always remember to shut off this valve first, otherwise you die. Once that is done, you can unscrew the old tank. Toss it aside—you can worry about it afterward. Pick up the new one and hold on to it tightly. Then latch it on. Make sure it is secure, or when you open up the latch ..."

"I die, I know."

"It's tricky doing your own oxygen. You have to maneuver it around and then place it back so it fits properly."

"Well, that isn't a problem," Ray said. "You can do mine, and I will do yours. That works out better anyway."

"You need to know how in case I'm not with you. Did you see?"

"Yes, I saw."

"Good." Finch started walking. They weren't sure exactly how much longer they had left before they would start to feel too woozy to go on, but they knew Ray wouldn't just leave them behind.

"Wait, what about your oxygen?" Ray said.

"I'm good. I don't need to change mine out yet."

"That doesn't seem right."

"I like to play things safe, but now is not the time for that. Our suits are very different. They gave you an old model. When they renew your grant, you need to make sure it includes the newest model. The corporation put you at risk. My suit has a failsafe that will keep me from suffocating for six hours even after my oxygen runs out. If they had given you better equipment, you wouldn't have almost died."

Ray fell quiet. Finch probably shouldn't have said anything, especially not now, while they were stuck on the surface without anywhere to go. Especially now, but they had to tell her because there wasn't going to be a later.

"How long did you say it would be to the station?" Ray asked.

"We've been walking about eight hours, so another day and a half should do it."

"There isn't enough oxygen for both of us for a day and a half."

Finch felt a flush of pride that she had figured it out so quickly. Ray had picked up so much in the last few weeks, hopefully enough to survive.

"What's your plan?" Ray asked.

Finch didn't answer. It was getting hard to think and words had never been easy for them.

"I won't let you die," Ray said. "You can't expect me to do that."

"I've lived so much longer than I was ever supposed to. I should have never made it to seventeen, let alone thirty-six. I've had a better life than I could have ever expected. I always knew I'd die out here."

"Maybe, but not today. You will just have to make it to forty and then fifty. You can become the first person to retire on the moon and sit around reading stories to all the children."

"That sounds ... horrible ..." It was getting harder to walk straight, and Finch decided that now was as good a place as any to lie down. "Take the oxygen. Get them to fix ... computer."

"You can't give up. That isn't fair to me."

"Fair." Finch couldn't help the laugh that escaped them. "Fair ... Funny ... Won't die ... Six hours."

"I can do the math. By the time I get to the station, you will be gone."

"No choice," Finch said. "So tired of living for others."

They closed their eyes and let their body finally relax.

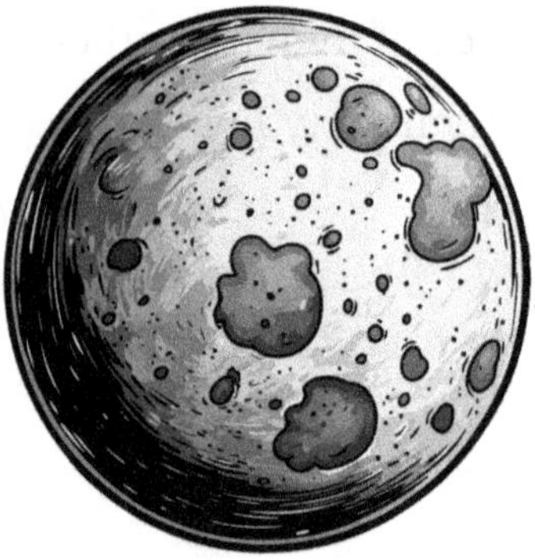

Ray

Chapter Thirty-six

"FUCK," Ray said. "Fuck, fuck, fuck." They kicked at the soil and watched as it seemed to hover before drifting back down to the surface.

Finch lay unresponsive on the ground. They didn't look dead, but they also didn't look like they were breathing.

"Fuck it," she said. It wasn't a choice. There was no way she would take another step, leaving Finch out here to die. She couldn't live with that knowledge—and she didn't care how selfish that was.

Ray reached into one of the bags and pulled out an oxygen canister. She hadn't been paying enough attention when Finch had replaced hers. She had assumed Finch would be there to help her through it like they had helped her through everything else.

The top of the canister had a covering. She hadn't seen

Finch take it off, but surely they must have. She twisted it, her gloves clasping on to a longer piece that had been designed for just such a reason.

The empty canister was still connected to Finch's suit, and Ray realized too late that she should have detached it first. Instead, she awkwardly put back on the protective piece and then took off the empty canister.

"They had better not have been lying about the six hours," she mumbled as she started to take off the empty canister, remembering at the last second to close the oxygen valve. She put the empty one back in the bag, balking at littering on the moon's surface, and then screwed on the full container.

Finch didn't move. Remembering, Ray opened the valve back up and let air flow into the suit. It had only been a few minutes, not enough to kill them—she hoped.

When Finch still didn't move, she grew worried, going over every part of the process, trying to figure out what she could have missed.

Finch let out a groan, and Ray stepped back, staying outside Finch's immediate reach.

"Why am I still alive?" they asked.

Finch moved their gloved hand over their body as if checking to make sure it was, in fact, still there. It finally paused on their helmet, as if feeling the solid material was enough confirmation. Slowly, they sat up, and Ray backed up a few more paces.

"How long was I out?" they asked.

"A few minutes. It took me a bit to remember how to put the oxygen on."

Finch stood, then twisted their body around, as if to see the tank strapped to the side of their suit. "You weren't supposed to do this. You were the one who was supposed to survive this time."

"You don't get to make those choices for me." Ray backed up a few more steps. "I won't keep going knowing that I let you die instead of us both trying to survive. I can't live like that."

"I did." Finch's voice came out quiet, the barest whisper picked up by the microphone.

"This isn't the same," Ray said. "You didn't leave people behind to die. Other people killed them. You chose to honor them by keeping going. There was nothing you could have done to save them."

"Maybe not in the camps, but the canaries ... they all died."

"That wasn't any different. They brought you up here to do untested procedures. You all were a cost-cutting measure by the corporations. The canaries died to line the pockets of people who already had more money than they knew what to do with. Surviving all that isn't your fault—it is a miracle."

"I should have been able to save at least one of them, but I never could. At least you were going to survive. Now ... now we are both going to die out here."

Ray approached Finch and clasped her hands on their shoulders. "We aren't dead yet. Let's go find the station so we can start petitioning to get that monument of yours created."

"There isn't enough oxygen."

"We will make it. I know that we will."

"Why ... how?"

"I have a lucky charm. I know that I just need to stick with you, and I will make it through. You're indestructible. I mean, look at you; you were dying minutes ago, and now you are ready to keep walking toward the station."

"I don't deserve it."

"To live?"

"Yes."

Ray leaned in close, putting her helmet right next to Finch's, even though neither could see the other through the sun visor. "You deserve to be here. What you don't deserve is what everyone has done to you. The others—they didn't deserve what happened to them. That isn't on you. That is on all those bullshit privileged Earthlings who think that one human life could be worth more than another. You know what I say? Fuck them. I'm not going to let them win."

"Don't let them win," Finch repeated.

"Exactly. Don't let the fuckers win."

Finch didn't say anything more, but they started toward the station and Ray fell in step beside them. They walked in silence, one step in front of the other. Every time Ray heard Finch let out a sigh or start to slow down she would scream into her helmet, "Don't let the fuckers win!" and Finch would pick up their pace, shoulders squared once more.

She wasn't going to let them give up. They had survived so much, and right here, right now, wasn't where their story was going to end. Ray wasn't sure how, but she knew it as the truth with every molecule of her being.

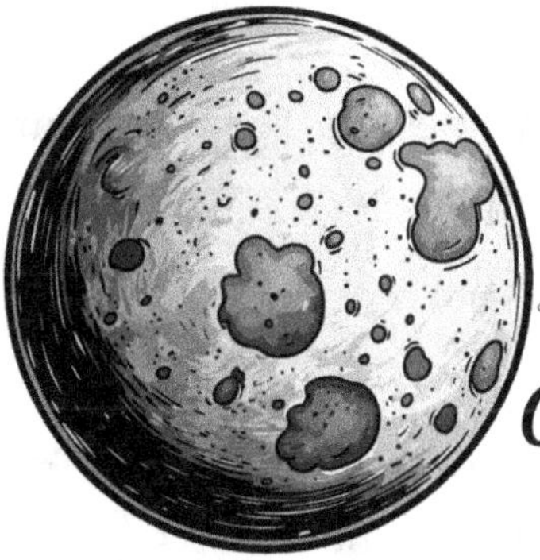

Finch

Chapter Thirty-seven

FINCH COULD FEEL the oxygen tank start to falter. That would put them out here at about sixteen hours, and still no sign of rescue. They weren't going to make it to the station, but every time they tried to let Ray know, the fool girl kept chanting, and they shut up. They couldn't dash her hope. Not if it was the last thing they could give her.

When Finch started feeling dizzy, they finally called Ray to a stop.

"We need to switch out tanks again," they said.

"Fine," Ray said, "but only if you switch yours out first."

Finch didn't fight it. There was no point now either way. They would either be rescued or they would both die. There wasn't enough oxygen left for another solution. They took the full canister and held it in their hands. It wasn't the first time they had realized how fragile human bodies were, how dependent they were on things like water, food, and oxygen.

"Don't let the fuckers win," Ray said.

Finch clinched their oxygen line and switched out the bottles like someone who had done it thousands of times before. Then they did the same to Ray.

"We are going to make it," Ray said.

Finch patted her shoulder, hoping the gesture gave her the right amount of encouragement. They didn't have it in them to speak anymore. Partly because they were afraid that Ray would hear the lie on their lips if they told her they were going to survive this. They had already prepared to die. It was Ray not surviving that gnawed at them. They just wanted to keep someone alive.

They started walking with Ray at their side, but stopped suddenly.

"Don't let the fuckers win," Ray said.

"Shh," Finch said.

It came out harsher than they intended, but Ray stayed quiet. Maybe she also heard the static that started to appear on the radio. Someone else was there.

"Hello," Finch said. "Can anyone hear us?"

The line stayed silent.

"Hello? This is Finch and Ray of Schmidt Station. Please come in."

There was something, a crackling, although not words. They must be on the edge of reception. Finch looked around for anything that might stand out and realized that their colorful suits would have to be enough. They started waving their arms around, turning in circles, uncertain which way the transport would be coming from. Ray caught on quickly and started doing the same.

"Is anyone there?" Ray said. She took over communication, announcing themselves over the radio.

"We hear you," the voice broke over the line, and Ray screamed in relief. "We see you also. You can stop waving your arms around."

Finch spotted a small cloud of dust approaching from the way they had just come.

"We are going to be okay," Ray said. She put her hand on Finch's shoulder and squeezed. "We are going to survive—both of us." Her voice cracked as she spoke.

Finch felt tears drench their face, an incredibly uncomfortable experience in a space suit, but at that moment, they didn't care. They both stood and watched as the transport started getting closer and closer, and when it stopped right next to them, Finch couldn't help but reach their hand out, making sure it wasn't an illusion. But the metal felt solid.

"Finch, I'm so glad we found you. We didn't think we were going to make it in time."

"Corporal Thompson? You came for us?"

"How are you all holding up? Do you have enough oxygen?"

"We just put on a new bottle," Ray said.

"Good, let's get headed back," Thompson said. "We have a long drive."

The transport was a Land Rover with four bucket seats and a metal roll frame. There wasn't much to it, but then, they weren't used for much anymore. It was a relic from the early days. Finch helped Ray climb into one of the back seats and put on her five-point harness seatbelt when her hands started fumbling on the restraints. They knew they should have been more patient and let Ray figure it out on her own, but all they could think about was getting her back to safety. She could learn after, at a real station, with real people to train her how to navigate the moon.

Finch climbed into their seat, and the transport took off while they were still buckling up. It turned right around and headed at a forty-five-degree angle from where they had come from.

"Where are you going?" Finch asked.

"Back to Johnson. What the hell happened to our home anyway?"

"Your home?" Ray asked.

"Corporal Thompson was one of the original crew," Finch said. "Your room used to be his before he transferred out a few years ago."

"You were the one who left Finch alone?" Ray asked.

"It wasn't supposed to happen that way," he said. "They were going to close down the station, but Finch wanted to stay, and the corporation liked the idea of having the extra ice. I put in a request to go back, but it was denied."

"You did?" Finch asked.

"Yes, no one liked the idea of you all alone out there."

"I thought I annoyed everyone."

"I'm sorry if I ever made you feel that way. But what the heck happened to the station?"

"We aren't sure," Ray said. "We think a solar flare caused dielectric breakdown to a scale greater than imagined, and somehow that caused the purification system to fry, which transferred over the powerlines to the station. It is just a theory that will need to be verified when we are able to analyze the site."

They continued to drive over the moon's surface, dipping in and out of the shadowed areas. They were traveling fast for an area that had no roads, and the ground kept them all bouncing, hitting their harnesses as they went.

"We didn't get a warning from Johnson," Finch said. "Before the computers went down, there was nothing. I thought that the storm was minor, and that they hadn't worried about sending out a message."

The men up front were quiet until the passenger spoke up. "It wasn't minor. We got feedback pretty fast that it was a major storm, and we went into lockdown. You should have gotten a notification—that is the procedure."

"Then the commander forgot about us," Finch said.

The words hung in the air until the man spoke again.

"We lost computers also. We think the satellites went out. The rest of the station is unharmed, though, no casualties. It wasn't until one of the communications officers came up to Thompson and mentioned that she couldn't get through that we realized something was wrong. She was worried about you, and the commander wasn't authorizing any outbound traffic."

"Then how are you here?" Ray asked.

"We, well, we went rogue," Thompson said. "No one was using this old thing, and we went looking for you. When we saw the show at the station, we were worried but decided to go around to the road instead of hightailing through the mess. Good thing we did. We saw the cab. That poor bugger looked like shit. We followed your arrow, but it took three trips around the crater before we saw your second one."

"You were headed in completely the wrong direction," the other man said. "We were even more worried, then, but carried on."

"I'm sorry about the station," Thompson said. "I know you loved it there, but I'm glad you both are all right."

"Me too," Ray said, causing them all to laugh.

Finch reached one of their hands out and held on to Ray. After everything, they had almost gotten her killed, after all. Finch hadn't even been leading them in the right direction. Ray squeezed Finch's hand. "All that matters is we made it," she said and then held on tight as the vehicle jostled them again.

Ray

Chapter Thirty-eight

RAY SAW the station when they started descending into another dark crater. Lights illuminated the area, highlighting the structure, and it was so much larger than the station they had just lost. She couldn't help but think it could easily hold thousands inside its walls. It was shaped almost like a dome with spokes leading off on all sides. Perched up high on the crater slope, floodlights showcased the various mining activities. These were not tiny bots going around picking up water, but large ones scooping up the surface soil and hauling it back to repositories.

The station was lucky that it hadn't had any incidents during the last solar storm, but as things continued, that would change. This was why she was here. It was her life's work to help keep humans from making the same irreparable damage to the moon as they had done to Earth. Schmidt

Station was a huge loss, especially to Finch, but it would propel the momentum for lasting change. And she knew that she would be able to sway the investors as well.

"It's so big," Finch said.

"It will be okay," Ray said. "We will be here together."

Ray stared, trying to take it all in as they drove closer to the station.

"Johnson Station, this is Thompson. We have found the missing occupants of Schmidt and are heading in."

"The commander is upset," Nalla's voice came over their radios. "You are cleared to park in Bay 8. Thompson and Murray are to report for reprimand in the morning, but the commander would like to see the Schmidt occupants straight away."

"You are going to get in trouble for rescuing us?" Ray asked.

"Here on the moon, it is important to follow commands," Thompson said. "But sometimes you have to disobey harmful orders and take the consequences."

"I'm glad you are both safe," Nalla said.

The rover pulled in through an open door with a giant black "8" on top of it, located off the side of one of the spokes. The men had unhooked their seat belts and started to do what appeared to be a routine. One went and closed the door, and the other plugged in the rover and started cleaning it off.

Finch unhooked their seatbelt, and Ray tried to hit the button that would disconnect hers. It was big enough to be hit with gloves on, but required her to press down instead of in, and it was harder than it looked. Thankfully, she got it disconnected before Finch had made it over to her side.

The belts hooked on her arms and caught on her legs, but she managed to get out of the rover with some dignity still left. Thankfully, everyone tried very hard not to pay attention to her. As they walked into the station, Murray came up to her and said, "Don't worry, we were all new once. You are doing great. Heck, you have survived more than most have experienced, so you are doing fantastic."

Ray's cheeks flushed, and she was grateful that no one could see it.

They all stepped into the airlock together.

"Grab on to a handle," Thompson said.

The airlock was longer than the one at Schmidt, with rows of eight handles stuck on the wall between each of the doors. The handles were permanent metal pieces coated with grippy material. She looked at Thompson to see him holding the bar with one of his hands, and Ray did the same. Once Finch had grabbed the handle next to Ray, Thompson hit the button to close the door and went to stand next to Murray.

As soon as the door closed, pressure started to build. It wasn't air, exactly—nothing pounded on her suit—but it pushed her away from the wall until she grabbed on to a second empty handle next to her.

All around them, tiny crystals of lunar soil started floating away toward the ceiling, where they were caught on metal plates. Only when the air had cleared did the pressure subside and the door inside open.

The men took off their helmets, holding them in their hands as they stepped into what looked like a gray tunnel. They stood there, waiting. Ray hesitated before finally removing her own helmet. The air tasted different—cleaner—and she closed her eyes as she breathed it in.

Finch still stood there, helmet on, staring at the men.

Ray tapped Finch's shoulder and pointed at the helmet. They all waited for several long seconds before Finch reached up and took their helmet off.

"Welcome to your new home," Thompson said.

Ray hurried to catch up as the men took off down the long tunnel. They passed other doors, each identical to the airlock they had just come through, until they eventually reached a large metal door.

"This is a secondary airlock in case the tunnel gets depressurized for any reason. Since we are good, we will just walk in and wait for the next door to open."

"Will it do—whatever it did last time?" Ray asked.

Thompson opened the door and waited until everyone was in before closing it again. "You can see there are two settings here. One allows the door to be used as an airlock, and the other will open it up." He pressed the green button, and the door swung open.

Ray studied the two buttons right next to each other. Sure, one was green and the other was red, but it seemed too easy to mess up and press the wrong button. But that was a future problem, because as soon as she stepped through, she wasn't thinking about the door anymore. They had entered a large room with platforms at least five levels up. The room itself looked like a workshop for machines, a place Finch would feel very at home in ... eventually. The gentlemen continued walking, and Ray hurried to keep up. They opened up another door, and this went into a hallway that led to two walls filled with shops and offices, with walkways connecting the two sides and stairs leading up several stories.

"The station was built in three sections, which helps if there is any sort of impact or disaster. The outside is the workspace. This middle section is full of offices and stores, while the next section is the living quarters."

"How high does it go up?" Ray asked.

"Ten floors, but the top two floors are the arboretum. That is where all our food is grown. I'll show you both later, but for now, we need to head over to the commander's office." They kept to the first floor, walking past some clothing shops and a small grocery store.

"Does everyone have to buy their own food?"

"No, cooking is only allowed in the kitchen, to help prevent fires, and all meals are provided in the cafeteria in the living area, but some people like to pick up a few extras. That is what the shops are for: to give people a little taste of home. But there are still those who send everything they earn back home and they get by just fine."

The shops fell away, and they entered an area that seemed closed off, with signs announcing various departments. They stopped in front of one labeled "Command."

"This is where we get off. We will have our comeuppance tomorrow. I'm sure the commander will be delighted that you are here."

The two men left, and Ray stared at the door. Finch stood still. They hadn't spoken a word since they had entered the station, and Ray suddenly noticed the harsh lights and all the sounds. It had revived her, being around so many people, but for Finch, it must be so overwhelming. So she took the lead and opened the door.

It opened into a waiting area with a reception desk that was currently empty. Behind it was a hallway with doors leading up and down it. All of them were closed.

Ray tried to wait, but she was also tired and had survived dying twice in less than a month, so she went up to the reception desk and shouted, "Hello, is there anyone here?"

There was no answer.

She shrugged and thought about sinking into one of the chairs in the waiting area. They were slightly cushioned with fabric material. It didn't seem made for space suits, so they both stood and waited, and all the while she resented that they hadn't been given a chance to rest before this meeting.

There wasn't much else to do. Neither of them had anyplace to go, but they had been outside for hours. Ray was hungry, thirsty, and suddenly really needed to pee. It was one thing to use the absorbent pad while she was out on a spacewalk, but quite another when standing in an office waiting for the person who was supposed to be in charge of the entire station.

Finch stood still, as if afraid to call any attention to themself, and that, more than anything, prompted Ray to go behind the reception area and start opening up the doors. The first one held a desk that looked like it had never been used. The second looked like a storage closet full of perfectly organized stationery. The third she opened to find the commander typing on a computer. He looked up at the intrusion. "We were told you wanted to see us."

"Rachel Bennett, so glad to see that you made it," the commander said.

"Commander, it is so nice to finally meet you. You can call me Ray."

"Is Finch here?"

At their name, Finch started forward.

"Sir," they said.

"I'm glad to see you survived once again. I am going to want a full report on everything that happened."

He went back to his computer, ignoring them completely.

"Excuse me, Commander," Ray said, "but the station we were on just burned down. We have spent a day walking on the surface of the moon, trying to survive long enough to be rescued. We were finally saved, only to find out that you didn't even authorize our rescue. So, if you could put down your computer for a few minutes to help us figure out what we are supposed to do next, we would both appreciate it."

He looked back up, his face full of annoyance. "I am glad you both survived. And the two who took out resources without permission during an emergency will be dealt with, but for now, you can find temporary residence here until you get sent back to Earth."

Finch tensed at that, their eyes wide with terror.

"Excuse me, sir, but who exactly are you suggesting is going back to Earth?" Ray asked.

"Now that the station is destroyed, you are no longer needed here," he said. "I am sure once satellites are restored and we have connected with the board, they will send you home."

"When I talk to the stakeholders," Ray said, "I will tell them that the company's negligence is exactly what led to the station's demise. This station will be next unless practices change. From just the first glance, I can tell you that you are overmining, and the same thing that happened at Schmidt will happen here. So, I would get used to seeing me around. We have a lot of meetings, conversations, and interactions still to come. And as for Finch, they just lost their home."

"I bet you never thought you would live longer than the station," he said.

Ray let the words process in her brain to make sure he had just said what she'd thought he'd said. Finch stood there, unmoving, completely mute. When the commander started laughing, as if he had just said the funniest joke, Ray found herself moving closer to his desk, putting down her helmet, and then leaning her body over his desk until her face was only a couple of inches from his.

"That was disgusting."

He rolled his eyes. "That was a joke between friends. Don't be so emotional."

"You know, it takes a special kind of man to pack a group of kids onto a space shuttle as collateral damage so he can gain all the glory for colonizing the moon. People on Earth may sing your praises, but I've been on the moon long enough to know that those living here recognize who the real heroes are. It isn't you. You are a coward. Thinking that your life is worth more than the canaries you brought here also makes you disgusting. From here on out, you will show Finch the respect they deserve."

"Are you threatening me?"

"I don't have to. I have heard about the firsts since I landed. They are legendary, and Finch is the last canary standing. Everyone out there would lay down their lives for them—two of your own people disobeyed your orders to make sure they were safe. Just imagine what would happen if they all knew that you didn't care enough to even send a communication letting us know what to expect, let alone refused to have them rescued. Up here, everyone depends on each other, but imagine if they found out that you didn't have their backs. What would happen then?"

The commander picked up a walkie-talkie next to his desk and pushed a button before speaking. "Amanda, we have new arrivals. I would like you to come and welcome our two newest residents. They will need housing and basic supplies."

Ray picked up her helmet and returned to Finch's side. They stood there until a very upbeat blonde walked into the office suite.

"Hi, I'm Amanda. Let's get you situated."

They turned to follow the woman when the commander spoke again. "It would do you well to remember who is in charge."

Ray didn't look back because they both knew that there, on the moon, the workers were in charge.

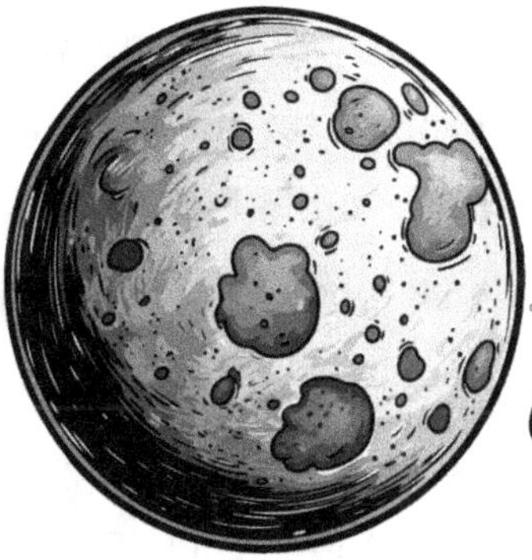

Finch

Chapter Thirty-nine

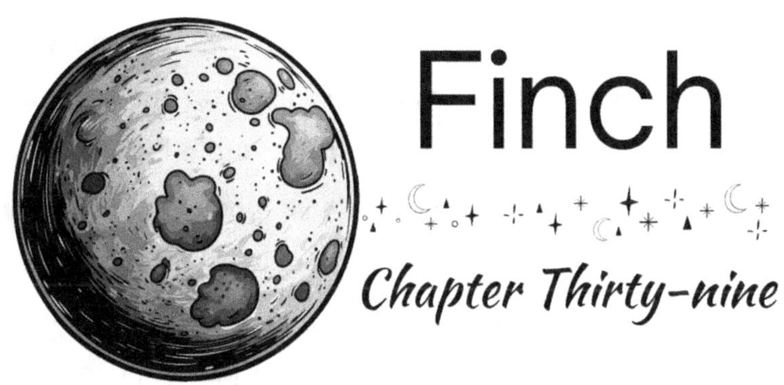

FINCH PULLED ON THEIR JUMPSUIT, trying to stop it from rubbing up against their collarbone. The material had caused them to break out in red bumps in the week that they had been required to wear it. They had thought about showing up one day in the T-shirt and sweats they had picked up from one of the shops. It was all-new material that hadn't faded from years of wear, but they had decided against it. Everyone on their team wore the coveralls. It was expected, and the last thing Finch wanted was to stand out even more.

A bell rang overhead, echoing through the room and causing Finch to drop the small solar panel they had been repairing. The rest of the team, seven other people, stood up, watching Finch as they left the room.

Finch didn't like being back on a team, especially not a team of eight. It felt ominous, even though they didn't believe in superstition. Also, they only worked eight hours, six days a week. There was too much unstructured time.

Finch put down the solar panel reluctantly and walked out the door to the mid-level. The noise hit them instantly. This was always the worst place in the station, with people's voices echoing off the walls and music playing in storefronts. They sprinted to the other side until they hit the residential area and collapsed against the wall in relief.

It was quieter here, at least mostly. A pair of people stared at them as they walked past, opening up the door to mid-level again. Finch took off away from the noise. They looked down at their hand where they had written their room number, rewriting it every day so they wouldn't forget. There were so many doors, and they all looked alike. Finally, they found their place—A145, and escaped inside.

Each quarter was self-contained in case of an emergency. It also worked to make them soundproof. This was the only place Finch could find relief, even if the room was too big.

When Amanda had first offered them a room, she had brought Finch to one three times the size. It had contained a full-size bed and a large desk. Finch had refused to even enter it. After some commotion, Amanda had finally allowed them to live with the crew instead of the officers.

Now they had a single bed, with a fluffy mattress a full two inches thick, and a desk a few feet long that was built into the wall, complete with a metal chair which slid easily across the floor.

There was a closet across from the desk that held several new outfits, enough for every day of the week, two more jumpsuits, and their space suit. They had tried to organize it as neatly as possible, but they missed their small slip on their station and the cubby built specifically for their suit. At the end of their bed was a storage locker. All it contained was the book that Ray had carried for them and the computer's storage drive.

That first night, they had crawled under their bed and hugged the book as they cried.

Now, they pulled off the jumpsuit before folding it carefully and putting it away. They looked down at their clothes. They couldn't remember if they had worn them yesterday, but there were no stains, so they knew that Ray would not say anything. They grabbed their new pad and headed off to the cafeteria.

With the shift change, the place was crowded, filled with the echoing sounds of people talking over their meals. The first week, Finch had stayed in their bedroom, eating the ration bars that Ray had brought. When they had run out, they had tried to request more, but the commander had claimed to be appalled that they had been eating them for the last year and had insisted that they eat three meals a day in the mess hall. At least it gave them something to do with all their extra time.

The place smelled, and each meal changed the room's overall scent. They grabbed a tray, proceeding through the line as people stood too close. Finch tried to grab things that seemed edible, but most days it was hard. They missed the bars, even the horrid aftertaste. At least each meal was still served with water.

They carried their tray to the farthest corner and sat down. The tray was covered in spaghetti with slimy noodles and wet sauce all glooped together. The bread was hard and covered in some sort of smelly butter. Next to it all was applesauce. Finch felt chills at the remembrance of the bite of applesauce they had tried to take—it had been just like gritty liquid—horrid stuff. They didn't understand how anyone could eat it. They missed their bars.

Finch pulled out their pad and tried to concentrate on the mechanics book they were supposed to read. They might have been put on a maintenance team, but they were expected to study and pass the same certifications that all the other team members already possessed. Finch didn't even know what half of the words in the book were. They missed the computer.

When Ray sat across from them, Finch practically threw the pad down on the table, grateful for an excuse not to have to look at it anymore.

"Things still aren't going well?" she asked.

Finch shook their head.

"You're still not talking to them?"

They shook their head again.

"Give them time. I bet they are just in awe that you joined their team."

Finch shrugged and then pointed at Ray.

"Well, I asked her out," she said. "We are officially going on a date this weekend. There is a dance club on Mid 6 that Jack said she would show me."

Finch smiled and then picked up their spoon and stirred their applesauce.

"Also, I heard back from the company, and they have officially extended my position to permanent, with no expectation of return. I am going to have a staff. I've already been poring over applications from lunarside, and there are a few candidates. I am going to have to bring some over from Earth as well. The first preliminary analysis is going to start next week. I'll look at the station and see if there is anything I can salvage."

"Thank you." Finch gave up on the applesauce and set their spoon down.

"How is the studying going?"

Finch looked around, making sure no one could overhear. "Not well."

"Is there any way I can help?"

Finch shrugged again. "The words, they are so big. The computer helped me before with all the reading."

Ray held out her hand. "Can I see your pad?"

Finch handed it over, watching as Ray tapped a few times on the screen. "These models have speakers on them. If you press this option, then it will read the book out to you, similar to what the computer did."

Finch took the pad back, looked at the option, and pressed the button. A robotic voice started reading out the text, highlighting each word as it went. Finch quickly pressed it to stop it from speaking anymore.

"I'm not sure how great it is at pronunciation, but it will hopefully help. I have another thing for you as well. Do you remember how we found the playlist of queer music?"

Finch nodded.

"Well ... it turns out that there is a movement Earthside to digitize all the books there and have them stored on the moon. Jack showed it to me. There are hundreds of thousands of books already on it, and everyone lunarside has access. Your book is the start of a trilogy. I already sent all three files to you, so you can finally find out what happens."

"Did you read them?" Finch asked.

"No way. Not until you do. I need to have someone to talk to about them."

Finch started poking at their spaghetti, trying to figure out how it would feel going down. They gave up, and instead scraped off the butter and slowly ate the hard bread—a small bite, followed by a sip of water to wash away the taste.

When Jack sat down with them, Finch tried not to react. They focused on their bread as the two women talked about their day. Thankfully, they used reserved tones, unlike the rest of the room.

"Are you going to eat that?" Jack asked.

It wasn't until the conversation stopped that Finch realized she had been talking to them. They finally looked up at the woman. She was petite but strong. The muscular miner's build was apparent in her arms, naked in the short-sleeved shirt. She had a nice smile, and Finch imagined she had kind eyes—but looking was more than they could handle. This was the first time she had sat down with them at a meal, but Finch knew this moment had been coming ever since Ray had first mentioned her name.

Finch shook their head and pushed their tray over to the woman. Jack reached out her hand, giving them her bread—the butter already scraped off. Finch took it with a slight nod and returned to looking at the table.

The room was full of people, Finch's new family. It was too much, too fast, but somehow, they would have to figure out how to make this work.

Continue the Lunar Abyss series!

Book Two

With Only the Starlight

Releases 3.31.2026

Order Now at mj-james.com

Get a FREE Short Story!

Join My Newsletter

Sign up at mj-james.com

ACKNOWLEDGMENTS

I started *Inside a Dark Space* about the time a new president had been elected. He hadn't even taken office, but what was coming was evident. Even so … everytime I saw something from my book happen in reality a bit of myself was lost. I want this book to be a reminder of why we need to help each other, be kind to each other, or at least not hate each other. As I kept writing it became more and more about resistence and reminding queer people that they have tried to eradicate us before, and we are still here.

A huge thank you to my editor, Sam. Thank you for loving my characters as much as I do. I am proud to know you and be able to work with you. And to Erica for helping to find all the last minute corrections. As alway, any errors are my own.

Thank you to my writing community who listens, provides feedback, and doesn't make me feel too much like the weird one.

My kids are a huge reason that I am here releasing this book, both for helping to make me who I am as well as listen to me prattle on about my stories because they know how much they mean to me.

A huge thank you to my readers. I've gotten a chance to start meeting you all in person, and you are lovely. This is book eight and I wouldn't have made it to this point without you.